PRAISE FOR DEBORAH HEMMING

PRAISE FOR *Goddess*

"*Goddess* is both a chronicle of the tentative young heart and an excoriating examination of the wellness and influencer industry. Written with sleek, smooth style and a sly sense of humour, Deborah Hemming is Canada's Sally Rooney."
— Christy Ann Conlin, author of *The Speed of Mercy*

"Tense and sinuous, *Goddess* dissects the insidiousness of wellness culture and celebrity with a keen eye. Hemming's story tightens its grip on readers, forcing us to examine our own doubts, desires, and search for belonging."
— Anna Maxymiw, author of *Minique*

"The storyline is engaging, and the pace of the exposition is well timed... For readers who enjoy well-described characters and setting, a female protagonist who gains confidence in herself, and a little magical realism to boot."
— *Booklist*

PRAISE FOR *Throw Down Your Shadows*

"*Throw Down Your Shadows* is a compulsive, intoxicating read. I cared for these characters, felt entranced and betrayed by them, as if they were my own friends. As the narration weaves between past and future, orbiting nearer to the black hole at its centre, Hemming proves herself to be a masterful storyteller. I lost sleep over this book, mostly because I couldn't put it down."
— Eliza Robertson, author of *Demi-Gods*

"*Throw Down Your Shadows* captures small town adolescence with unwavering veracity, Hemming's gracefully restrained prose gives us an intimate view of what it's like to come of age in the expansive lusciousness of rural Nova Scotia, amongst complicated relationships forged in a tight-knit, intergenerational community."

—Eva Crocker, author of *All I Ask*

"*Throw Down Your Shadows* blends psychological depth and menace to create a story that is both propulsive and thoughtful: a rich, character-driven novel with touches of the weird and the regional particularities of the Annapolis Valley. Hemming upends the conventions of coming-of-age novels while demonstrating that unique stories of adolescence crashing into adulthood can have universal resonance."

—Naben Ruthnum, author of *A Hero of Our Time*

"In her compelling debut, Deborah Hemming has written a haunting and moving story alight with memorable characters. Compulsively readable right to the shocking conclusion, I was completely enthralled with this novel."

—Nina Berkhout, author of *The Mosaic*

Goddess

ALSO BY DEBORAH HEMMING

Throw Down Your Shadows

Goddess

Deborah Hemming

ANANSI

Copyright © 2023 Deborah Hemming

Published in Canada in 2023 and the USA in 2023 by House of Anansi Press Inc.
houseofanansi.com

All rights reserved. No part of this publication may be reproduced or transmitted
in any form or by any means, electronic or mechanical, including photocopying,
recording, or any information storage and retrieval system, without permission in
writing from the publisher.

House of Anansi Press is committed to protecting our natural environment. This
book is made of material from well-managed FSC®-certified forests, recycled
materials, and other controlled sources.

House of Anansi Press is a Global Certified Accessible™ (GCA by Benetech)
publisher. The ebook version of this book meets stringent accessibility standards
and is available to readers with print disabilities.

27 26 25 24 23   1 2 3 4 5

Library and Archives Canada Cataloguing in Publication

Title: Goddess / Deborah Hemming.
Names: Hemming, Deborah, 1989- author.
Identifiers: Canadiana (print) 20220401675 | Canadiana (ebook) 20220401683 |
ISBN 9781487011116 (softcover) | ISBN 9781487011123 (EPUB)
Classification: LCC PS8615.E487 G63 2023 | DDC C813/.6—dc23

Cover and book design: Alysia Shewchuk

*House of Anansi Press respectfully acknowledges that the land on which we operate is the
Traditional Territory of many Nations, including the Anishinabeg, the Wendat, and the
Haudenosaunee. It is also the Treaty Lands of the Mississaugas of the Credit.*

 Canada Council Conseil des Arts
for the Arts du Canada

ONTARIO ARTS COUNCIL
CONSEIL DES ARTS DE L'ONTARIO
an Ontario government agency
un organisme du gouvernement de l'Ontario

With the participation of the Government of Canada
Avec la participation du gouvernement du Canada | Canadä

*We acknowledge for their financial support of our publishing program the Canada Council
for the Arts, the Ontario Arts Council, and the Government of Canada.*

Printed and bound in Canada

MIX
Paper from
responsible sources
FSC® C103567

Goddess

Prologue

VERMONT

I went outside because I needed to breathe. Back then, the air in our house often felt thick with tension, and in response I would put on a jacket and scramble into my boots. I would ease open the back door, slip outside, and close it gently behind me so no one would hear me leave. Then, I would run. We lived in the woods, surrounded by dense forest, and I was the only one in my family who ever ventured past the driveway. I was the black sheep, the outdoor cat.

I remember it had rained that day. The ground was still damp, and everything looked fresh and green. Alive. I ran until I was past the treeline, far enough into the hidden darkness of the forest that I felt completely *alone*. I stopped to rest, gulping down the clean air of the woods like I was chugging water. A familiar calm enveloped me. This was where I was meant to be. Not with them. Not with my mother, especially.

I was eight at the time. I had been seeking refuge in the woods for as long as I could remember; my ritual when the mood turned dark at home. Now that I was refreshed, I walked on, following a familiar path until I came to the spot where I liked to sit, my back against a large maple. I crossed my legs and looked around. A cool gust of wind swept through the trees, sending branches waving. In the distance I heard a woodpecker tapping on an unknown trunk.

I must have closed my eyes for a moment because the next thing I knew, it was all around me — a substance in the air I had never encountered before. Not smoke or fog or mist, but something else. Something yellow and sparkling in the air, like magic dust. I looked around in search of an explanation. Where was it coming from?

It took me a moment to locate its source. The substance was coming from the trees themselves, as if evaporating from all the leaves of the forest. It was like each plant was casting a spell. But to what end?

Panic rose in my chest, and I felt a strong urge to run home. I tried to stand, pressing my hands into the cool earth to push up from the ground, but as I did, the maple behind me released another puff of its glittering haze. Almost immediately, my fear faltered. I settled once again, resting my head against the tree trunk, and against all my previous instincts, I slept.

PART 1

The Goddess Allure

The forest is never quiet. All around creatures large and small, of fur and feather, announce their presence. A growl, a sniff, a chirp. The soft thud of a paw to earth or the sharp whip of a beak to bark. But out of the din rises a slow trill. My whooping call, unlike any other. Look up and you'll see me. The cardinal. A flash of red; otherworldly, beautiful.

— *Violets in Her Lap* by Agnes Oliver

1

In the airport bookstore I avoided the fiction section and headed straight for the magazines. I told myself I needed the latest copy of *The New Yorker*; I was headed to New York after all. I took the long way to the back of the store, skirting around a display of candy bars and averting my gaze from the books. But at the last moment, I glanced sideways. I couldn't help it. I never could.

My chest lifted and my stomach lurched. There it was. My book. My first and quite possibly only novel. There was a stack of copies on the bestsellers table, and someone was even holding one, flipping through its pages: a woman in chic wedge heels and a floral wrap dress.

I moved closer to the magazines, keeping an eye on the woman—there was something French about her; the red lipstick maybe—who seemed to be deciding whether *Violets in Her Lap* by Agnes Oliver was worth the hardcover price. She turned to the back flap where my author photo lived and I quickly looked away, letting my blond hair fall into my face. Not that she'd recognize me. Two months of being on the road, or rather, in the air, meant bags under my eyes and yesterday's T-shirt.

When I chanced another glimpse, I saw that she was getting in line, my book in hand. Again, my body reacted as if in conflict with itself. Relief flooded my limbs, but fear festered low in my gut. She was buying my book (good). That meant she was going to read it (good in theory — but what if she didn't like it?).

I grabbed a copy of *The New Yorker* and hurried to get in line behind her. I was immediately met by a wave of her perfume, surprisingly woodsy, like pine, white cedar, and water lily. For a moment, I was back in the woods, a child again, dangling my legs in the cool pond west of our house. I felt completely at ease. But then the sounds of the airport brought me back to the present.

The woman paid, and when she turned to go, she looked at me and smiled politely. I thought about saying, "That's my book! I'm the author!" but the moment passed and the woman was gone, taking the scents of my childhood with her.

Had I ever imagined it would be like this? Stalking readers in airports? No, of course not. But publishing *Violets in Her Lap* had been nothing like I'd expected. From the high six-figure advance they'd given me for my "fairy-tale book deal" to the fact that I was still waiting to feel like I was everything everyone said I was: talented, original, a fresh voice.

I was the first to admit I owed most of my success to Robert, my publicist. Robert was definitely a genius. He had convinced the media I was some kind of literary "It" girl ("Big advance!" "A complete unknown!" "Only thirty years old!"), and in no time I was being featured in newspapers and magazines and on blogs and podcasts. People didn't only want to know about my writing, they wanted to know about me: my morning routine, my skincare regimen, what I liked to wear and eat and drink. Apparently, that's what was expected of young female authors these days: a lifestyle, a brand. I had to invent a skincare regimen to be able to talk about it; I now had a toiletries bag stuffed with serums and moisturizers I almost always forgot to use.

I hurried to pay for the magazine, afraid I would lose sight of the woman in the floral dress—my future reader—but outside the store, I spotted her walking down the wide airport concourse. She had stashed my book in her bag, no longer clutching it for all to see. I followed her for several minutes, keeping my distance, and then watched as she turned into a nail kiosk. Without thinking, I followed her inside. By the time I reached the kiosk, she was already seated before a manicurist, choosing her colour from the polish options. She didn't look up when I entered.

There were four manicurists working. I sat down in front of the one farthest away from the woman. What was I doing? I had no idea. A part of me hoped she would pull out my book and start reading. Then maybe I could see her reaction to the first few pages. Or maybe I just liked how she looked, the smell of her perfume. She seemed so feminine and put together. She definitely had a skincare regimen, one she followed religiously. It intrigued me that she'd want to read my book. I was nothing like her.

"What will you have?" the manicurist asked me.

It took me a moment to understand the question. I had never actually had a manicure before. I looked down at my nails, picked at and uneven. Could she even do anything with these?

"A manicure?" I said, my voice croaky and coarse sounding in the white serenity of the kiosk.

"Yes, but what kind? Gels?"

I frowned. "Just the regular kind."

"Colour?"

I looked sideways. The woman had chosen poppy red. Bright and cheerful. Bold. I searched for it in the display of bottles.

"That one." I pointed.

The manicurist nodded and immediately got to work. She started by clipping my nails, which surprised me. I'd always thought they were too short, but here she was, making them shorter, evening them out.

The woman, I saw, was not reading my book. Of course she wasn't. Her hands were occupied. Didn't think that one through, did you, Agnes?

"Where are you headed?" the manicurist asked.

I pulled my gaze from the woman. Is this what we were supposed to do, make small talk? I told the manicurist I was on my way to New York, and she raised her eyebrows in approval.

"Work or play?"

"Work," I said, distracted. The woman was laughing easily with her own manicurist, as if they were old friends.

"And what do you do?"

"I'm a writer."

The manicurist frowned. "Why are you whispering?"

Was I whispering? An awkward laugh slipped out as I shook my head. "Sorry."

"What do you write?" She was now filing the edge of each nail, rounding them to match the natural shape of my fingers.

"Fiction. Novels. Well, *a* novel."

"Oh." Her eyebrows rose again. "Romance?"

"No, not romance. It's a book about nature. Well, not about nature. It's told from the perspective of nature."

"So, like, animals?"

I hesitated. I had never been very good at explaining *Violets in Her Lap*. You'd think being on a book tour for two months would have helped, but I still struggled with my elevator pitch. "Animals, yes, but also plants. Trees and flowers. Moss."

"Moss?" Her brow furrowed.

"It's hard to describe." I looked sideways again, wishing I had never started talking. Clearly the woman in the floral dress thought my book sounded good. Maybe I should ask her what she thought it was about.

"Hm." The manicurist fell silent, though her brow remained wrinkled; it seemed talking time was over. I imagined her telling her friends after work about the crazy woman she met who wrote a book about talking moss and appeared to be stalking another client. Nice one, Agnes.

It's true, mine wasn't a normal book — not many contemporary novels have no human characters, only talking plants and animals, like some kind of children's story with more complicated language — but apparently people liked it. Robert said it was timing. My book was topical. The felt effects of climate change: floods, wildfires, hurricanes... people wanted to understand the powerful forces they had long taken for granted. They wanted to feel connected to the natural world that had turned on them. That made sense, but I hadn't thought about any of that when I was writing it, which meant I probably didn't deserve all this credit. The book hardly seemed to belong to me anymore, anyway. It belonged to other people: its readers and its critics. There were even translations of it in languages that I would never be able to read. It was like I had made this thing and now that it was in other people's hands, I didn't recognize it anymore.

The manicurist began painting my nails. The polish smelled like any other I had encountered in my life: vaguely toxic. I was struck by the irony. Manicures were considered a form of self-care, a small way for women to pamper themselves, but they were actually killing us, cancer-causing chemicals slowly leaching into our skin. I wondered if breathing in the fumes every day took a toll on the manicurist's health. Maybe at this point she didn't even notice the smell. So familiar, she mistook it for benign.

Toxins aside, I should have done this at the beginning of my tour: my hands already looked better. I had never really thought about my nails, to be honest, but that was my mother's fault. She'd never taught me these things. "Who has time for manicures?" I could imagine her saying, perplexed by the thought.

I had been looking forward to my book tour ever since Robert had announced it. I had thought it would make my success feel more real — readings in bookstores seemed more tangible than my name on bestseller lists — but it had mostly been stressful and lonely, a blur of vending machine snacks and unfamiliar hotel rooms. At each stop, I met more people — all strangers who knew my name, who held my book in their hands or on their laps, who wanted me to personalize their copy — and in my mind they formed a collective I wasn't a part of. They were fans, readers; they had each other. I was the author, an outsider; alone, isolated.

I watched as the manicurist applied a second coat to my nails. I noticed how she dipped the brush into the polish then carefully swiped it on the edge of the bottle, leaving behind the excess.

"Let that dry," the manicurist said, pulling out her phone, "and then we'll do the topcoat."

I nodded, looking sideways again. The woman who had bought my book was already getting her topcoat. She looked completely at ease, like she did this all the time, like she belonged here.

For three stops on my tour, I'd been paired up with another writer. He was mid-career, with four books to his name, and practiced at the whole thing: reading aloud from his book in front of large groups with perfect delivery — that NPR voice everyone loves — and chatting with bookstore staff like they were old friends. He had a smile that never seemed to tire. He wore blazers and made people feel comfortable. He was the real deal, a Genuine Writer as imagined by the masses. I had watched him, wondering how he made it look so easy.

One night, after a reading in Charleston, we walked back

to our hotel together. It had rained while we were in the bookstore. The streets were slick, the old trees dripping. As we walked, he went on and on about this award and that writer's residency and all the markers of success he had secured and surpassed in his career. I knew for a fact I had received a larger advance than he had for any of his books, but I kept quiet. I wasn't one to brag.

He invited me to his room for a nightcap and asked me what I was working on next, my so-called work-in-progress, which currently had a word count of zero. But I didn't want to talk about work. Instead, I kissed him. I didn't really find him attractive, but I wanted to feel better about myself, and it worked, for a minute. When it came to men, that's all I made room for these days. Minutes. Anything more and my writing suffered.

The woman in the floral dress stood up, her nails dry, her manicure complete. She was ready to go. I took a short, quick breath. Again, I felt the urge to say something, to indicate that I was the writer whose book she had just bought — I could even sign it if she was interested — but she gave me the same impersonal smile as before and I chickened out. As she walked away, I looked down at my hands, my new poppy-red nails, and didn't recognize them.

2

I found my seat in first class (I was still getting used to that). Immediately, the flight attendant handed me a glass of champagne, and though I'd promised myself I wouldn't have a drink before arriving in New York — I needed to be fresh for my reading that night — I couldn't bring myself to say no. First-class perks. Enjoy them while they last, Agnes.

I sipped my champagne and stretched out my legs. Outside my window, the Chicago tarmac steamed with heat. I reached for my magazine and turned a few pages. Right, this was why I didn't read *The New Yorker*. I liked words, but all that uninterrupted, tiny text made my eyes immediately glaze over.

I forced myself to read a review of a new Broadway play — if it sounded good, maybe I'd go see it while I was in the city — but it sounded awful. A comedic period piece starring two Hollywood actors. "Dickens meets *The Hangover*," the reviewer wrote. What did that even mean?

I skipped ahead and read a few of the cartoons, flashes of poppy-red catching the light as I turned the pages. Eventually, I landed on a profile of Geia Stone, the famous actress turned wellness guru who was inescapable on social media these days. The photo, a close-up of Geia's angular face looking straight into the camera, took up an entire page, with the write-up on the page opposite. She was all icy blue eyes and long, dark, wavy hair, a few perfectly placed freckles on her nose and cheeks. She was regularly referred to as the Most Beautiful Woman in the World, and also as a quack, using pseudoscience to sell millions of dollars' worth of wellness products to women through her lifestyle brand Goddess™. Self-care and inner nourishment were the guiding principles of the Goddess™ woman. The profile was promoting a new podcast her brand was launching, Goddess™ Cast, which Geia wouldn't actually host.

"I have two amazing editors for that!" she was quoted as saying. "Though I will make an appearance when we cover topics particularly close to my heart."

I skimmed ahead, stopping at a question from the interviewer about *The Opposites*, the sci-fi–thriller movie series she'd created with her ex-husband, British director Jack Verity. I knew the series well; I'd been a fan back in college. Though the films only ever had a niche audience, *The Opposites* was lauded by critics for being an intricate, feminist mind-bender. Each movie posed more questions than it answered, and fans became consumed with trying to solve the layers of riddles embedded in the narrative. I once spent three hours going down a rabbit hole of fan theories on Reddit.

The series was supposed to consist of four movies—Geia and Jack had outlined all four before writing the script for the first film—but they only managed to make three before their marriage dissolved. Their obsessive fans were devastated, left hanging and desperately wanting more. I suspected this interviewer was one of those fans. It had been six years since the last film; the tragic non-conclusion of *The Opposites* should have been old news by now.

"You know," Geia responded in the article. "It's not about any kind of animosity between Jack and me. We're still very close. We co-parent our two children together, and really, we go beyond that. I would call him a dear friend, almost like a brother. But the kind of intimacy required to create art together is not healthy for our friendship or our family right now. Never say never, but no, we have no plans to bring back *The Opposites* any time soon."

Many critics questioned Geia's close relationship with her ex-husband. The couple claimed to have simply decided to remain in each other's lives after splitting up five years ago. Former lovers and partners, now the best of friends. They made overcoming personal messiness and resentment look easy. Too easy. Divorce was supposed to be difficult. I thought of my own parents, long divorced, each of them better off without the other. The idea of them staying friends post-marriage was laughable; they'd barely tolerated each other when they were together.

I turned the page without finishing the profile. I hadn't paid much attention to Geia since she sold out. After *The Opposites*, she'd transformed from indie darling to big-budget actress by starring in a handful of mainstream films, and then one day she quit acting and launched Goddess™ out of nowhere. To her early fans, the move was baffling. The only through line I could see was that Geia's character in *The Opposites* was a supernatural healer, and now here she was, a corporate mogul with millions of fans touting products that promised to heal and detoxify the modern woman.

I looked up as a few final passengers boarded the plane. They walked past me and the others sitting in first class, toting bulky carry-on luggage that looked like it just met the size restrictions. I smiled at a young girl with wonky straight-across bangs that I imagined she'd cut herself. She grinned back. I glanced up at her mother. She looked exhausted, ready to break. Her mouth stayed slack despite my offer of a smile. I shifted in my seat, looking away. I remembered being someone who resented people like me. I was still that person, I told myself. I was just sitting somewhere else.

The aisle seat next to me remained empty, which felt lucky. Maybe today would go well, the next few days too. I was going to be in New York for close to a week. Though most of the events on my book tour had been well attended so far, New York seemed like the ultimate challenge. Home to the literary elite. I had been imagining empty rooms, silent audiences. But maybe not.

I finished the last of my champagne. Several minutes had passed since the last passengers boarded the plane, and still nothing was happening. We weren't moving and the captain hadn't made any announcements explaining why. The champagne bubbles went right to my head and a familiar numbness crept over me. I set the empty glass and my magazine on the table of the seat next to me and closed my eyes. Then, silence. Everyone around me stopped talking. I opened my eyes and saw a man had just boarded the plane, a final passenger. He carried a brown leather bag slung over one shoulder and he grinned and shook his head as if to apologize for his lateness as he chatted to one of the flight attendants, who looked completely charmed.

I recognized him immediately. But how could that be?

Jack Verity was wearing a grey hoodie and jeans. He was tall with a slim build and dark hair. As he walked down the aisle to my row, he smiled cheerfully at the other passengers, a close-cut beard framing his full lips, and I decided he looked even more handsome in person than he did in all those magazines. He stopped and looked at me, my empty champagne glass, my copy of *The New Yorker*.

"I think I'm here," he said, his British accent lengthening the vowels.

"Oh, sorry!"

I reached for my stuff, moving the magazine onto my lap and clutching the champagne glass in my fist. I watched him easily hike his bag up into the overhead bin. Then he sat down. Right away, I noticed he had a kind face, almost boyish, despite his age and dark beard. I pulled my gaze to my lap while he finished putting away his things. Stop staring, Agnes.

"I'm glad they waited," he said, sighing, looking right at me. His eyes were the colour of burnt caramel: a deep golden brown. "I don't think there's another flight until tonight."

I nodded, totally star-struck.

Stay cool. You don't want to make him uncomfortable.

"Do I know you?" he asked suddenly, titling his head, looking at me more closely.

Of course he didn't know me. Was he just trying to be nice?

"I don't think so."

"Wait a minute." His face lit up. "Are you Agnes Oliver?"

When he said my name, the world around us seemed to shimmer. I nodded slowly in response, thoroughly confused. How did he know who I was?

He laughed. "I'm reading *Violets in Her Lap* right now. I recognize you from the jacket photo."

I swallowed, my stomach fluttering. I was at a total loss.

"You're the reason I almost missed my flight. I was reading in the lounge, and it was like time had stopped. I didn't even hear them paging me. Someone had to come find me."

The right side of his mouth crept upwards into an adorable crooked smile. I swallowed again.

"I'm Jack." He reached out a hand. "I might just be your new biggest fan."

3

The man I had been reading about moments before — critically acclaimed director and ex-husband of Geia Stone, Jack Verity — was so close I could touch him. His scent made the back of my neck tingle. It was clean and bright, like cracking open the peel of a lemon. He had continued to shower my book with praise all through takeoff and was now insisting on more champagne. I blinked but the scene remained the same. I wasn't making this up.

The flight attendant jumped into action, as one does in the face of celebrity, and the champagne quickly arrived. I couldn't be sure, but it seemed like a different kind than the one I was first offered, better somehow. Colder and cleaner. Maybe they saved the good stuff for people like Jack. We were up in the air now, on our way to New York, the mottled tops of white clouds visible outside my window. Somewhere in the cabin I heard a woman say, "I think that's her ex-husband! Geia Stone!" The woman pronounced Geia's name incorrectly, saying *Guy-ah* rather than *Jee-ah*. If Jack heard, he didn't let on.

I kept sneaking glances at him as if he might disappear. Did he seem different than regular people? He had that effortless look I associated with famous people. The casual, brandless clothing—hoodie, jeans, sneakers; all impeccable quality—and the good looks that made you keep going back for more. He spoke with a confidence that suggested no one scared him. He crossed one long leg, his ankle resting on his knee so that it extended into the aisle: he took up as much space as he pleased. When he wanted more champagne, he raised a hand and waved at the flight attendant, saying "Hey, chap!" louder than was polite.

But he was also very kind, not as untouchable as I would have expected. In any paparazzi photos I had seen of Jack and Geia with their two children, Jack had looked angry, shielding the faces of their twin daughters from prying cameras. But when the flight attendant stumbled over his words, outing himself as a huge fan, Jack quickly put him at ease. He said he looked exactly like a friend of his from back home.

"No, really, you could be related. Do you have any family in England?"

The attendant said no, completely tickled.

"Maybe you do and you don't know it. Hey, how about a photo? I've got to send it to my mate. He's gonna flip."

I watched as Jack took a selfie with the flight attendant, using his own phone, and then casually suggested they do one with the man's phone as well. It all happened in seconds. The flight attendant walked away beaming.

"Cheers," Jack said, clinking his glass against mine.

"Cheers." I smiled, entirely charmed.

"So, you're on your way to New York too. Is that home for you?"

I took a quick, short breath. Was I really going to just sit here and talk to Jack Verity like it was nothing?

I gulped down some champagne. "Montreal. I've lived there since college."

His face lit up. "I love Montreal. I was there in March looking for a place to shoot my next film. In retrospect, probably not the best time of year to go location scouting. It was bloody freezing and there were two snowstorms in five days."

I laughed. I remembered the storms he was referring to. I didn't leave my apartment for close to a week, save for a trip to the dépanneur for emergency sustenance: wine and potato chips.

"So what brings you to New York?" he asked.

"The book. I'm finishing off my tour."

"Of course." Jack re-crossed his legs. Now his other knee was propped up, hanging out dangerously close to my own. "So, tell me. How on earth did you come up with this story? No human characters, just talking trees and fungi. Bit of a risk, no?"

I shook my head. "Insane, right?"

"No, not insane. But definitely a risk." He paused. "What is it about nature that speaks to you like that?"

I pretended to pause too, but I already knew what to say; I had answered this question a lot on tour, and I knew what people wanted to hear.

"I grew up in rural Vermont," I said evenly. "And I spent a lot of time in the woods as a child. I think a part of me always knew my first book would be set there, back among those red pines. There's something about the forest that really gets the imagination going. There's a sense of both mystery and possibility. The freedom of an untouched space. I wanted to explore that in a way I hadn't seen any other book do before."

Jack nodded thoughtfully, but he didn't look satisfied. "Sure, okay. But it must have been more than that. The way you write, it's like you have this special connection to nature. Like you feel at home there. Is that fair?"

I nodded.

"Why do you think that's the case?"

I hesitated. He was taking me off-script.

"Okay, let me rephrase." Jack looked away for a moment, as if choosing his words carefully. "What pulled you to the woods to begin with? Did your parents take you for hikes? Did you play in the woods with your friends?"

"No," I said, slowly. "I was always alone."

That piqued his interest. "Always?"

I shrugged. "It was my safe place."

He raised one eyebrow. "Interesting."

"Why is that interesting?" I was suddenly growing hot.

"I don't mean to pry. It's just, your book is rocking my world right now, and I'm trying to figure out why. It's not every day I get a personal interview with my new favourite author."

The right side of his mouth again lifted into a lopsided grin as he looked down for a moment. I felt myself blush. I wanted to give him what he wanted—he was being so nice about my book, and I could tell he was genuinely curious—but I never talked about my childhood with anyone. "Well, I guess if I'm being honest, I was usually running away when I went into the woods."

Jack watched me closely, his face now solemn.

I exhaled. I was never going to see Jack Verity again. Just go with it, Agnes. I took another gulp of champagne.

"My parents fought a lot. And my mother was really difficult. She's, like, a perfectionist on steroids. Even when we were really young, she had the highest expectations for me and my brother, especially when it came to school. There wasn't a lot of room for fun in our house. My parents never got along really. Home wasn't a happy place."

My pulse sped up just talking about it. I pictured my mother's disappointed head shaking; her insistence that I sit at the small desk in my bedroom until I got it right, whatever it was, a math problem or some stupid homework assignment. Her absurd standards paralyzed me, but they motivated my brother, who was seven years older and smarter than me in the ways that counted. Having her looking over my shoulder, both literally and metaphorically, I learned to second-guess my every thought and idea, until I had no sense of what I really thought anymore.

I pushed the memory from my mind.

"When things got to be too much," I continued. "I'd go outside and escape to the woods. I felt more like myself there...totally free from judgement. Something I never felt around my mom." I smiled faintly. "It's my favourite thing about trees. They don't judge."

Jack beamed at me, and I noticed his eyes contained flecks of amber. "I wish my kids could have that relationship with nature."

"What about you?" I asked, hoping to move the conversation away from me. "Where did you grow up?"

"London."

"And you're based in New York now?"

"L.A., mostly. But we spend every summer in the Hamptons and I have a place to crash in the city if I need it."

We spend every summer. Did that mean he spent all summer, every year, with Geia? I'd assumed the myth of their post-divorce closeness was mostly a branding exercise. It was very Goddess™ to make the transcendent choice to befriend your ex. Was it actually real?

"So," he said, "when do you write? What's your routine, your process?"

I cringed. We were back on me again. "Right now, I don't write."

"No?"

I sighed heavily. Another topic I didn't like to talk about. "Since I finished my book, I haven't been able to write anything else. I try, but I just...can't. It's a problem. My book deal was for two novels, with a firm deadline for book two. I'm supposed to hand in a first draft by the end of the summer. If I don't deliver...well, let's just say it won't be good." I shook my head, surprised by the emotion in my voice. I had never said any of this out loud.

My fear of failing at the only thing I'd ever loved to do was made worse by the possibility of letting down my publishing team if book two never came to be. And I'd have to pay back my generous advance on the second book, some of which I'd already spent.

"My agent and editor are really nervous. I swear they can sense my lack of progress. But no one's more nervous than me."

Jack's smile faded. He was watching me so closely I had to look away.

"I don't believe in writer's block," he said, after a moment.

I didn't either, not in theory.

"Yeah, I don't know. There's just been a lot going on. The book tour and all."

"I get that. Publicity isn't very inspiring."

I nodded, though I knew there was more to it than that. Some nights when I couldn't sleep, I worried I might never write again. I felt broken, like my inner voice had been silenced. I had recently googled "how to write a novel" and then promptly deleted my browser history, imagining someone hacking my computer, exposing me for a fraud.

Jack rested his chin on his hand, turning closer to me. "So, who are your influences? Who do you like to read? Who are your people?"

I hesitated. Questions like these made me squirm. What if I said something or someone he hated?

"I would count you as an influence," I said, realizing it was the safest answer. "I've seen all your films. Some of them multiple times."

"And?" he asked, leaning an inch closer. I noticed a few flecks of grey in his dark hair. It looked like it might be curly if he didn't cut it short.

"And what?"

"What did you think?"

I smiled. "I wouldn't have watched them so many times if I didn't like them." I wasn't sure what he was getting at.

Jack set his empty champagne flute on the arm table and folded his hands in his lap. "It's funny. I find myself rewatching the films I hate more than the films I love. There's a lot to be learned from bad films. What doesn't work. What I don't want to do. That's influential too."

I considered that.

"I prefer to learn from artists I admire," I said. "I remember when the first *Opposites* movie came out. I walked out of the theatre and my heart was literally racing. I felt like I could fly."

Jack laughed. "Really?"

"I felt this need to move. I went back to my dorm room and danced like I hadn't...maybe, ever? I remember thinking these people, you and Geia, were really on to something."

I blushed at the memory, but Jack shook his head and gave me his lopsided grin again. "You see, that right there is my favourite thing about telling stories. It's a collaboration. Between us, the creators, and you, the viewer. We never imagined that kind of response. You, dancing in your dorm room. But it's beautiful, and it adds to the story the film is telling."

"I love that," I said.

We both fell silent. I could feel our time together slipping away. I knew I shouldn't even be looking at men right now—book two wasn't going to write itself—but being up in the air with Jack, in this liminal space, far from the regular flow of time and my responsibilities back on the ground, had its appeal.

"So, you have an event tonight?" he asked, scratching his beard below his cheek.

"A reading at Orchard House Books. You know it?"

He nodded.

"They've got Eliza Cohen to interview me."

"Wow. Awesome."

"You say awesome, I say terrifying. I've loved her forever. I'll probably lose my ability to speak as soon as she walks in."

"You won't," Jack said. "You'll be awesome too."

I imagined him reaching over to squeeze my hand, but he remained still, his own hands clasped in his lap.

As the plane began its descent into JFK, it was like a spell had been broken. The champagne was gone; we both had other places to be; we'd never see each other again. I looked out the window. The island city glinted in the afternoon sun, looming below us, shiny and uninviting.

Then we were on the ground, packing up, and Jack was checking his phone. I checked mine too. I had a text from Robert.

Can't wait for tonight! he wrote, which only made me more nervous. I knew he was just trying to be supportive, but I preferred to pretend these events weren't happening until minutes before they began.

I stuffed my magazine and laptop into my backpack and held it on my lap, feeling like a little kid. I watched Jack retrieve his bag from the overhead storage. He pointed at my suitcase, a question. I nodded and he pulled it down for me, tucking it in front of his seat. He looked at me and smiled, close-lipped. I smiled back.

I followed him off the plane, dragging my suitcase, but I soon began to fear I was following too close. I walked slower, keeping a few paces behind. I stared at his back. He had put his grey hoodie back on. It was smooth, free of wrinkles. Good quality. Expensive.

My heart was pounding. What was I supposed to do in this situation? I wasn't quite ready to let him go.

He turned around, looking sheepish. "Is this awkward or what?"

I nodded.

"Well, come on." He waved me forward. "I don't care if they take pictures."

Oh, god. I was giving him space because I assumed he was already elsewhere in his mind, onto bigger and better things, but of course: paparazzi, fans. People might see us and think we were together. They might take pictures.

I wondered who would see the photos. Old friends, family, the people I used to work with at the café. And what about Geia? Would Jack care if she saw him photographed with another woman? I imagined my own ex-boyfriends seeing the photos. Their confusion and questions.

As we navigated the airport, I noticed a few people pointing, but not as many as I expected. Jack was famous, but he wasn't as famous as Geia. He was the man *behind* the camera, the director, mostly known for being the father of Geia's children, her former husband. People knew him but they might not notice him if they weren't really looking.

I was sure if Geia were here, walking beside him, they'd recognize him immediately.

We approached the exit. Neither of us had checked luggage and I could feel our time together coming to an end. He's Jack Verity, Agnes. You got to talk to him for two hours. Leave the man alone.

But I couldn't help myself. I spotted a line of yellow cabs and my stomach did a somersault at the idea of us sharing one into the city. Then we could continue our conversation. Or maybe start a new one. Now that we were off the plane, now that we had walked together through crowds of people, had our connection become more substantial than the random collision of assigned seats?

"I'm this way," Jack said, before I could ask him to split a cab.

I looked up at him. He squinted one eye in the sunlight.

"It was great to meet you, Agnes. I can't wait to finish your book."

"I hope you hate the ending," I said. "Then maybe you'll reread it."

He laughed, his lips parting into a wide smile. "Good luck at your reading tonight." And then, just like that, he was walking towards the line of black cars in the distance. Private service.

"Miss? Miss?"

A taxi driver was shouting at me through an open window. "You need a ride?"

"Yes," I said, coughing. Behind me, a long line of yellow cabs idled, creating a haze of exhaust that made my throat burn.

4

The cab started and stopped, whizzing when the traffic let up and coming to impatient halts at every impasse on our way into the city. The driver tapped the brakes with a restless foot. I imagined Jack's driver knew a secret route, one that ensured he and other celebrities made it into Manhattan faster and more smoothly, a secret tunnel perhaps. I wondered if Jack liked the city. I had a theory that where you grew up imprinted on your very being, affecting how you would experience place forever. I could enjoy cities, but they would never feel like home because of where I was raised. Montreal was familiar now, after living there for so many years, but I'd never really get used to all the people and concrete. Jack was from London. He probably didn't even notice the noise and pollution of urban life anymore.

I closed my eyes as we came to another jerky stop, and took myself back to the woods — imagining the coolness of the tree cover, the fresh smell of pine needles. My earliest impulse to write was born in that forest. My first stories were about gnomes and fairies, who were only visible to children and who lived in homes made of moss and bark mere footsteps from my own back door.

I often wondered who lived in our old house now. My parents sold it after the divorce, but I never learned who had bought it ... a young family, or a retired couple maybe? It was a funny angled wooden thing, with lots of tall windows and a long, twisting driveway that kept it hidden from the road. Deer wandered across the property regularly, setting off the security lights; the occasional bear too. Though we lived in that house my whole childhood, neither of my parents seemed to like it much. My mother was always on assignment for her newspaper, and my father often complained about his commute — how much easier it would be if we lived closer to the small liberal arts college where he taught.

The cab took off again and my backpack slid onto the floor. I reached to set it upright, my stomach churning from the champagne. These days I felt so far away from those woods, and it made my chest ache. I had written about them in my novel, bringing them to life through words, giving them their own voice, but I still longed for the way they used to make me feel.

Did my mother ever venture into the forest? Maybe if she had, things would have been different. Maybe she would have loosened up a bit, taken a breath, paused for a minute. When I proudly showed her my earliest woodland stories — tales of a fairy named Isabel and her gnome friend Ansel — I remember the look of concern on her face. They made her worry about my soundness of mind, my future. This when I was still a child, little more than six or seven. I should have been able to exist in a dreamworld if I wanted to — most parents encouraged make-believe, didn't they? — but she made me feel like there was something wrong with me for writing stories like that. My wild imagination, she called it, shaking her head and rolling her eyes in my brother's direction. They often had a good laugh at my expense.

My mother was an exotic creature to me back then, always coming and going, leaving us with our father for days at a time when she was working on a new story. She was an investigative journalist, which translated loosely in my young mind to detective. I found this endlessly glamorous. I imagined she wore a trench coat and carried a flip-top notebook. I pictured her uncovering clichéd clues: fingerprints and drops of blood. In reality, she spent most of her time interviewing anyone who held the right information, searching for the truth about bad businesses and corrupt politicians, building her story. My mother was obsessed with injustice. She saw herself as a warrior against oppression, using words to save people who didn't have a voice of their own. Of course, at home, she was blind to the ways she herself could be oppressive, to me or to my father.

Unlike me, my brother, Max, could do no wrong in her eyes. He worked hard and got good grades and kept a steady eye on a career in computer science, an up-and-coming field at the time. My mother praised him for his discipline. Not only was Max always at the top of his class, he was also captain of the basketball team. He'd go on to get a big scholarship at a college my mother hand-picked for him.

I felt like I was made of different material than my family. My hair was sunny; theirs were different shades of dark. I was short; they were tall. I tanned easily in the summer; they stayed fair, burning if they weren't careful, my father in particular, with his freckles. Lots of lonely kids think they're adopted, but I knew my mother would have never chosen me if there had been other options. I was simply an aberration, a bad egg.

MY PUBLISHER HAD put me up in a boutique hotel in the Flatiron District. My room was small with high ceilings, a large window, and gorgeous wallpaper: lapis blue covered in sprawling green ferns. When I first took in the room I could swear the ferns were moving, the vibrant ends furling and unfurling with the faintest quiver. But on second look, it was just a trick of the eye.

I untangled myself from my backpack, stripped off my cardigan, and leaned on the windowsill. Below, Broadway was clogged with traffic. The cars moved slowly and though I couldn't actually hear their honking — the walls must have been soundproofed — I felt like I could. I'd seen enough movies to know what a busy New York street sounded like.

I checked my phone. It was just after two and I was starving. I ordered room service: fries to quell the effects of the champagne and a salad that sounded filling. While I waited for my lunch to arrive, I slipped off my shoes and lay down on the bed. The white linens were cool and soft to the touch. I reached for my phone again and looked up Jack on Instagram. I wasn't following him. I guess I hadn't thought much about Jack Verity for a few years. My interest in *The Opposites* was pre-Instagram.

I scrolled through Jack's account. His last post was from a week ago and the one before that almost a month prior. I scrolled some more. None of Jack's photos were of him. There were a few photos of his twin daughters, tastefully taken so you could only see them from behind or the side, never face on. The rest of the photos were either stills from other people's films or photos of unrecognizable people in what he called the "edit room." Large computer monitors, dark lighting. I realized I hadn't even asked what he was working on. Our conversation had been entirely about my work.

Next, I looked up Geia. I wasn't following her either. I distinctly remembered doing so at some point, but I wasn't into the whole wellness thing and I'd grown tired of the guilt her posts made me feel. No one could ever look or feel or be as good as Geia Stone. Some people found that motivating. I found it depressing.

Geia didn't post every day either, but she added to her feed more often than Jack. In the last little while she had shared photos of her dance-cardio workout, of her niçoise salad — a recipe from her first cookbook — of her Five Favourite Goddess™ Skincare Products for Summer, and — my heart skipped a beat — of Jack.

There he was, sitting at a big harvest table, wearing the same grey hoodie he'd worn on the plane and grinning like crazy, with his chin cradled in one hand. In front of him sat a big plate of pancakes.

Brunch with baby daddy, the caption read.

I wondered if brunch together was a common occurrence. I wasn't friends with any of my exes. Kids made it different of course, but Jack and Geia's ability to morph their connection from romantic to platonic seemed superhuman. I zoomed in on Jack's face. He wore the same grin, a bit lopsided, just like on the plane.

I scrolled further down. There was a photo of Geia standing naked outside in a garden, her breasts covered by an arm, one leg propped up. She looked incredible. But who had taken the photo? Jack?

I googled them. Jack and Geia. Their relationship. I read all the sordid details, many of which I had come across before, but now I paid them new attention. There was actually an article that tracked the timeline of their relationship: meeting for the first time, getting together, getting married, creating *The Opposites*, having children, breaking up. Who got paid to write this stuff? It was total fluff.

I didn't learn much in my search that I didn't already know, but I got to see lots of photos of them together. They had met seventeen years ago, when Jack was twenty-three and Geia twenty-eight. In the early photos, they looked slim and fresh-faced, jeans slung low, holding hands as they walked the streets of London, New York, Paris. Neither of them had aged much since, but Jack's face and body had filled out and his beard had a touch of grey. I preferred forty-year-old Jack. He looked more solid, less wide-eyed and impressionable.

Geia looked exactly the same at forty-five as she did when she was twenty-eight. I was only looking at photos online — maybe she looked different in person — but she seemed nearly ageless. These weren't airbrushed photos either. I scrolled through dozens of paparazzi shots, meant to catch celebs when they were looking their worst; no wonder women clamoured for her beauty and skincare products. They wanted what she had. Dewy, plump skin that seemed like it was lit from the inside.

I watched an interview on YouTube that Geia and Jack had given shortly after *The Opposites* first came out. I had seen this interview before — years ago — but I watched it now with new eyes. While Geia spoke, Jack gazed at her. He looked completely smitten, borderline hypnotized.

There was a knock at the door: my food. I ate at the little table by the window, leaving my phone on the bed. The fries were crisp and salty and just what I needed. I doubted Geia Stone ever allowed herself to eat food like this, fatty and indulgent. The thought made me smile, and I devoured the plate quicker, dunking each fry in silky aioli spiked with Dijon mustard. My salad sat untouched.

5

After lunch, I wandered outside in search of something to wear to that night's event. It had been cold and rainy when I left Montreal at the start of the tour, so I'd packed with that in mind. But late May had brought with it a fierce heat wave. I had done the best I could with the clothes I had in my suitcase, but the heat promised to continue through the week. I needed to find a good outfit for my reading, and maybe a few others for lunches and meetings with my agent and publishing team.

I didn't know Manhattan well, but I figured if I headed south and west, I'd hit the West Village. There'd be plenty of boutique shops there.

I grew sweaty immediately. It was desperately humid, and despite all the tall buildings, it was hard to find shade. It felt good to walk though. I put on my sunglasses and tried to embrace the day, though the crowds and noise made my skin crawl.

Ahead, I spotted the Flatiron Building and stopped to take a photo. There were tables and chairs set up in a pedestrian plaza out front, a wedge of space bordered by the building's adjoining streets. I sat down briefly to post the photo on Instagram. Robert was always telling me I needed to produce more content for my "socials." This would make him happy.

I was only thirty but Robert, at twenty-three, made me feel ancient. When we first met, he seemed desperately hip: constantly on his phone, wearing intensely tailored suits, always talking about people and restaurants and gossip I knew nothing about. I remember thinking my publisher was dumping me on a rookie by assigning my book to a recent college grad. But Robert knew exactly what he was doing. He had a real knack for packaging people and books in such a way that made the world want to unwrap them.

Sitting in front of the Flatiron, I hesitated. I never had any idea what to write for a photo caption. Why was this so hard? I was supposed to be a writer.

I settled on three emojis: an apple, a city building, and a blonde girl waving. I posted it and the likes immediately started flooding in. Because of all the recent press about my book, I now had tens of thousands of followers.

Right away, I received a notification that someone wanted to send me a direct message. I almost dropped my phone when I saw it was Jack.

Look to your right, he wrote. *Best pistachio gelato in the city.*

I turned and spotted Eataly on the northwest corner, a huge Italian marketplace that took up a whole city block. I grinned. Then I got a notification that Jack was now following me. I followed him back and replied to his message.

Isn't pistachio an old man flavour?

I waited for his response but the app told me he was no longer active. I crossed the street, clutching my phone in case he wrote back.

Eataly was bustling, people navigating the aisles stocked with cheese and bread and various Italian delicacies. Biscotti, panettone. Thankfully, the gelato counter was close to the entrance. I waited in line, watching the chaos, and ordered the pistachio. Jack was right. It tasted like heaven.

I continued to walk, passing the Flatiron and then a park. The park's tall oak trees stood motionless in the non-existent breeze, stretching for the heavens but easily outdone by all the towering buildings nearby. At the playground, I watched a child slip down a metal slide, another soar into the air on a swing.

I sat down on one of the benches to eat my ice cream. City parks weren't nature per se, but they were something, and I felt myself relax a little, looking up at the leafy tree cover, cooled by the speckled shade. Nearby, one grey squirrel chased another, looping up and around the trunk of a tree. As they descended back down, the pursuing squirrel paused to look in my direction, letting the other escape. The small creature raised its bushy tail, gazing at me for several moments, as if trying to understand my presence — *she doesn't belong here*, I imagined it thinking — and then continued on its way.

THE WEST VILLAGE was quieter. The streets were narrow and the buildings weren't as tall. There was a quaintness about it, a charm. If I ever moved to New York, I imagined I would live here amongst the bistros and trees. Maybe I could get some writing done here.

I wandered into a store with a promising dress hanging in the window: breezy, sleeveless, periwinkle blue. Inside, the shop was cool from the air conditioning and they were playing a folksy indie record I vaguely recognized.

"Can I try on that dress in the window?" I asked the woman behind the counter, a tall redhead with purple eyeliner and a protruding collarbone. "The blue one."

Briefly, she glanced up at me from her laptop. She nodded, unsmiling, and promptly looked back down at the screen.

I found the dress on a rack myself and picked out a few more, not sure what I was really looking for. In the past, I'd never had much money to spend on clothes, and now, even with plenty of money to play with, I still felt like I didn't know what I was doing. Women who worked in boutiques always seemed so cool, so put together, like they held some innate knowledge of style and poise I would never gain access to, like the woman in the airport who'd bought my book. I sifted through the racks, selecting colourful pieces without looking at the price tags. I imagined the tall redhead had written me off as a tourist immediately. A tourist with old sneakers and no style. Not that she'd be wrong.

The dressing room was small and cramped, with a floor-to-ceiling mirror. I peeled off my jeans and sweaty T-shirt, thankful for the momentary freedom of being naked in a cool space. My feet smelled from the day of travel, and I decided I should probably find a pair of flats or sandals for tonight too.

I tried on the dresses, one after the other. They all seemed the same to me: equally appealing but also probably ugly. I couldn't tell. I assumed there was something wrong with each dress that I just wasn't seeing. Shopping had never been a part of my childhood because my mother didn't have the time or interest to take me, so I never really learned what looked good on me. She herself dressed mostly in black and grey. I remember a lot of slacks and turtlenecks, modest leather loafers: her uniform. I had my own uniform now of jeans and T-shirts, the occasional button-up tucked under a sweater.

In the mirror, I looked at myself in the periwinkle dress that first drew me into the store. It looked fine. Maybe a bit boring? Maybe the colour wasn't right?

I settled on a short coral-coloured shift dress for that night, though I wondered vaguely if it was authorial enough. I thought of my tourmate, the blowhard writer with the blazer, how he always looked the part. But I looked like I was playing dress-up when I wore a blazer.

I checked the price tag. The dress was more expensive than any clothing item I'd ever bought. I took a deep breath. You have the money, Agnes, I reminded myself.

I bought the coral dress. I also purchased a few other dresses in similar shapes but different colours, including a pale-blue linen one that wouldn't be good for an event, but which I really liked, more than any of the others. When I

41

approached the counter, arms laden with items, I remembered the issue of shoes.

"What about footwear?" I asked, turning my head to look around the store.

The redhead blinked. "Yes, we have footwear."

"No, I mean I need a pair of shoes, something nice to go with these dresses."

"All of them?" she asked, brow furrowed.

Did she think I was being cheap or unstylish? I swore she was wrinkling her nose. She could probably smell my feet.

"I'm travelling, so I don't have a lot of luggage room." I mimed the size of my small suitcase with my hands, trying to explain away whatever she was currently thinking about me, but her expression remained unchanged. "I'll just be a minute." I laid the dresses on the counter and dashed to the table of shoes in the middle of the room. I grabbed the first sandal that looked neutral enough to go with everything. A tan, flat, strappy thing.

"This, in a seven."

I didn't even bother to try them on.

BACK AT THE HOTEL, I sat on the edge of the bathtub in a fluffy white robe that was far too big for me. I cuffed the sleeves twice, and still they reached down past my wrists. Unlike the rest of my towering family, I was short and easy to overlook. People often bumped into me, and it took forever to get a bartender's attention. As a child, I was often running to catch up.

I had taken a shower as soon as I got through the door.

I wrung out my wet hair and then opened up my earlier message from Jack. Still no response to my attempt at a tease: "old-man ice cream." He couldn't possibly be insulted, could he? He was only ten years older than me. Maybe it just wasn't a funny thing to say.

According to the app, he hadn't "seen" the message yet, but I often read messages as they appeared in notifications and kept the app closed. This was a privacy thing. I received a lot of messages from people who had read my book, and only replied to some of them. People loved to tell me everything they liked and didn't like about it. Maybe Jack put *me* in the same category: a random fan. But no, he had messaged me first. We had talked the whole flight. He was reading my novel.

I didn't have a lot of time before the event. I dried my hair, strands flying in all directions, and thought about what I would say to Eliza Cohen when I met her at the reading. Eliza had risen to fame in the sixties writing political fiction. She was often referred to as the voice of her generation. I still had no idea why they had paired her with me for this event.

I unearthed a reading copy of my book from my suitcase. Even if the sight of it still made me feel a bit dizzy, it was the most tangible thing about this journey so far. The weight of its pages and a cover with my name on it. Everything I had read online about publishing your first book told me I should expect to hate my cover design, but I didn't. At first, I was underwhelmed by it, but I'd grown to really love it. The image was a bird's-eye view of a forest with *Violets in Her Lap* and my name, Agnes Oliver, in bold white letters, tucked between treetops in varied shades of green. A single red bird, a cardinal, soared out from the branches.

At events like the one tonight, I would usually read from the first few pages, because they set the scene for the book and I didn't have to provide any explanation of what was happening. The pages explained themselves. But tonight, I wanted to try something different. I decided to read a passage from the middle of the book. Time to pull out the big guns, Agnes.

I took a sip of water and read the section through three times, standing in front of the window, the city alight below me. The third time sounded pretty good. I underlined a few words so I remembered what to emphasize. Did other writers do this? I had no idea.

A text came in from my agent, Zelda: *New review on LitHub!*

She sent the link but I closed out the message without opening it. I wasn't reading any more reviews. When *Violets in Her Lap* first came out, I couldn't help myself. Other authors had warned me against it, but Zelda would bring them to my attention, and I was so desperate for validation back then that I devoured them. They were mostly positive, but I had a way of reading between the lines, picking up on subtle dissatisfactions or hesitancies on the part of the reviewers. If they said the book was a "page-turner," I worried they meant it lacked substance. If they said the book was "ambitious," I assumed they meant I didn't succeed in doing all I had set out to do. There was always something negative lurking below the surface, and soon reading my reviews felt like I was watching my mother read my report cards as a child, taking issue with the smallest things. And that was just the positive reviews. The first really negative review made me want to stay in bed forever. It confirmed everything I had feared about my book, all the ways I imagined it was lacking.

I was in a hotel in Boston at the time, the city where my mother lives, and I immediately wondered if she had read the review too, a one-star critique. It was published in a newspaper—not the one where she worked, thankfully—so it was possible. I imagined her nodding along in agreement with the reviewer's scathing assessment, even though she herself hadn't read the book. Or had she? We didn't talk anymore so I had no way of knowing.

The thought of her seeing the review had made me burrow deeper under the covers. The hotel room grew dark as the day faded and I had only pulled myself away from my nest of blankets when it was time to head to the bookstore for my reading.

I was shaky when reading that night. At one point, I looked up and thought I saw my mother at the back of the room. But it was just another tall woman with dark hair, and when I finished, she smiled and clapped along with everyone else.

6

I should have tried on the sandals. By the time I reached the hotel lobby, they were already pinching my heels. I'd have blisters on both feet by the end of the night. I emerged onto the sidewalk and wondered if my worn backpack lessened the effect of the coral dress. I should have remembered to buy a better bag today; even a tote of some kind would have worked. Maybe the backpack would seem writerly, like I couldn't be away from my writing tools for too long—my notebooks, my pencils, my non-existent book two—not even for an evening. Or maybe, probably, no one noticed stuff like that. Enough, Agnes.

I hopped in the first cab I saw. The driver wasn't talkative and I was grateful. I needed to focus, to get in the zone. My stomach was a writhing ball of nerves that flipped like snakes, constantly slithering over and under each other. Great. Now I couldn't get that image out of my head. I felt even more ill. I opened the window and rested both hands on my stomach. I was always nervous before a reading, but tonight — a New York event with my publishing team in the audience — was a whole new level of pressure. I took a deep breath.

The city was quieter at this time of night. The heat had finally broken and shade now crept between the buildings, making the streets feel cool and serene. My cab passed by Eataly and the Flatiron Building. I thought of Jack but resisted the urge to check my phone. I took more deep breaths.

After a few minutes, the cab pulled up in front of Orchard House Books. It had a large display window and a red front door, which was propped open. I could see copies of *Violets in Her Lap* in the window, along with my photo and a sign announcing I'd be reading there tonight. The snakes writhed faster in response.

I paid the cabbie and stood in front of the window. My sandals were already killing me. I checked my phone. I was early. Too early.

"Agnes!"

I turned and saw Zelda waving at me from down the sidewalk, increasing the pace of her stomping. She always wore chunky Fly London heels. At her agency you could hear her coming down the hallway, loud and unapologetic. Tonight, she also wore various pieces of oversized clothing: huge round sunglasses; wide-legged black trousers; a weightless white shirt that fell elegantly from her body.

Zelda pulled me into a hug. "Tonight's going to be fantastic!" she said, knowing that I needed to hear it. "You read the *LitHub* review?"

I shook my head.

"Well, it's another rave! People are so excited about this book, Agnes. It's incredible. You should be so proud of yourself."

I smiled and nodded, an urge to cry swelling inside me. It was hard to have someone be so nice.

"Let's go inside. We can't have the author standing on the sidewalk when people arrive."

Zelda ushered me into the bookstore, which was charming and narrow and packed to the gills with books. At the back was a small space for readings: a stage and seats for thirty or so people. When we were planning promotions for the book, I had insisted the readings should all happen at small, independent bookstores. Robert wasn't thrilled by the idea—he'd wanted to hold the launch in the Brooklyn Botanic Garden, surrounded by nature, with an audience of two hundred—but he eventually gave in.

"We'll do an event like that later," he had said, winking at his intern, "when you're feeling more comfortable with the public-facing aspects of your career."

Zelda introduced me to Clinton, the owner of Orchard House. My first thought was that he looked like a 1970s serial killer: thin blond hair that was sparse on top and big, empty eyes accentuated by aviator glasses. Without smiling, he told me he had finished my book last night and was eager to hear me speak.

"Are you expecting many people?" I asked, attempting to sound casual.

"We get a good crowd for events like this. We're a very literary neighbourhood. People like to come out and show their support for writers."

That was reassuring, though another part of me hoped no one would show up and I could just go back to the hotel early.

Clinton showed us to a small room at the back of the store, which appeared to be his office. It wasn't glamorous. There was a desk with a computer against one wall and a sagging brown couch opposite. Clinton told us to help ourselves to water — there were half a dozen bottles on his desk — and that he'd bring Eliza in when she arrived. The way he said it, I got the sense he already knew Eliza Cohen. Maybe she had launched books here too. I sat down on the couch. Eyeing the old, brown cushions, Zelda said she preferred to stand.

Zelda retrieved her phone from her purse and started scrolling. "Clinton's a funny one. He's slept with practically every man and woman in New York publishing, and still everyone continues to love him. And no one expects him to call because he has a way of making you feel like one night with him is enough."

I raised my eyebrows.

"Apparently," she said with a shrug, and we both laughed.

Zelda continued to amaze me; she seemed endlessly confident. When I signed with her, I immediately knew I was in good hands. She was exactly what I needed, someone to act as my guide, to steer me in the right direction.

Zelda put her phone in the pocket of her pants, opened a bottle of water, and took a sip. She put the bottle on Clinton's desk. "You feeling okay about tonight?"

"Sure. I mean, I'm nervous to meet Eliza. She's a legend. But I'm grateful for the opportunity."

"You don't have to do that, you know."

"What?"

"You don't have to act so grateful all the time. You're the reason all of this is happening. You and your book. You deserve it."

I smiled faintly. "Have you met her before?"

Zelda leaned against the desk and then, re-thinking that decision — the surface looked sticky — stood up straight and crossed her arms. "Twice. Though I doubt she remembers me. She's kind. You'll be okay."

She returned to her phone, scrolling more intently this time. I realized we didn't actually have a lot to say to each other right now, with book one done and book two nowhere to be seen. Our conversation flowed better when we had a project to work on, a problem to solve. At least she wasn't asking about book two. Yet.

"Do you know who Jack Verity is?" I asked.

Zelda looked up immediately. "Of course."

"I sat next to him on my flight today."

"Seriously?" She looked impressed. "What was he like?"

"He was . . . nice. We talked, like, the whole two hours."

"I love his films."

"Me too. And he was reading my book."

"Really?"

"He heard about it somewhere. Picked up a copy."

"Fantastic," Zelda said brightly. "Maybe he's considering turning it into a film."

For a moment, the snakes halted their frantic dance; that possibility hadn't even occurred to me, though it made more sense than Jack simply enjoying my company.

"He didn't say anything to suggest that he was, but yeah, maybe. How cool would that be?" I hid my disappointment. That would be a good thing, Agnes. No, a great thing.

There was a knock at the door and Clinton entered, followed by Robert, Jessica, my editor, and . . . Eliza Cohen.

"Agnes Oliver," Clinton said, maintaining his monotone from earlier, "this is Eliza Cohen, your interviewer for the evening."

I stood up and reached out my hand. Eliza's was cold to the touch. She was incredibly thin, birdlike, and even shorter than me. She must have been close to eighty — her iconic bob, complete with severe bangs, was pure white — but her green eyes had a spark about them. She clearly wasn't slowing down any time soon. She had put out two books in the last sixteen months, both of them bestsellers.

"It's wonderful to meet you, Agnes," Eliza said in a croaky voice. "I enjoyed your book immensely."

"Thank you." I surprised myself with the steadiness of my own voice. "Your work means so much to me. Tonight feels very special."

Eliza smiled and nodded politely. Then, she opened a water bottle and took a big gulp before sitting down on the couch. We were all watching her and she knew it, but she handled it gracefully.

"I like to read before public speaking to calm my nerves," she said, unearthing a Kindle from her purse. "Please feel free to go on talking. I don't need quiet to concentrate."

She started reading. Zelda, Robert, Jessica, Clinton, and I all looked at each other. What was there to say?

Robert cleared his throat. "Looks like a good line forming outside, Clinton. When do you let them in?"

Clinton looked at his watch. "Now seems as good a time as any."

He disappeared. I exchanged looks with my team. It was impossible to talk freely with this literary legend sitting a few feet away. I was desperate to know what she was reading. I couldn't believe she used a Kindle.

Robert was wearing a khaki-green linen suit, wrinkled in a stylish way. I was glad he was here. Throughout this whole process of promotion and publicity he had been endlessly patient and enthusiastic.

Jessica, however, still intimidated me. Even after working together on the book for over eight months, our interactions had never transitioned from professional to friendly. She was in her early fifties, a well-known figure in publishing who had edited countless books much more important than mine. Tonight, she wore a short, tailored black dress and stilettos, her salt-and-pepper hair long and wavy down her back. Zelda and I secretly called her Eagle Eye because she had been relentless at nitpicking the tiniest discrepancies in my manuscript. She had offered little praise throughout the editorial process; her comments were almost always critical. Which of course did wonders for my self-esteem. But I knew I was lucky to have her. *Violets in Her Lap* was a million times better because of her edits.

"Agnes was just telling me about a very interesting seat companion on her flight in today," Zelda said.

Robert looked up from his phone and Jessica raised her

eyebrows, mildly curious. Zelda looked at me; she wanted me to say his name.

"Jack Verity."

Jessica's brow rose a notch higher.

"Geia Stone's ex?" Robert asked, jaw dropping. "The director?"

Zelda and I both nodded.

"Apparently," Zelda said, crossing her arms, "he's reading her book and loving it."

Robert's jaw dropped even further. "Agnes's book?"

Zelda nodded deeply.

"Are you thinking what I'm thinking?" he asked.

Again, Zelda nodded.

Robert turned to me and squeezed my forearm. His eyes looked gigantic. "This could be huge, Agnes! I wondered about selling film rights because your book is so ... unusual. Who's going to want to make a film full of non-human characters? But yeah, Jack Verity would."

Even Jessica offered a small smile, tilting her head as if to say: Yes, that could work.

"He didn't say anything about turning my book into a film." I needed to make sure this was understood. Robert had a way of running away with half-formed hunches. I didn't want him starting any rumours.

Clinton poked his head back into the office. "Five minutes until showtime, folks."

I glanced over at Eliza, still not really believing she was sitting right there. She continued to read intently, her head bent over her Kindle. I could see the bones of her shoulders poking through her pink button-up.

"Who's doing the introduction?" I asked Robert, who was typing madly on his phone.

Without stopping, he explained that Clinton would introduce Eliza and then Eliza would introduce me. Again, I glanced over at her. What could this icon possibly have to say about me?

"Okay," Robert said, slipping his phone into the pocket of his pants. "I just texted a friend of a friend who works with someone in Jack's circle."

"What?" I asked, my insides shifting.

Robert put his palms up, claiming innocence. "I just asked if she knows what Jack's working on these days. Nothing specifically about you."

"I think Agnes has a crush on our director," Zelda said with a smirk.

"I don't," I lied, feeling my cheeks flush. "I literally just met him. I just don't want him to think I'm some opportunist or something."

"You need to be a little *more* opportunistic, if you ask me," Robert said.

Clinton appeared in the doorway. "Eliza, Agnes, we're ready for you."

I nodded to indicate I understood, but the ground suddenly felt unstable. I hadn't even had time to look over the passage I was going to read. Eliza stood up, stashing away her Kindle, and walked towards the door. My palms flooded with sweat. Robert and Zelda were both staring at me. I must have looked as bad as I felt.

"Hold it together, kid," Robert said.

"I'm okay." I heard the *whoosh* of blood rushing in my

ears. What if I got out there and fainted? Or peed my pants? Or found myself unable to speak? What if I forgot how to read? What if I couldn't answer Eliza's questions?

I glanced at Jessica. I knew she'd think I was being ridiculous. But she nodded in my direction.

"You got this," she said calmly.

"Come on." Robert gestured for me to follow. He and Zelda had already moved towards the doorway. "You first."

I swallowed and stepped forward. I didn't have any other choice.

7

Eliza's introduction was beyond generous. She called me a "wonder" with "singular talent" and a "voice that is quiet but defiantly inventive." She said she couldn't wait to read what I wrote next. That last line made me feel weak.

My reading went okay. I stood at the podium, clutching my book like it might save me, and hoped no one could see my hands shaking. I hadn't put enough thought into how to best set up the passage from the middle of the book, so I was a bit meandering at first. But once I began to read, I loosened up. The words took hold of me like they did when I was writing, and I was just a means through which the story could flow. The book had nothing to do with me, nothing to do with any one person. Apparently, that's why people liked it so much.

When I finished reading, the crowd erupted with applause. I finally took a real look at the people assembled in the room. Every chair was occupied and there were even people standing at the back. I shook my head, smiling, and sat down next to Eliza.

She was nodding thoughtfully. The applause stopped and she looked over at me.

"Agnes," she said. "How are you doing?"

I laughed nervously. "I'm okay. I'm good."

"Are you though?" She looked out at the audience. "People don't realize this but most writers hate public speaking. We get nervous, like anyone else, maybe more than anyone else. Writers are indoor cats. We prefer the company of our books."

I chuckled along with the crowd, but I could feel a flush bursting in my cheeks. Did I seem so nervous that she had to explain it to these people?

"But we like our readers, don't we, Agnes?" She turned back to me. "That's what makes being up here worth all the pain, right?"

I nodded. I realized, though it was terribly intimidating, it was good they had paired me with a seasoned pro for tonight. Eliza knew what she was doing. She was putting everyone at ease right from the start, including me.

"So," she said, when the laughter had died. "Let's start with the title. *Violets in Her Lap*. It's unexpected in today's literary landscape. It's almost whimsical. Where does it come from?"

I'd been asked about the title before, but no one had put it quite that way. She said "whimsical" like it was a good thing, which I appreciated.

"It comes from Sappho, the Greek lyric poet," I said between two quick sips of water. I remembered how my father, the Classics professor, used to read me her poetry before bed. "I found the phrase in a translation of her fragments and it just stuck with me. Sappho used it to describe a bride with 'violets in her lap,' like she was holding flowers, a bouquet, but it seemed to me it was appropriate for a book about the natural world. To evoke all that lives and grows in the lap of Mother Earth."

Eliza smiled. "I love that." She paused, as if thinking. "Now, changing gears slightly. I wonder if you could talk a bit about the birch trees in the book. They were my favourite of the trees you depicted. Tell me how you found their voice."

I took another sip of water while I tried to think of the right answer. With questions like these, there was always the honest answer and then the answer I thought the interviewer and audience wanted to hear. But based on how Eliza was watching me with those keen green eyes, I knew she would see through any attempt at subterfuge.

"There's something really special about birch trees," I said cautiously, trying to see how my words were landing. "They're beautiful of course, tall and elegant, almost silver in colour. But," I paused, "their beauty seems to me to be a product of their tendency towards reinvention."

Eliza's face lit up with a rare grin. "Reinvention. What do you mean by that?"

I looked briefly at my lap. "They're one of the few trees that shed their own skin," I said, still cautious. I had thought about this a lot but never expressed it out loud. "A bit like a snake. The bark peels off in these delicate, beautiful pieces. Like paper shavings. There's a practical reason for this.

Birch trees photosynthesize through their bark and that process of peeling allows more sunlight to get in. But I've also always thought about that process as a form of refinement. A way of trying to get to an essential core. Shedding dead weight, being born anew. I think that's so beautiful."

Eliza nodded. "It is beautiful, definitely, but I'm more intrigued by how you think about these things. Birch trees, animals. You seem to understand the natural world in a way few of us do. Where does that come from?"

I gazed at her. She was sounding like Jack, but I wasn't willing to go there in front of an audience like I had with him on the plane. No childhood talk; nothing too personal. That was my number-one rule for interviews.

"I'm not sure that's true."

"But it is!" Eliza said emphatically. "When I finished this book I thought to myself, this woman sees a different world than I do."

I swallowed. "I don't know." I searched for the words to respond. I thought of my mother, her disapproval of my more fantastical side. "I've certainly always had a wild imagination."

The crowd laughed.

"But it's more than that, isn't it?" Eliza pressed. "It seems to me that you're attuned to the world in an unusual way, almost like you have a special sensitivity. For example," Eliza continued, "you write from the perspective of a mole, but instead of focusing on his lack of sight, you focus on all he feels and understands that we humans have never considered. You empower these creatures. That makes me think you're privy to something the rest of us aren't."

"Maybe," I said uncertainly. I had promised myself a long time ago I would never tell anyone what I had experienced in the woods as a child. The glittering dust. They would think there was something wrong with me. "I think I see myself reflected in the natural world, so there's a kinship there. To me, nature seems very misunderstood."

"And you feel similar?"

"I do." I nodded. "I always have. And what's strange about feeling misunderstood is that it often makes you try harder to understand others. Maybe if I get them, they'll get me."

"Interesting."

"I don't think the natural world is indifferent to us, like some people say," I continued, glancing at the crowd and then back at Eliza. Maybe I could go there without fully explaining. "I think, when I walk through a forest, nature is actively trying to figure me out. It's responding to my scent, the sound of my footsteps, my presence. Just like I'm trying to figure *it* out, and other people out, every day. I'm responding to cues. I'm paying attention. I'm adapting in response, much like a tree branch that winds its way around a power line to reach the sun. The natural world and I have that in common."

"So, you're saying you believe the natural world is aware of us?"

I swallowed. Would it sound too weird to say yes? That's how I'd always understood the dust. It was a form of communication. A way for the trees in the forest to talk to each other and to me. A way to deter pests, or warn other trees of an encroaching fungus, or even to calm down an upset little girl.

"I do," I said, after a moment. "But only insofar as the natural world is aware of everything that constitutes itself. I guess I count myself a part of it."

Eliza grinned. "I love that answer."

The audience clapped loudly and I reached for my water. I couldn't help but smile.

AFTER ELIZA FINISHED her part of the interview, she opened the Q&A to the audience.

The first person had a question for Eliza, not me. I was grateful—I needed a break from speaking—but also a little hurt. This was my book. My event. Funny how I could want something and not want it at the same time. I was experiencing a lot of that lately.

Eliza, as I said, was a pro. She found a way to turn the question around and shoot it back in my direction.

"What do you think, Agnes?" she asked, and I sat up straighter as I responded, fumbling for an answer.

The second person asked me what I was working on next.

"I wish I could say I was already writing my next novel, but promoting this book is pretty much a full-time job right now," I said, avoiding the gaze of Zelda, Robert, and Jessica standing at the back. "I'm hoping to start writing again soon though."

The person nodded, though they looked disappointed.

"One more question," Eliza said. She pointed. "You, at the back."

I didn't hear the woman's question and had to ask her to repeat it. I was distracted by the person who was standing next to her. I spotted the grey hoodie first, then the lopsided smile. My face turned warm as Jack Verity grinned at me from the back of the room.

I SIGNED A LOT of books, unsure what to write for people beyond my signature. Robert had taught me to ask readers, "Would you like me to personalize it?" and then they could provide direction. Usually, they just told me to include their name. But then it was their name plus my name and that looked silly. It was all a bit awkward. Most people didn't know what to say to me when they came up to get their book signed. They didn't know me, aside from the interview they had just heard or maybe some review they had read. Many hadn't even read my book yet.

One woman said she liked my dress. Another asked me what I was reading right now. That was about as big as the small talk got.

Jack stood in line with everyone else. Because he'd been watching from the back of the room, he joined at the very end of the line. I kept looking up discreetly, watching him get closer. No one directly around him seemed to recognize him; they were all looking forward, at me. I wondered how that made him feel. Turn around! I kept thinking. A great filmmaker with a signature much more valuable than mine is standing just a few feet away from you!

At one point, Clinton approached Jack and they shook hands. I couldn't hear what they were saying but I suspected Clinton was expressing his admiration for Jack's work.

By the time it was Jack's turn, the room had pretty much emptied out. Robert hung around chatting with Clinton, but both Jessica and Zelda had left. Eliza had gone too, after shaking my hand and wishing me luck at the end of the interview. I had thanked her and now wished I'd had my wits about me to say more. That might have been the only time in my life I got the chance to speak one-on-one with Eliza Cohen.

"My hand hurts," I said, as Jack approached.

He laughed and I felt a bit weak. I couldn't get over his face. It seemed nearly perfect. I hadn't known what a perfect face looked like until now.

"Does that mean I get a second-string signature?"

"It might mean you get the real thing."

I reached for his book. I signed my name and considered writing my number inside, but decided that was stupid. Zelda was right; he was probably after film rights. I could see him wanting to get to know a writer before adapting her work. What had Geia said in that *New Yorker* piece? "Creating art with someone requires intimacy."

"What are you doing after this?" Jack asked quietly as I passed back his book.

"No plans."

"Fancy a drink?" he asked with a little shrug.

I nodded, lightheaded again. Who cared if he wanted my story and not me? He was Jack fucking Verity. I would take what I could get.

8

Jack fucking Verity took me to a bar "a few blocks away," which felt like twenty thanks to the tight straps of my expensive new sandals. I tried my best to hide my hobble, but with every step, my heels rebelled against their new prison.

We were silent for the first block, sneaking quick side glances at each other. When we both looked over at the same time, we laughed.

"It's been a while since I've hung out with anyone," he said. "I mean, not for work."

I wondered if he meant it had been a while since he had hung out with another *woman*. From what I'd read online, apparently he was single.

"I'm glad you came tonight," I said. And then, watching to see how he would react, "I didn't think I would ever see you again."

"Even after our chance meeting on the plane? I feel like the universe has thrown us together for some reason."

My heart skipped. Did he mean romantically or creatively? Or both? Was it my story he wanted, or me? I realized I wouldn't be upset if it was both. I imagined us holed up in a secluded cabin somewhere in the forest. Writing a screenplay, taking off our clothes.

I tried to sound nonchalant. "What would be the reason to throw us together?"

He looked at me and smiled. "I guess we'll have to find out."

We rounded a corner and I saw a sign for a bar up ahead. Hopefully that was our destination. If not, I was going to have to take off these sandals. Barefoot on a New York City sidewalk would be better than monster blisters tomorrow. Jack headed towards the bar, thank god, and told me he thought I had done great tonight.

"You're a good reader," he said. "I like your style."

"Really?"

He turned to look me in the eye. "I go to a lot of readings. They can often feel contrived, like, performances? Practiced, you know, over-rehearsed. But you weren't performing tonight. You were actually reading the words on the page. You even seemed surprised by the text at certain moments, like you were open to its, I don't know, wonder?"

Jack pushed open the door to the bar. It was dark, moody, and I was immediately hit by the smell of beer and sweat. A large bar ran along one side of the room and a pool table stood opposite. Booths lined the windows, full of punky-looking people who didn't glance up when we walked in.

Jack led me to the bar, where we sat on stools. The bartender nodded at Jack, who asked me what I wanted.

"Beer's fine."

Jack ordered two of what he had "last time."

Silently, the bartender poured us each a pint. I took a big gulp. I needed this after the reading and the painful walk. I slipped the straps of my sandals off the backs of my heels, freeing my feet.

"So, you've been here before?" I gestured at the room with my beer.

"My place is nearby."

"I like this neighbourhood," I said, though I wasn't really sure where we were. I tried to imagine what his place might look like. An airy loft? An impressive brownstone? Did he share it with Geia? "You mentioned you have a place in the Hamptons too?"

"Kind of. It's Geia's house, but I have my own space there. Same with our place in L.A. 'Jack's quarters,' we call it. My own little wing of the property. But my flat here in the city is mine alone." He took a gulp of his beer and went on. "It's actually the first apartment I rented when I moved here for film school. It was a total shithole back then. Me and my two roommates, all of us eighteen and on scholarships. We had no money, but it was amazing living there, all together. Some of the best times of my life. All we did was work — a new film project every few months." He caught my eye briefly, as if to see if I was interested in hearing all of this, and when I smiled, he continued. "We were figuring out who we were as artists and helping each other along the way. One of us would write a script, another would produce, rounding up actors and scouting locations, and the third would direct. Next project, we'd switch roles. I miss those days. That's why I bought the place. To hold onto my glory days, I guess. Sounds stupid, but it's true. Life was so slapdash back then. We created a lot of crap. But I've never felt more alive or more creative. I was never more confident that this was what I was supposed to be doing."

"And now you get to do that for a living. Make films, I mean."

He frowned, watching the bartender change a keg. "Kind of. It's not the same as it was back then though. That's the thing about filmmaking: as soon as you're successful, you lose your freedom. The studios you wanted so desperately to back your projects finally do, but they want input, to intervene, to change things. Back then, living in that flat with my mates, I felt like I could make anything I wanted. Now...my options are limited. It's frustrating, you know? There are a lot of stories I want to tell, but before I even start outlining, I have these voices in my head saying, 'That's too expensive, that's uncommercial, that's impossible.' Practicality is the death of creativity."

"That's a great line. You should put that in a film."

He smiled.

"But I know what you're saying." I traced shapes in the condensation on my pint glass. "About the other voices? I'm dealing with that now, trying to come up with an idea for my next book. There are people waiting for it—my agent, my editor, my readers—and that means I'm writing for an audience. Before, I never thought I would actually get published. I was just writing for me. Now I keep anticipating what my agent will hate, what my editor will want to cut, what readers are going to nitpick. I feel blocked on all sides, like I can't move."

My heart was racing, but saying these things out loud made me feel lighter.

"That sucks," he said, and I glanced at his mouth. I felt an urge to kiss him. To be kissed by him. I swallowed and he continued. "But I guess it's just the nature of the beast. As artists, we can't exist in isolation. We just have to figure out how to mute certain voices at certain times."

I nodded. I knew he was right, but that was easier said than done.

"Do you know what you want to write for the next book?" he asked.

I settled my attention on my glass. "Sort of."

That was a lie. I'd had many ideas in the last year, but none of them had stuck.

Seeming to understand this, Jack reached over and squeezed my hand. I shifted my fingers so they were intertwined in his for a moment. He grinned and then pulled away to reach for his beer. Inside, my very being fluttered.

WE TALKED MORE about my reading, about New York. We ordered another round of beers and then another after that. Jack was lively, bursting with energy. One leg bounced up and down at a constant, frantic speed, and he used his index fingers as drumsticks to tap on the bar. He did all this while he talked, the energy of these tiny movements seeming to feed the vigour of his speech. At one point, we realized we were hungry — neither of us had eaten dinner — and

Jack ordered fried cauliflower from the bartender. I thought he must have been mistaken — they wouldn't sell snacks like that in a dive like this — but the bartender put in the order and soon the dish arrived, the best cauliflower I had ever eaten, with a ginger dipping sauce. We devoured the whole thing in seconds. It was salty and hot and wonderfully greasy. It crossed my mind that Geia likely wouldn't approve of this, like my fries from earlier, but Jack was into it, and that made me like him even more.

I wasn't used to a man being so vulnerable with me, talking about his art, his frustrations, his past. Most of the men I had been with posed a challenge: they were closed off, impossible to read, a locked door I was obsessed with trying to open. But Jack wasn't a challenge. He was completely open.

Jack asked me questions about my family. I told him how my parents split up when I was seventeen and sold the family home in Vermont. How ever since, we'd been a fractured unit, all dispersed to different cities.

"Do you have any siblings?" Jack asked.

I nodded. "A brother. Max. We talk sometimes, birthdays mostly, but we've always had a weird relationship." I looked away for a moment, scanning the drinks list on the wall behind the bar. None of this was easy to talk about. "I told you earlier my mom was hard on me, and Max was very much her favourite, the preferred child. Still is. We're just very different. He's brilliant in a science-y kind of way. He went to MIT. Now he has this big, important job in tech I don't understand. And then there's me. I've always been more interested in reading books and writing stories. We just never found a way to connect."

"And your dad?"

"He and I were buddies," I said. "My mom was hard on him like she was hard on me, so I think we bonded over that. But he's not perfect either. We're not as close anymore."

My father was always my ally at home. Like me, he was in touch with the more dreamy aspects of life. My mother banned fairy tales and Disney movies from our house because they told a story about femininity that she didn't want me to hear. But when I was seven, my father gave me a book of Greek mythology and it activated something in me. Beyond the forest outside our home, it was my first creative influence, opening up new possibilities in my imagination.

I thought back to how I used to knock on his study door after an argument with my mom, tears forming at the corners of my eyes, and he'd let me in without question. He understood what I was feeling because she was mean to him too—in different ways, but with the same harsh tone, the same underlying current of disappointment. Neither of us met her expectations of what a daughter or a husband should be. It was like she was angry that we existed—but it was her fault that we were here. She had married him; she had given birth to me.

"What do your parents do? Are they writers too?" Jack asked.

"Kind of. I mean, they both write."

"Meaning?"

"My dad is a professor. He writes academic stuff. And my mom, she's a journalist. So, yes, she's very much a writer, but she would hate to be put in the same category as me."

Jack laughed.

"No, I'm serious," I said firmly. "To my mother, fiction is a total waste of time. Politics and current affairs, that's what matters. Those are the only stories worth telling."

"Why was your mom so hard on you both?"

I shrugged, surprised at how candid I was being. These were memories I didn't even like to think about, let alone share with anyone else. But something about Jack—his own openness, perhaps—made me want to be honest about my past. "With my dad, I think she resented him. He's charming and outgoing, everyone loves him, and she was jealous or something. She could never be quite so...effortless? It's also just her general outlook on the world. Her work requires her to exist in a very dark place. She doesn't investigate happy stories. She goes after the big, bad wolves. The corrupt politicians, the entitled elite. People who abuse their power and make others suffer. So, imagine you spend your life committed to all of that and then you have a daughter like me. Writing stories about things that don't exist. Back when I was a kid, it was fairies and gnomes. Now, it's talking plants and animals." I shook my head. "I don't think she's ever understood me, and there's nothing she hates more than puzzles she can't solve. So, instead of accepting me in all my weirdness, she criticized me instead. When I was little, I used to just take it, but as I got older, you know, I fought back."

I fell silent, exhaling slowly. Now that I had started, I felt like I couldn't stop. The memories flared up in my mind as Jack kept his eyes on me. He seemed to be hanging on my every word.

"When I was a teenager, Max was already out of the house and my parents were living completely separate lives.

71

My mom was on the road a lot and Dad spent more and more time at work. When she was home, my mother no longer had her sparring partner, so I got all the heat. She'd attack me for not living up to my potential, only getting passable marks in school, partying too much, and I'd bite back. It wasn't pretty."

I exhaled deeply again. How long had it been since I had said any of that out loud?

"Wait," Jack said. "Agnes Oliver...Is your mother Vivian Oliver?"

I nodded.

"She broke that story about the mayor of Boston, right?"

I nodded again. It was her biggest story. The takedown of a mayor who had been accepting bribes from the New England Mafia for nearly two decades. My mother had worked closely with an undercover cop for over three years to gather evidence. That meant lots of nights away from us, her family.

"We haven't spoken since I finished college," I continued. "When I decided to write my novel. I got a job at a café to support myself while she wanted me to take some stupid internship at her newspaper instead. She said no one makes a living writing fiction anymore. Well, Mom," I raised my glass, "here's to you being wrong."

Jack swallowed, watching me. I knew I sounded angry. Maybe I had gone too far, said too much.

"Sorry," I said, backtracking. "I never really go there."

"No, no. I asked. It's okay."

I shook my head and let go of a brittle laugh. "This is why I don't usually talk about this stuff."

"Maybe this is why you *should* talk about this stuff."

I smiled. "Can we change the subject?"

"Of course."

"Tell me about *your* family," I said. "I've talked more than enough about mine. You said you grew up in London?"

He took a slow drink from his pint. "North London. My parents still live there, in the same tiny flat I grew up in. We didn't have a lot of money when I was a kid and they insist on living like we still don't. I mean, they don't, but I do. I want to buy them a new place, but they keep saying no."

I wondered how his family got along with Geia. Since she had become rich and famous, she was known for living an incredibly extravagant lifestyle: private planes, massive houses, the best of everything.

"It's tough. They just can't relate, you know? They think I've gone soft. They don't seem to realize it's still hard for me. I'm not going to say I struggle. I know how privileged I am. But if it wasn't for Geia, I'd probably still be totally unknown. That's a reality I have to live with."

"I don't think that's true. Your work speaks for itself."

"I hope so. But it's weird, you know, kind of living in the shadow of your ex-wife. She's amazing and I'm grateful for everything she's done for my career, but I sometimes wonder if people back my projects because of my connection to her."

"But you don't even work together anymore."

"Still." His shoulders slumped forward, betraying an inner lack of confidence I would never have expected from Jack Verity. "I often ask myself where I would be if I had never met her. Maybe I'd still be renting my little flat around the corner, still living with my roommates. Well, no." He cracked a smile. "It wasn't rent-controlled. We probably wouldn't be able to afford it now."

I laughed, but I felt a swell of sympathy for him. I hadn't imagined he would feel like he existed in Geia's shadow. He was one half of their creative partnership, a key player, but it was true she had become more successful since they broke up, whereas he'd only made one more film that I could think of.

"What are you working on now?" I asked.

Jack told me about his new film, a character study set in Chicago. It was currently in editing. He had spent two months shadowing a homeless man for research, he explained, and they had become good friends. The man's name was Joe.

Jack showed me a photo of him with Joe, both of them wearing big, toothy smiles.

"Do you keep in touch?"

"A bit. I look him up whenever I'm in town. We're planning to do the premiere in Chicago so he can be there."

"He looks happy."

"He is," Jack agreed. "One of the happiest people I've ever met, in fact, and that's despite some really shitty stuff he's had to deal with." He paused. "I tried to help him... you know, find him a place to live, get him set up and everything. But he's allergic to charity. He's like my parents. Doesn't want to owe anything to anybody. But he makes out okay, I guess."

I stared at the photo a moment longer and then handed Jack his phone. That was when he noticed the time.

"Shit. It's late. Should we go?"

WE EMERGED FROM the bar. The street was quiet but else-where the city was still very much alive. Distant noise, a car horn, someone yelling. We lingered outside the bar. I wasn't sure what we were waiting for, but I didn't want the night to end, just like I hadn't wanted the flight to end earlier.

"Are you okay to get back to your hotel?"

I nodded, though really, I had no idea where we were. I'd just hop in a cab.

"Okay, cool."

I could tell he was hesitating. He was shifting from foot to foot. He wanted to say something.

Say it, I thought. Whatever it is.

"I have to go to the Hamptons tomorrow," he said, after an eternity. "I'll be there for the next few weeks, maybe longer."

"Oh." I felt like I was sinking into the sidewalk. He was saying that this was the end of whatever this was. He was leaving town.

"It's my birthday this weekend, actually. Geia's throw-ing me a party."

What was I supposed to say to that?

"Nice."

A grin crept across his face. "Any chance you'd want to come?"

I blinked. "Sure. I mean, yes. Definitely. I have the week-end off, no events, so that works."

"Great." He looked delighted. "Can I give you my number? I'll arrange a car for you."

I nodded as I unlocked my phone and handed it to him.

"Cool. It was really great hanging out tonight, Agnes.

Tomorrow, I'm going to sit by the pool and finish your book."

He walked me to the corner, where I signalled to a passing taxi. When we said goodbye, his body bent towards mine just slightly, like maybe he wanted to hug me, but he didn't. On the ride home, I imagined us hugging. The vision morphed—from us hugging, to us falling into my cab, to our bodies crashing together through my hotel room door—and I let it.

9

A black SUV was waiting for me outside my hotel on the morning of Jack's birthday. It was only 10 a.m. but already sweltering hot. After three days of exploring the city, I was ready for a change of scene. I had visited the Met and MoMA, eaten oysters at Grand Central and more pistachio gelato at Eataly, and sat at countless cafés and bars, doodling in the notebook meant for working on book two. New York was amazing, no denying it, but it was also very stressful. The pulse of the city throbbed in a way I wasn't used to, and I found myself going to bed with a headache, my energy spent from traipsing around town all day. My neighbourhood back home in Montreal, full of artists and musicians who worked irregular hours, was much more relaxed.

My driver opened the rear door to let me in, calling me "Ms. Oliver" without missing a beat. I asked him how long we'd be on the road, and he told me it wouldn't be more than an hour and forty minutes.

"Traffic isn't bad," he said in a deep voice. "It's still early."

I nodded and then fell silent, watching the city go by through my window.

Since the reading at Orchard House and my night at the bar with Jack, I'd attended two meetings about my second book. The first, with Zelda, took place at a rooftop bar in Chelsea. Over Campari sodas, Zelda had told me to "get real." I was being vague about my progress, and she could tell I was far from having a draft completed.

"The end-of-summer deadline will simply need to be extended. Not so far as to upset anyone," she said, "just enough to give you a bit of wiggle room." My chest lifted. I was grateful and relieved Zelda was willing to buy me more time. And so, the next day, Zelda and I met with Jessica and Robert for lunch. Zelda suggested pushing the deadline to the end of October, which would give me one extra month, and though Jessica looked like she had just swallowed a cockroach and Robert like he was momentarily having a heart attack, they eventually agreed. That deadline was firm though. There would be no more extensions, which meant I had to get writing fast. Or rather, I had to settle on an idea fast, and then get writing faster.

As we were leaving the restaurant, Zelda felt the need to mention to the team that I was now a "close acquaintance" of Jack Verity, and a possible collaboration was in the works. I gaped at her. I'd told her I was going to the Hamptons in confidence; I hadn't said anything about Jack and I working together.

"Is that true, Agnes?" Jessica asked, surprised. Did she maybe even sound impressed?

I knew what Zelda was doing: distracting them with good news. And it seemed like it was working.

"We'll see." I smiled, close-lipped.

So now there was that to worry about too. I couldn't just go to Jack's birthday party and enjoy myself. I had to convince him to turn my book into a film. Did I even want that? I wasn't so sure.

I didn't know what to pack for my day in the Hamptons (What does one bring to Geia Stone's summer house?), so I didn't pack much: a bathing suit (Jack had mentioned a pool), a sweater, and a book I had bought for Jack as a birthday gift. Jack had assured me that the party would be casual, so I wore the blue linen dress and a new pair of white Vans I had picked up to replace my old, smelly ones. I lathered on sunscreen and struggled with my hair, which had become a cloud of frizz in the humidity of the city. I was nervous. In the car, I drank too much water for something to do, so that soon after leaving the hotel I already had to pee.

I opened my phone and reread the last few messages from Jack. We'd been texting every day, and one night we'd even stayed up late talking on the phone. He had told me more about the film he was working on, what his days looked like now. The film was deep in "edit land" and he said he could lose hours subtly shifting the focus of the narrative by making miniscule cuts to scenes or by changing the music. His collaborators were in L.A., so they worked together from a distance, which was a challenge; but he felt he needed to be close to his daughters right now. It was a tradition, he explained. Every summer, his modern family spent four weeks together in the Hamptons.

I asked him about the other months of the year. What did they look like?

"It varies," he said. "If I'm in L.A., I'm with Geia and the girls. That means family has to come first. But if I'm on location or in New York, I'm on my own, which means all work all the time."

"Wow."

"Do I sound obsessed?"

"A bit."

"My friends say I need a girlfriend."

I laughed. He had already dropped a few similarly flirty hints into our conversations. He commented on my photo on the jacket of my book, how he had flipped to it after reading the first chapter, curious to see what I looked like.

"I wasn't expecting you to be so gorgeous," he said, making me blush all alone in my hotel room.

He had finished my book, and though he texted two fire-works emojis by way of a reaction, he said he didn't want to talk about it until we were together in person. My pulse hammered in response.

So excited you're coming to the party! he had texted yesterday. He sent a lot of exclamation marks, which I wasn't used to from a guy, but I liked.

Me too. By the way, what kind of party is it? Ball gown required? I wrote, only half joking.

Small family thing, he responded. *BBQ, casual*.

That sounded manageable, though a part of me had been expecting to encounter Hollywood's elite at this thing. I was relieved. I wasn't ready for that; meeting Geia Stone would be enough.

What can I bring? I asked.

Just yourself!

I smiled, rereading the message. But no. Bad, Agnes. I wasn't supposed to be getting involved with anyone. The evening before, I'd sat at the hotel bar with my notebook and a martini, feeling very sophisticated and writerly, but all I could think about was Jack, about seeing him in the Hamptons today, which was exactly what I needed to protect myself from if I was ever going to write book two. I told myself I would go to the party — how could I not? — but I needed to see it as a one-time thing, a fling perhaps. With a possible professional spin-off in the form of a film adaptation.

THE DRIVE FELT long and then too short, my nerves about going to Geia Stone's house mounting into full-body anxiety: sweaty palms, full-to-bursting bladder, stomach snakes alive and well. As we drove into a small, yuppie-looking town, I asked the driver to pull over and dashed into a café full of tanned, attractive people drinking green juice and matcha lattes — Geia's people — and found the bathroom at the back. I reached the toilet and pee gushed out of me, a shuddering relief.

I washed my hands and glanced at myself in the mirror. I wiped away flakes of mascara from underneath my eyes and tried to smooth down my hair. I had no idea what I was doing. Was I just supposed to walk into Geia Stone's

Hamptons mansion and attend a birthday party for Jack Verity like it was nothing?

The prospect of meeting Geia was the scariest part. I imagined standing in front of her, looking into her beautiful blue eyes, with nothing to say. She was known for being very tall. Tall and gorgeous. I'd always thought of actresses as existing in a different category of beautiful. They didn't look like normal people, because they weren't normal people. They were a cut above, made of different matter entirely. That meant comparisons between yourself and them, though inevitable, were futile. I should focus on that. But wouldn't the difference between Geia and me be all the more starkly obvious when we were standing next to each other? I imagined the scene: me looking girlish next to her, unkempt and plain. Jack would see. He would realize I wasn't what he thought I was.

I GAZED OUT the car window at the Nancy Meyers–inspired estates lining a quiet, leafy street, all with neat lawns and tasteful but very solid fences, and felt a twisting low in my stomach. This was it. Arrival imminent. The driver put on his turn signal in front of a large, charcoal grey home with a goldenrod-yellow front door. The security gate opened as we approached, and the driver pulled the car up a cobblestone driveway.

"We've arrived," he said, stopping the car next to the house. The doors to the garage at the end of the driveway were open, and I could see another black SUV parked next to a cherry-red antique sports car.

The driver hopped out and opened my door. I hesitated, slowly unbuckling my seatbelt. I felt just like I had at Orchard House Books my first night in New York: terrified. What did I do now? Knock on the front door? Introduce myself? I looked down at my phone. Maybe I'd text Jack to come out and meet me.

"Everything okay?" the driver asked.

I nodded and smiled, stepping onto the driveway. He shut the door behind me and got back into the suv.

"Goodbye, Ms. Oliver," he said. In seconds, he'd backed out of the driveway and was gone. I was alone, immobile with fear.

I realized I couldn't stand there long. Security might mistake me for a trespasser, a crazed fan trying to get to Geia. I looked down at my phone and started writing a message to Jack, but before I could finish typing *I'm here!* a man appeared from the side of the house. He wore loafers and khaki pants, cuffed at the ankles, with a bright pink gingham shirt.

"Agnes?" he asked.

"Yes."

"I'm Benjamin, Geia's assistant. Would you like to come inside? They're in the backyard."

I nodded, wondering who he meant by "they."

Benjamin was short, only an inch or two taller than me, with thinning dark hair. He wore a neutral expression, his face relaxed in a look of endless patience. I followed him up the driveway and around the side of the house. He walked quickly but silently. Graceful, like a dancer.

We went through another gate, which led into the huge backyard. A long, green lawn stretched on forever, lined on both sides by birch trees, their bark gleaming in the sunlight. In the faint breeze, I caught a whiff of sweet clover, and somewhere in the distance, wild rose. Over to the left, there was a large, rectangular pool. My heart lifted when I spotted Jack in the water, a little girl held above his head. I scanned the rest of the garden, but couldn't see Geia anywhere.

"Jack," Benjamin called, raising his voice but not changing his placid tone. "Agnes is here."

Jack turned, beaming, and threw the little girl playfully into the water. Benjamin and I strode across the lawn as Jack and his daughter climbed out of the pool, wrapping their bodies in giant white towels.

"You made it," Jack said, when we reached them. "How was the drive?"

"Great!" I said a little too loudly, but he didn't seem to notice.

"Agnes." Jack put his hand on the little girl's shoulder. "This is Sage, my first-born."

Sage rolled her eyes. "By two minutes."

Jack laughed. "Those two minutes felt like forever."

"It's nice to meet you." I reached out a hand and she shook it.

Sage looked at me with her father's eyes.

"Agnes," Benjamin said. "Can I get you something to drink?"

"Water would be great."

"Same for me," Jack said.

Benjamin headed for the house. The lawn sloped upwards to an elaborate outdoor kitchen complete with a long, stone dining table. The back of the house was all windows. I wondered if Geia was inside, if she could see us.

"Shall we sit?" Jack asked.

We moved to two loungers near the edge of the pool. Sage promptly jumped back into the water.

"So, is this weird?" he asked.

"No. Not at all." I shook my head, but after a beat we both laughed.

"It's gotta be. I mean, it's kind of early to be meeting my kids and my ex-wife."

Kind of early? Did that mean he saw this as the beginning of a longer relationship?

"Yup. And also..."

"Right. My ex-wife is a movie star."

I laughed again and it felt good. I wasn't so nervous now that I was here, in front of Jack again. I was used to men making me feel confused and distraught, but Jack made me feel at ease.

"I just really wanted you to be here, Agnes. And Geia's great. I know it's strange to be so close with your ex but it's because of who she is that we can be such good friends."

I nodded, unsure how to respond.

"Did you bring a bathing suit?"

"Yup."

"It's hot. Let's swim. And then we can chat about your book."

10

Jack led me towards the house while Sage ran ahead of us, her long dark hair dripping wet. Jack had told her to stay out of the water until we returned to the pool, and she announced she needed to find Sparrow—who I knew from my online research was her twin sister—and Kathari, a name I didn't recognize.

Sage slid open a large glass door and disappeared inside. Jack was telling me who was coming to the party, but I was having a hard time listening. I was entering Geia Stone's summer home for the first time. We entered a large living room, sparsely decorated, with white walls and oversized furniture. My first thought was of heaven. The space was divine, tranquil. Tall, vaulted ceilings and a sense of light and levity. The art on the walls was all abstract, heavily textured, also mostly white. I gazed around in a circle and then realized Jack was watching me.

"Sorry," I said. "It's really nice."

He squeezed the back of my arm. "It's okay. I had the same reaction when I first saw it." He pointed down a long hallway. "Bathroom's down there. I'm gonna see where Benjamin is with those waters and maybe find us a snack."

I wandered down the light-filled hallway. Floor-to-ceiling windows lined one side, looking onto the backyard. There were several doorways on the other wall. I found the bathroom. Surprisingly, it wasn't white—brilliant teal tiles covered the walls and floor. I changed quickly into my bathing suit. My hair seemed less frizzy now. Probably the cooler Hamptons air. I opened the cabinet under the sink and found it well-stocked with Goddess™ products: soaps and cleansers and serums and masks. I was tempted to take one and then realized how weird that would be. Stealing was something a stranger would do. I'd been invited into Geia's home. I was here for a party. Bad, Agnes.

I put my dress back on over my bathing suit, self-conscious about walking through the house half-naked—what if I ran into Geia?—and returned to the hallway. I could hear laughter. Sage's or Sparrow's, or maybe both. I paused, listening. They must be in the next room, just through the closest doorway. They sounded like they were having fun, but I didn't want to introduce myself to Sparrow without Jack there.

"Kathari!" one of them called. "Where are you going?"

I was about to walk away—whoever Kathari was, they were going to catch me eavesdropping—but my heart stopped and I was suddenly unable to move. Was I hallucinating? A large green snake appeared in the doorway. Liquid, yellow eyes. Body as thick as my calf. It raised its head to watch me, unblinking. What the hell was this? Were the girls playing with this reptile?

"There you are!" Jack joined us in the hallway. "I see you've met Kathari."

"What?" I asked, not turning my head. The snake was staring right at me, and I wasn't very well going to break eye contact. I wasn't scared, exactly, more shocked, surprised even. A giant snake roaming free in this clean, beautiful space.

Jack stood next to me. "Oh, sorry. Are you afraid? It's okay. He's completely safe. Kathari is part of the family."

I swallowed. Kathari the snake was still staring at me. I had a strong sense he knew I had been eavesdropping. Now, he was less than six feet away. He had an odd white mark on his back, near his head, like a misshapen X.

Jack leaned down to stroke the top of Kathari's head. "See? He's a pet. Just less furry."

I nodded, still a little unsure.

"Do you want to pet him?"

I shook my head. "No, thanks."

I wasn't usually unnerved by any kind of animal, no matter how menacing their reputation—I grew up knowing how to smell a bear and what to do if you found yourself face-to-face with a coyote—but there was something different about this snake. It felt like he could understand what we were saying. But how could that be?

Kathari finally broke his staring contest with me and gazed up at Jack for a moment, seeming to enjoy the affection, and then disappeared back through the doorway. The girls squealed in delight at his return.

"Come on," Jack said. "I told Benjamin to make us a real drink."

BENJAMIN MADE A mean mojito. Jack and I sat on pool loungers under the shade of an umbrella, both in our bathing suits. We had taken a quick swim to cool off and now he was telling me what he thought about the ending of my book. I was trying very hard to listen, but I kept thinking about Kathari. Those eyes. The way he seemed to know I had been listening to the girls. I'd never seen a reptile up close like that, except in a zoo through a glass partition. This was completely different. And Geia and Jack let their daughters play with this creature? Shouldn't there at least be a handler or something?

"As soon as I finished," Jack said earnestly, "I wanted to reread it. And I'm not just saying that because I want to sleep with you."

I looked up. That had gotten my attention.

"Everything okay? You seem a bit spaced out."

"Sorry." I took a sip of my mojito. "I've just never seen a snake like that before."

Jack nodded. "I should have warned you. He's been in the family for years, so I'm used to him. But I can see how that would be startling."

I raised my eyebrows.

"Okay, startling is putting it mildly. How about batshit crazy?"

I laughed. "Getting warmer. So, he's Geia's pet?"

"Yeah, she's had him since before we met."

That surprised me. That meant Kathari was at least seventeen years old. (It's creepy that you know how long Jack and Geia have been together, Agnes. Don't ever share that with him.)

"What's the lifespan of a snake?" I asked.

"No idea. I think they can live pretty long though. Why?"

"Just curious." I hadn't thought about it before, but it made sense that snakes lived a long time. There was something almost mythical about them. I tried to imagine Jack meeting Kathari for the first time. How had Geia explained her penchant for this giant reptile to him back then? And why hadn't I read anything about Kathari online? That snake seemed to be Geia's best-kept secret. It didn't really suit the Goddess™ brand, but I could see a creature like that appearing in *The Opposites* movies. There was a great scene with a colony of bats in film two.

That was when Jack leaned forward and kissed me. It was short and soft, but wonderful. I opened my eyes and grinned. He was grinning too, our faces closer than they'd ever been.

"I've been wanting to do that since the plane," he said. He leaned back into the lounger. "Geia started it yesterday. She's really enjoying it so far."

"What?"

"Your book. I gave it to her to read after I finished."

Hearing her name interrupted the moment. I was reminded of Geia, in the background. Where was she, anyway?

"I have something for you," I said, reaching for my

backpack. "For your birthday." I passed him the book, wrapped in brown paper.

He looked genuinely surprised. "You didn't have to get me a gift."

"I wanted to."

He unwrapped the book. *The Penelopiad* by Margaret Atwood.

A funny look crossed his face.

"Have you read it already?"

"No," he turned it over and read the back copy.

"It's a retelling of *The Odyssey* from Penelope's perspective. I've been reading the original stories since I was kid. One of the first books that made me want to be a writer was a book of Greek myths for children that my dad gave me. But this is something else altogether."

The funny look was gone. "It sounds awesome," he said. "Thank you, Agnes."

JACK AND I took a walk down to the edge of the property, holding hands. I was surprised Geia's home wasn't right on the water, but Jack told me the beach was just a short walk away.

"We can go there tomorrow," he said. "If you want."

"Tomorrow? Am I spending the night?"

He looked embarrassed. "Oh, right. I mean, only if you want to. I just figured the party would go late and you'd be too tired to head back tonight. You have another day off, right?"

"I do, yeah. But I didn't pack for an overnight stay."

"I'm sure we can find you a toothbrush. Seriously though, no pressure."

I let him lead me down the lawn, digesting this new information. A sleepover? I wondered where exactly I would be sleeping. Had Geia okayed this?

The back of the property was bordered by a clump of dense forest. Jack pulled me in between the trees. Immediately, I felt calmer amidst all the green.

"This is nice," I said, sighing.

"I love this part of the property. I come down here just to sit and think sometimes."

I took in the trees: a mix of evergreens and maples and more birches. I watched a chipmunk run up a high branch, and two chickadees twitter about, looking for bugs in the bark. Then Jack pulled me towards him, kissing me again. I allowed myself to fall into him. He pushed me gently up against a tree and put his hands in my hair. The shiver of longing I'd been feeling since that night on the sidewalk morphed into a full-body quake. After a few minutes, he pulled away. His brown eyes looked amber, catching the sunlight that spilled between the trees. He exhaled slowly.

"We should get back." He grabbed my hand, intertwining our fingers. "It'll be lunch soon."

I nodded and we turned to go. I wondered why we had to come all the way down here to make out. Didn't he have his own space in the house? Were we hiding? I had done enough of that in the past. I wasn't interested in sneaking around again.

I pulled my hand from his, but he didn't seem to notice. Somewhere nearby, a branch cracked loudly in the forest, making me jump.

11

When Jack and I got back to the house, there was a man sitting by the pool. He looked young, maybe twenty-five, with the body and face of a model. He was shirtless, eating grilled vegetable kebabs, Wayfarers hiding his eyes. Up by the house, I could see another man working the barbecue in the outdoor kitchen. Their at-home chef, maybe?

Jack introduced the shirtless man as Luke, though he provided no explanation of who Luke was or why he was here. No "my friend" or "Geia's nephew" or anything like that. Luke nodded in my direction when Jack told him my name. He seemed generally bored with everything: the weather, the pool, his lunch. He kept looking down at his phone while Jack and I talked to him, like we were boring too. We sat down on the loungers and Jack started telling Luke about my first encounter with Kathari.

"Can I get a beer?" Luke yelled suddenly, but there was no one else around. I almost felt like he was asking me, that I should run up to the house and find the fridge.

Within moments Benjamin appeared with a beer and a plate of more vegetable kebabs. He handed us the food while I wondered if the pool area was mic-ed somehow. We were far enough away from the house that Benjamin shouldn't have been able to hear Luke yelling. Did that mean he had heard Jack and me talking earlier too? Is that why Jack had led me to the back of the property?

"Where's Geia?" Jack asked, retrieving the book I had given him from the spot where he left it earlier.

"Out on her bike," Luke said, not looking up from his phone.

Jack nodded and then started to read. I realized I should have brought a book for myself too. I didn't think there would be time for that.

I grabbed my phone and sat on the edge of the pool, dangling my legs in the water. I wished I had someone to text about the snake, the kiss, the prospect of a sleepover, but the only person I could think of was my college roommate Kate. She'd also been a fan of *The Opposites*, but we had fallen out of touch years ago. I wasn't even sure I had her current number.

I put my phone down and swayed my legs in the water. The sun was high and hot in a cloudless sky. I slipped out of my sundress and slid into the pool, dunking my head under, and swam to the other end. The cool water was a relief. I did a few more laps, exchanging looks with Jack whenever I reached the end of the pool close to where he was sitting.

"How is it?" I asked him.

"Definitely intrigued," he said.

95

I swam back to the far end and floated on my back with my eyes closed. The sun was warm on my face. I felt very far from home. I thought about Jack kissing me. The smell of him, his warm grip, his hands on my back, in my hair. It made me a bit dizzy to feel wanted like that. Wanted by someone I could actually see myself being with beyond a night or two. But though Jack was different than anyone I'd ever been with, he came with an ex-wife. Did that make her the other woman, or me? I had played that role in my last relationship, and I wasn't interested in doing so again. I had sworn I never would.

No one sets out to have a relationship with a married man, it just happens. At first, maybe you convince yourself you didn't notice his wedding ring. Then, you listen closely when he says it's not working with his wife. You fall in love. As you fall, you trust that things will change. That he will leave her and you will be together. Faith is a powerful force, especially when it's tangled up with romance.

I MET OWEN at a backyard party my first summer after graduating from college. A co-worker from the café had invited me. It was desperately humid, even for June in Montreal, and people gathered in the garden, lit by fairy lights, drinking beer and white wine.

I had spotted Owen immediately. He was the tallest person there, hard to miss, wearing dark-framed glasses and a pale-green button-up. He must have spotted me immediately too. I noticed him looking at me while he was talking to someone else, which I liked.

Eventually, we moved through the garden and towards each other until we stood side by side at the far end of the drinks table in the semi-dark.

"I'll take some of that," I said to him.

He topped up my wine glass from the bottle in his hand.

"Are you a student?" he asked, taking a small sip of wine. The crowd was mostly academic. My co-worker was doing his master's in cultural studies.

"No," I said. Not as of three weeks ago. "I'm just here with a friend."

We were standing close and I had to tilt my chin up to look at him. My neck felt very exposed.

"Good," he said with a charming smirk.

He told me he was a post-doc, that he worked on mid-twentieth-century media and Freud's theory of the uncanny. I told him I was a writer, proud of my recent commitment to finally write the novel I'd always dreamed of.

I had moved into a new apartment on my own so I'd have quiet and space to work. I had a job at the café with flexible hours. And I had cleansed my life of my mother after her last-ditch effort to turn me into a journalist through that dumb internship.

But then Owen asked me what I had written. I blinked, realizing my mistake. I hadn't published anything. Not even a bad short story in a student arts magazine. My notebooks at home didn't count.

"Well, I'm working on it," I said, backtracking. "I *want* to be a writer."

He smirked again. I'm not sure why I found that smirking so appealing.

We ended up talking all night, about Montreal, the university, his work. At one point, we circled back to my earlier mistake. He asked why I'd said I was a writer when I hadn't written anything.

"I've written stuff."

"Just nothing anyone has read."

"Well..." I faltered, looking for an explanation. I felt I was meant to write. I always had. "Maybe the writing itself is only part of it. Being a writer is also about how you see yourself and the world. Watching, listening, observing."

"Right." He nodded and I was pleased I had said something smart. But then he switched gears: "So, how many people have I slept with?"

I laughed. "What?"

"If you're so observant, you must have insight into my character. How many would you say I've slept with?"

I panicked. Was this what he considered flirting? I had no idea how to answer that question, but I threw out a number. "Twenty?"

He shook his head. "You're not even trying."

I began calculating. Married young, I thought. I had noticed his wedding band, even if I'd deny it later. Probably didn't come into his own until college. That ruled out high-school sex. "Nine?"

"Closer." That smirk. "For you, I'd say fifteen. There's something restless about you. You get bored easily."

I swallowed. How could he possibly know that? Who was the writer here, me or him?

It took a few weeks for anything to happen. I'd told Owen where I worked, and he started coming in with his laptop and his books, sitting by the window in the corner. I often caught him watching me as I wiped down tables or served people coffee.

One day, he stayed at the café until closing. My co-worker James had to tell him we were locking up. Owen nodded and I watched him pack up his things and then sit on the bench out front.

"What's that guy's deal?" James asked. He was nineteen, a musician, like every other guy in Montreal.

I shrugged and shook my head. I didn't know how to explain, or if there was even anything *to* explain.

James left first. When I went outside a few minutes later, Owen stood up.

I locked the café door behind me.

"Do you live close?"

"Not far." I gestured vaguely west, to where Mile End met Little Italy. My new apartment.

"Can I walk you home?" he asked.

"Sure."

We stayed quiet while we walked. I wasn't sure what was going to happen. He was married, with a prestigious post-doc. I worked at a café and often felt like a child. Then we were at my building. He just stood there, not saying anything, looking up as if he knew which windows were mine. My apartment actually faced the back alley. You couldn't see it from here.

"Do you want to . . . ?" I asked, unsure if I should finish the question. I didn't want to scare him away, make him think I was the type of person who seduced married men. But I wanted him to come up. I wanted more of his attention, that feeling I had enjoyed while he watched me in the café.

"Yes," he said firmly.

We went upstairs to my apartment. I opened two beers and we sat on the couch. I felt itchy, nervous. Something needed to happen. At least the beer was cold.

Through the silence he put his hand on my arm. Then we were kissing, in my room, on my bed. It all happened very fast. It was intense, a lot of grasping and heavy breathing. When we broke apart, he stared up at the ceiling and shook his head. I imagined he was thinking this was all a mistake, that it couldn't happen again, that it wasn't worth the risk. But then he reached for my hand, squeezing hard, and it felt like he didn't want to let go.

THIS WAS DIFFERENT, I told myself, as I finished swimming another lap. Jack was different. Sure, Geia was still a big part of his life, but it sounded like they were more friends than anything else. But could anyone ever really fall out of love with Geia Stone?

"Agnes." Jack was calling my name. "Agnes!"

I turned in the water and there she was. Standing between Jack and Luke, wearing a gigantic sunhat. Geia Stone was waving at me.

12

"It's so good to meet you, Agnes," Geia said, pulling my wet body into a hug.

I was hugging Geia Stone. She smelled like strawberries, and she was so tall I had to turn my face so it wasn't smooshed into her breasts.

"You too. Oh, I'm sorry. I've gotten you all wet."

She let me go and smiled like it was nothing. "I'll be dry in two seconds. It's so fucking hot! Anyone else dying for a drink?"

"Way ahead of you," Luke said, raising his empty beer bottle.

In the distance, I noticed Benjamin hurrying down the lawn towards us. "Drinks?" he asked Geia as he reached us.

The pool area had to be mic-ed. How else could he have known? Or maybe he came running whenever she appeared.

"Maybe some wine?" Geia said, fanning herself with her sun hat. I noticed her freckles were more pronounced than in the photos I had seen online. "Something cold and white."

Benjamin nodded and began filing through wine options in his brain. "The Rosaki? Domaine de Kalathas?"

"Sounds wonderful, Benjamin. And bring some potato chips, please. I'm starving."

Potato chips? Geia Stone ate potato chips? Benjamin hurried back to the house.

"I would be lost without him," she told me. "He's not just an assistant, he's my lifeline."

I smiled like I understood what that meant.

"Shall we sit?" she asked, and we all followed her to a long, low table set back from the pool. It was shaded by a large yellow umbrella, the same colour as the front door.

We sat down and I made a conscious effort not to stare at Geia. I found her beauty unnerving. Pictures didn't capture the crystalline blue of her eyes or the rich chestnut of her hair, lightened by the sun in soft streaks near her face — the effect other women strived for when they asked for natural-looking highlights at the salon. She wasn't wearing jewellery or a lick of makeup. She sat cross-legged in her chair, her back straight. Her tanned limbs were incredibly long and delicate, peeking out from under a floaty floral dress. That dress would have looked like a nightgown on anyone else. But on Geia, it looked magnificent.

Geia took a deep yoga breath and then looked expectantly at us. "So, what have we all been doing?" She sounded like a mother inquiring after her children.

"I went for a run," Luke said in the same bored tone as earlier. To my surprise, Geia reached over and drew circles with her finger on his bare shoulder. Was Luke her boyfriend? If so, the media wasn't aware. I hadn't come across anything online about Geia's new man. "Then I came down here and these two appeared."

Geia's head whipped back around to Jack and me. "You appeared? Where did you disappear to?"

"We just went for a walk," Jack said with a little shrug.

"Did you meet the girls?" Geia asked me.

"I met one of them, Sage. She was swimming when I first arrived."

Geia nodded. "You'll meet Sparrow soon."

Benjamin returned with the wine, which he poured for all of us, leaving the bottle in a bucket of ice nearby. I wondered if every summer day was like this here. Drinking and sitting and not much else. It seemed very un-Goddess™. Shouldn't we be meditating or drinking celery juice or something?

Geia explained that the wine was Greek, like her. She told me she was born on a small island called Mastika, not unlike the island where this wine was made.

"Home," she said with a little sigh. "I miss it, but I'm going back soon."

"When?" Jack asked. He sounded surprised.

"July. I told you, didn't I? The work thing." Geia looked at me. "This one's got an awful memory, I'm warning you now."

"Right. I forgot," Jack said with a frown. He sounded unconvinced but quickly changed the subject. "What did you get up to this morning?"

Geia's face lit up. "Oh my god, you guys. There's this incredible patch of wild strawberries down the road. Remember we found them last year? I almost forgot and then I woke up this morning and I was like we *need* strawberries for Jack's dinner. How does strawberry shortcake sound, by the way?"

"Sounds great," Jack said. He looked over at me. "You're in for a treat. Geia's making the whole dinner herself."

She beamed. "I love to cook."

"I love your cookbooks," I said, and immediately regretted it. I sounded like a fangirl and it wasn't even the truth. I'd had a roommate who loved her cookbooks back in college, but I'd never even flipped through one. Why was I lying? To impress her?

"Oh, god. Those were a pain in the ass, weren't they?" She looked at Jack and then back at me. "You have to test each recipe, like, seventeen times."

"We ate well that year," Jack grinned, and the former couple seemed to share a moment, a memory of meals neither Luke nor I were a part of.

Luke noticed the moment too. He reached over and placed his hand on Geia's thigh, but she didn't react.

"But what am I saying?" Geia exclaimed, setting down her wine. "Here I am talking about how onerous it is to test recipes when we have a novelist in our midst. Now that has to be tedious — writing fiction!"

For a moment I forgot who she was referring to, but all three of them looked at me, waiting for a reply.

"It can be," I said slowly. "But you know, tedium is part of the process."

Geia nodded. "Good attitude. Very Zen. Are you a Buddhist?"

I laughed. "No."

"Luke and I did this incredible silent retreat with Buddhist monks in Tibet last year. It was life-changing. It really makes you appreciate the value of quiet. I think I choose my words more carefully now because I realize how each one can interrupt peace for someone else."

Luke moved his hand from her thigh up to the side of her face. She looked over at him, smiling sweetly the way lovers do. I wondered if seeing Geia and Luke affectionate with each other bothered Jack. Even if Geia and Jack were only friends, it still must be weird. Seeing your ex with someone else always was.

But when I stole a glance at him, Jack seemed unmoved, his face relaxed. At one point, he even reached over and grabbed my hand, holding it while we all talked. I noticed Geia's gaze flit down to our joined palms but she too, seemed perfectly okay bearing witness to our blossoming intimacy.

THE WINE KEPT COMING. Soon we were all tipsy, and it was only midafternoon. I wondered what Geia's followers would think of that. She who preached moderation and all things detoxifying. It was very off-brand.

But really, Geia was nothing like you'd expect, given the ethos of her empire. She swore like a sailor and she finished off the large bowl of potato chips basically on her own. In general, she seemed pretty low-key. Beyond the mention of Buddhism, no Goddess™ talk made its way into our conversation. I had been expecting her to be high-strung; Type A with a dash of New Age pretension. But she was actually fun to be around.

Eventually, Geia announced she needed to continue cooking—apparently, she'd been preparing the food for days—and Luke mumbled something about taking a nap before the party. That left Jack and me alone again. He said he could show me to my room if I wanted. I nodded, my head light from all the wine.

It turned out that the east wing of the house, though joined to the rest of the property, was set up to be Jack's private space. His "quarters." He had a small kitchen and his own living room, both looking out over the yard. No wonder he felt like he lived in Geia's shadow; he did, literally.

Silently, he pulled me through the space, holding my hand, eventually leading me upstairs.

"This is your bedroom," he said, showing me a white room with a big bed and its own ensuite bathroom.

I wasn't sure how to feel about this: separate bedrooms. It made me wonder if maybe I had fooled myself, that he didn't like me after all.

"Where do *you* sleep?" I asked, looking down the hall. I felt a familiar need for certainty. I wanted to feel like I had outside, when he kissed me. I wanted to know how he really felt.

"Down the hall."

We passed by an office outfitted with large flat-screen monitors—the "edit room" I had seen photos of on Instagram—and then he opened the door to his own bedroom, its walls the same light blue as my dress. A large painting hung over the bed: another textured abstract in muted tones like the ones in Geia's living room.

"Nice," I said, glancing around briefly. And then I went

for it. I kissed him and he kissed me back, his hands moving from my face down to my arms and then my hips, lifting up my dress just slightly.

"Whoa," he said, pulling back. "Is this okay?"

"Yes," I breathed, leaning forward.

"Wait." He pulled back further. "Are you sure? We've had all that wine and we're only just getting to know each other."

Now *I* pulled back. I felt like he had slapped me. What was all that kissing for then? I stared at him for a moment, confused. I wasn't used to being asked to pause and think before sex. I remembered Owen tearing off my clothes, sometimes entering me before we'd even made it to the bedroom. A fast and reckless passion. Urgent, immediate, bordering on uncomfortable because we just couldn't help ourselves.

I sat down on the bed, growing warm with embarrassment. "I'm sure," I said. "I want this. But if you don't —"

"No, I do. I just wanted to make sure we were on the same page."

He pushed me back on the bed. Finally. This was what I liked. Not checking in, not making sure we weren't making a mistake.

We were kissing again and he was taking off his shirt and his hands were moving slowly up my thighs. I wasn't used to that either. Could he feel how my body shuddered? Trembling from the inside out. He removed my dress and began kissing me all over. When his mouth found its way between my legs, I gasped.

And then he was moving upward, towards me. He moved

slowly inside me, like he was searching for something. He wouldn't stop looking at me. I suddenly felt very shy. I looked away and then back at his face.

His eyebrows were knitted with concern. "Are you crying?" he asked.

"No," I said, but he caught me wiping away a tear.

13

I stood in the shower in my ensuite bathroom. The shower head was shaped like a square, positioned directly over me, and water fell from it like rain. Soft but effective.

The shelf was stocked with Goddess™ products and I decided to try the Buff It Off Body Scrub. I scooped out some of the grainy mixture, cool in my hand, taking satisfaction from knowing it was very expensive. I scooped some more. It smelled like rose and coconut. I applied it to one leg, rubbing in a circular motion as instructed by the label, then rinsed it clean, feeling to see if it made any difference. I was shocked by the smoothness, the subtle sheen. My skin felt like silk.

I repeated this on the other leg and then both my arms, scrubbing desperately, wanting to slough away whatever had just happened with Jack.

After he'd noticed me crying, everything had stopped. He lay down beside me, held me, made space for my tears.

"What can I do?" he asked, but that only made me cry harder.

I was mortified. I had never cried during sex before. But the way he kept looking at me, the slowness of it all, the intimacy—it was just too much.

When I eventually stopped crying, we lay there for a while. Jack told me it was okay. He thought it was too soon too. But that's not what I thought. It wasn't too soon. This was what I had wanted, wasn't it? Maybe this was my body's way of telling me to stay away from him. Focus on the book, Agnes. Don't get distracted.

Rather than try to explain myself I quickly suggested we get ready for the party. He kissed me and I headed to my own room. I was shaking as I stepped into the bathroom.

When I got out of the shower, I found the drawers of my bathroom were also stocked with Goddess™ products. Serums and moisturizers and even the clean makeup line Geia had recently launched. Who had put these here? Not Jack. Geia? Benjamin?

Was it weird to wear Jack's ex-wife's makeup to his birthday party? I didn't really have any other option, and it wasn't like he'd know anyway.

I distracted myself by playing with the products. I pressed the orange-scented Endless Moisture Face Oil into my skin and it seemed to absorb it immediately, leaving my face with a rosy glow. I mixed two different cream blushes, dabbing them onto my cheeks, and admired the effect. I looked like I had just returned from a brisk country walk. Flushed and alive. I guess this stuff really worked.

I heard a knock at my bedroom door.

I wrapped a towel loosely around myself. I liked the idea of Jack encountering this image of me when he opened the door. Maybe we could try again. "Come in," I said. "Not quite ready yet."

But when the door opened, it was Geia. Her long hair was tied up in a full bun and she was wearing a striking burnt orange jumpsuit.

"Oh," I said, pulling my towel tighter. "Hi."

Geia was holding a yellow gingham dress.

"Hey, Agnes. Sorry to catch you just out of the shower. Jack mentioned you could maybe use a party dress for tonight. I guess you didn't realize you'd be staying into the evening? This is a sample from our summer capsule collection at Goddess. I thought it looked like you."

Geia laid it on the bed and smiled. "You look amazing, by the way. You're glowing. The sun really agrees with you."

"Thanks." I looked away, embarrassed. I knew it wasn't the sun. It was either her face oil or the almost-sex with her ex-husband. I wondered if she knew that.

"I'll leave you to it."

"Thanks," I said again.

As she left, I noticed the outline of her perfect, peach-like bottom in her jumpsuit.

I couldn't compete with that. What was I even doing here? I wasn't cut out for any of this.

I assessed the dress and was annoyed to discover I loved it. It was exactly my style. The same shift-shape of the dresses I'd bought in New York but in a vintage-inspired print I wouldn't have chosen for myself. I tried it on. Then I put on the blue linen dress I'd been wearing all day. They were both nice, but the yellow one was much better. The blue also smelled like sweat and sunscreen. Fine, Geia, you win.

Then I remembered my footwear. Geia had only brought the dress, so my sneakers would have to do. I slipped them on my feet and sat on the bed to wait for Jack, scrolling through Instagram, not digesting any of the photos as they passed by my eyes. So, Geia wanders into Jack's wing as she pleases, even when he has a guest? What if she had walked in earlier when we were in bed together? I didn't like how blurry their boundaries were.

Geia had been nothing but kind and generous though, lending me the dress, inviting me to spend the night. No, Jack had invited me. But I couldn't imagine he had done it without an okay from her first.

I stopped scrolling. There was a new post from Jack: a photo of *The Penelopiad* by Margaret Atwood, the book I'd given him for his birthday. I smiled. A gift from me, posted for the whole world to see.

THERE WERE TWELVE people at the party, including me. This led me to speculate that someone had either been uninvited — unlikely — or, like me, added to the guest list at the last moment. Twelve was a perfect dinner party number. Some magic had been worked to make that happen.

Jack had described the party as a casual barbecue, but though it was happening outdoors, it was neither casual nor a barbecue. The grill appeared to be off and people stood in small clumps on the patio, sipping champagne and cocktails, chatting and laughing. The women wore chic summer dresses and most of the men wore shirts with collars. Jack was the only one in a T-shirt.

As we approached the guests, I whispered to Jack, "Who are these people?"

"Just some friends," he replied. "People from the neighbourhood. A few from the city."

The long stone table was set with candles of various heights and vases of gorgeous purple flowers: a mix of iris, lilac, and anemone. As we passed by, I noticed each plate held a handwritten menu for the evening's dinner. Did Geia write those?

The others watched us as we walked over to join them, and I imagined they were confused by my presence. Who is that woman, and why is she wearing sneakers?

I wondered how Jack would introduce me. As a new friend? Maybe he would tell the funny story of how we met on the plane. I doubted he wanted these people to know about our budding fling, especially after the tearful sex.

To my surprise though, he grabbed two flutes of champagne, gave one to me, and then grasped my empty hand. As he said hi to various guests, he introduced me as "Agnes Oliver, a brilliant writer," and recommended my book to them all, which was lovely but made me want to run and hide.

If these people were surprised that Jack had a new love interest, they didn't show it. They said it was nice to meet me and a few of the women complimented me on my dress. I told them it was Geia's, to which they raised their eyebrows in surprise.

Many of Jack's friends were famous. The first one I met was one of the most beloved American comedians of all time—and who, I learned, had a property two doors down. Unexpectedly, he came across as shy; his pint-sized wife did most of the talking.

There was also an actress from that HBO series I'd watched religiously in my twenties. She played the neurotic best friend of a narcissistic writer, and like Geia, she was even more beautiful in person. I wondered if this was the case with all celebrities. She struck me as excessively polite. Twice, she apologized profusely to me and the comedian's wife; first when she reached over to get a napkin and then again when she took a glass of champagne. She stayed quiet for the rest of the cocktail hour, as if not wanting to bother us again.

I met a journalist from the *New York Times*—I recognized his voice more than his face because I listened to his news podcast almost every morning—and a performance artist from Montreal, which we bonded over. I also talked to a chef with a food-travel show on Netflix and a young Korean-American fashion designer.

Everyone was very, very nice. They all seemed to love Jack and so they made space for me, asking me questions about my book and assuring me they would get a copy.

The conversation moved to summer travel plans. The comedian and his wife had a trip booked to Spain. Jack shared what we had learned earlier, that Geia would be spending time in Greece for some Goddess™ event, but mentioned no trips of his own. Maybe that was because he was always on the move: London, Chicago, New York, L.A.

While the others talked, I tried to stay present. I listened to them speak and tried not to stare at the faces of those who were so strangely familiar, the comedian in particular. I used to watch his TV show when I was a kid in the nineties. He was so much older now. It seemed like the face I knew had morphed, but I still knew it better than my own. I'd spent more time looking at him on screen than I ever had looking in the mirror. Occasionally, my mind wandered, unable to process where I was and who was speaking. I looked towards the trees at the back of the property, their leaves twitching in the slight breeze, and imagined running for cover like I had as a child.

If it wasn't for Jack's hand holding my own, I felt I might have floated away.

BENJAMIN ANNOUNCED IT was time to sit down and eat. Everyone looked towards the table, where Geia stood smiling, skin glowing in the fading evening light. That orange jumpsuit really was a showstopper.

Jack was seated at the head of the table. From the place cards, I saw that I was to his right. On my other side was the NYT journalist, and across from me was a quiet couple who I'd met briefly before dinner. They lived in the neighbourhood, and while they weren't famous, they seemed comfortable around the celebrities.

Geia sat at the far end of the table with Luke by her side. He still looked bored, but he was wearing a shirt now, a nice white button-up with mint-green stripes. I wondered what the other guests thought of Luke. His chiselled good looks, his languor, his age.

Servers appeared out of nowhere carrying the first course—a pea soup spiked with vermouth and topped with butter-poached lobster.

Before we could dig in though, Geia stood to make a toast. She towered over the table, raising her glass. Her hair looked like it was made of satin. She had taken it down from her bun, soft waves framing her unmistakable cheekbones, her delicate chin. "To Jack, father of my children, genius creator. You bring such light into all our lives. You are not just the man of our dreams, you are the man who makes dreams come true. I can't wait to see what you do next, my love. Happy birthday!"

We all clinked our glasses and Jack beamed. I shifted in my seat, feeling hot with jealousy. Was he still in love with her? How could he not be?

I tasted the soup. Of course it was heavenly. There was nothing Geia couldn't do, it seemed.

"You okay?" Jack squeezed my knee under the table.

"Mm-hm," I lied.

14

The party didn't go late. After dessert, the other guests started wandering home, everyone wishing Jack a happy birthday again and thanking Geia for the lovely evening. She put her palms together and bowed her head to each guest in response.

When it was only the four of us left, Jack suggested we turn in for the night. I nodded, feeling tipsy. I had downed a lot of wine in a short period of time. During dinner, I had found myself watching Geia more than anyone else. Her laugh was loud and intoxicating—everyone wanted to coax it out—and her stories were surprisingly wild. She talked openly about sex, encouraging everyone to share the craziest places they'd ever done the deed, and when it was her turn, she told us about the time she and Luke had managed to have sex in a wicker beach bed at a resort in Barbados in the middle of the afternoon. I noticed Jack poured himself more wine during her story. Thankfully, she didn't recount any steamy memories involving Jack, though I wouldn't have put it past her. She was an open book.

We said good night to Geia and Luke and made our way back towards the house, the grass wet with fresh dew, the air finally cool. When Jack opened the sliding doors, I started, heart in my throat. Kathari was slithering across the room towards us, yellow eyes flashing as they reflected the patio light.

"It's okay," Jack told me. "He won't hurt you."

Jack opened the door wider and let Kathari out. I watched the snake glide towards Geia and Luke through the grass. There was something very strange about that snake. He seemed unlike other animals, unnatural somehow. I couldn't put my finger on it. Maybe it was the way he moved? Or how they all treated him? He seemed almost human, so integrated into their family.

"He's allowed out like that?" I whispered. "What if he gets off the property?"

"Oh, that's not an issue. He doesn't do anything Geia doesn't want him to."

I wondered how that could be possible. Could you really train a snake like you could a dog?

SLEEP CAME QUICKLY in Jack's bed. We didn't discuss sleeping arrangements, it was just understood that I would spend the night there, which I liked.

I awoke around two in the morning, forgetting for a moment where I was. The shaded outlines of Jack's room didn't register until I heard his light snoring and felt the warmth of his body next to mine. My head was foggy, but my wine buzz had mostly worn off.

Within seconds though, I was wide awake — my mind racing through all that had happened that day. Being here, meeting all those people, crying. Did I say anything I shouldn't have? Did I stare too much?

I cringed at the familiar darkness. I knew these empty hours well. As a child, nightmares were never my problem. It was lying awake in bed that scared me. Long stretches of time, unable to sleep, only my mind for company. I always insisted my bedroom door had to stay open, the light in the hallway on, but even then I would often appear back downstairs in my pyjamas, asking whoever was around — my father, my mother, Max — to tuck me in again just so I could spend a little less time alone. Alone, I scared myself. Thinking of ghosts, mostly, but other terrors too: monsters, demons, zombies. Those categories seem so general now, but I was talented at creating specificity. Elaborate back-stories, evil schemes. I imagined dark creatures in my closet or lurking in the shadowed corners of my room. I envisioned them hanging from the ceiling, waiting to drop on top of me as soon as I closed my eyes. The ghosts of other children, little boys and girls with pale faces and singsong voices, were my specialty. My wild imagination got me in a lot of trouble.

My mother, when she was home, had no time for my nighttime fears.

"Don't be so stupid," was her refrain when I showed up downstairs in need of comfort.

Then she'd usher me back to my room and firmly shut the door. The light in the hallway became invisible, and I was plunged into pitch black. She said I needed to grow up. I was being silly, and it wasn't cute.

That's when I began to bargain with the darkness. I dreamed up negotiations to protect myself: If I blinked ten times, it couldn't get me; if I slept facing the wall, without moving, it couldn't see me. Sometimes this even worked.

I got up and wandered over to the window. Jack's room looked onto the backyard. The lawn glistened in the moonlight. As I gazed out at the trees lining the back of the property, swaying in the faint wind, a movement in the swimming pool caught my eye.

It was Geia, swimming laps. On the edge of the pool, I spotted Kathari, curled up in a tight coil. No sign of Luke. What was she still doing up? And swimming, at this hour?

After a few more laps, Geia dove down into the water and re-emerged on the stairs at the far end of the pool. As she stepped out of the water, I realized she was completely naked. Her long limbs gleamed in the moonlight.

She walked past the pool area onto the lawn. Kathari didn't follow, only raised his head to watch her go. When she got to the centre of the lawn, she stopped and looked up at the sky. The moon was bright and full above her. She lay down in the grass and spread her limbs wide, like she was making a snow angel. What was she doing? Was this some sort of Goddess™-approved moonbathing?

She lay there for many minutes, and the moonlight shining upon her seemed to intensify until her body was fully aglow, almost like she was absorbing the light. I looked up at the sky, but the moon appeared normal. It was Geia who had changed. I blinked, trying to make sense of what I was seeing.

Movement from the pool area again. Kathari slithered towards Geia across the lawn. When he reached her, he encircled her ankle, looping around it like a vine. I was too far away to make out Geia's expression, but she didn't seem startled by Kathari's presence at all; she didn't even flinch. Winding around her leg, Kathari's head passed her knee, her thigh, her lower abdomen. Here, he paused, and Geia reached down to caress his head, as you would do to a lover.

Kathari continued upwards, coming to rest on Geia's chest, most of his length still wrapped around her leg. The snake's body began to glow like Geia's. Both of them were gleaming—a strange, rosy light. Was I dreaming? Was I still drunk? My skin wouldn't do that if I lay naked in the grass under the moon. Was it some sort of chemical reaction, perhaps, between some product of hers and the light?

The glow seemed to intensify the longer they lay there. Then, all at once, a bright flash erupted from Geia's body, sending radiant waves of light in all directions—across the lawn, into the trees, towards the house. For a moment, it was like daylight.

15

I was never sure about the things I witnessed in the forest that couldn't be explained. The strange dust when I was a child was only the beginning. After my encounter with the shimmering substance, I started to experience the natural world in a new way. Walking in the woods, my sense of smell changed; as if by magic, one day I noticed an explosion of new scents all around me. I no longer smelled only flowers and trees, but also the earthy fungi and moss that crept along the forest floor, the tang of the algae that lived in the pond, the musk of animal fur belonging to creatures that were surely miles away. It felt so real, but could I trust it?

I certainly couldn't share it with anyone, that much I knew. After reading my fairy stories, my mother had made me feel like there was something wrong with me, something deeply weird and abnormal. What would she do if I told her what I was seeing and smelling in the woods? I feared she'd send me away, maybe to boarding school, maybe somewhere worse. So I kept it all inside me, secret, hidden.

Eventually, as I grew older, my "new senses" — as I'd taken to calling them — began to fade, but I never forgot them. I reasoned that my early experiences of nature, real or not, had a purpose in my life. I would use them as inspiration in my storytelling. I had told Owen that being a writer wasn't just about writing; it was about how I saw the world. And while I was trying to be clever at the time, I realized as I said it that I believed it.

But the morning after Jack's birthday party, as I lay in bed listening to him in the shower, I struggled to rationalize what I had seen through the window the night before. I knew it wasn't a dream. I had never felt more awake than I had watching Geia and her snake under the moon. But where did my strange mind end and reality begin? I sat up and gulped down the glass of water on my bedside table to clear my mind. Still, it spun in circles.

"You're awake," Jack said, emerging from the bathroom, hair wet and fully dressed. "How did you sleep?"

I held the empty water glass in my lap, clasped in both hands. "Fine," I said, my voice hoarse. I was still thirsty.

"Breakfast?"

I watched Jack put on his watch and unplug his phone, scrolling briefly through something I couldn't see. Did he know what Geia did when the rest of us were sleeping? Had he watched Kathari wind his way up her body before? Had he ever seen the same flash of light?

"Sure." I got up slowly from the bed. "I'll go get dressed."

Jack nodded, still looking at his phone.

I headed for my room, but I paused in the doorway, turning to look at him.

"Jack?" I said quietly.

He glanced up. "Yeah?"

Should I ask him about what I'd seen? What could I even say that wouldn't make me seem completely unhinged?

"What is it, Agnes?"

I hesitated. I couldn't find the words. Jack had a way of making me feel like I had known him forever, but we had only just met. I didn't want to scare him away, especially after my emotional outburst yesterday. Maybe I *had* been dreaming? Or sleepwalking? That made more sense than what I thought I had seen last night.

"It's nothing," I said, shaking my head. "I think I just need a cup of coffee."

He smiled. "That, I can do."

DOWNSTAIRS, WE WERE met by the smell of pancakes. Geia was back at the stovetop, whipping up breakfast and looking every bit the goddess in a crisp white shirt-dress that showed off her tan. I smoothed the front of my own wrinkled dress, wishing I had thought to pack more clothes.

"Morning," Geia said brightly. The twins were seated at the large kitchen island, drawing pictures in between bites of blueberry pancake. Kathari, I noted, was nowhere in sight.

"Coffee? Matcha? Shot of whisky?"

I stared at Geia, trying to reconcile the woman standing before me with what I'd witnessed the night before.

"Only kidding!" She laughed. "God, Agnes, don't look

so serious. We only drink in the morning around here on Christmas. And New Year's. And, well, my birthday. So, what will it be? Lattes? What's your milk preference?"

"Sorry?"

"Are you non-dairy? We have oat, almond, cashew, soy. I think we might even have pea."

Pea? As in pea milk?

"Dairy's fine," I said.

Geia pressed a button on a giant, shiny espresso machine next to the stove, and within seconds presented Jack and me each with a perfect latte. I took a sip. It was better than anything I'd made in all my years at the café.

"Sit, sit," she said, gesturing to the kitchen island. "This batch is almost ready."

Jack introduced me to Sparrow, who had a slightly rounder face than her twin, and then started asking the girls questions about their drawings. I looked from Geia to Jack and back again. It seemed they really were one big, happy family. She was humming cheerfully while she flipped our pancakes, sipping her own latte like she made breakfast for her ex-husband's new love interest every day. Could she really be this perfect, so exactly like the flawless image she presented on social media? A real-life goddess?

"So Agnes, I have to tell you, I'm loving *Violets in Her Lap*. I read the first hundred pages last night before bed and picked it up again this morning as soon as I was awake."

I must have looked surprised because she smiled knowingly. "Jack told me you were humble." Geia shook her head. "If I teach you anything, Agnes, it's that you should own your talent, your special contribution to the world. Who has time to be humble?"

She stacked pancakes on two plates and drizzled them artfully with maple syrup. I wasn't surprised she was reading my book — Jack had mentioned it yesterday — but I wondered how she'd had time to read last night after her midnight swim and moon–snake communion on the lawn. Did the woman sleep at all? Or was this proof that I'd dreamed the whole thing?

"Not me!" Sparrow spoke up proudly, grinning at her mother. "Look what I drew, Mommy. Isn't it beautiful?"

Geia tucked a lock of Sparrow's dark hair behind her ear and assessed the drawing. "It's gorgeous! Agnes, don't you think it's gorgeous?"

I looked up, mouth full of delicious, perfectly golden pancake, and nearly spat it out. Sparrow held up her rendering of the night sky, complete with a big, bright, full moon.

Keep chewing, Agnes.

"Beautiful," I said, taking a swig of coffee to clear my throat. "It was a full moon last night, wasn't it?"

I waited to see if this would get a reaction, but Geia was back at the stovetop and didn't seem to hear to me. The vision of her sprawled on the lawn, body aglow, returned to my mind. She seemed perfectly normal this morning though. Well, perfectly normal by Geia Stone's standards.

"I'm thinking today's a beach day," she said, her back to us. "Agnes, you'll join us, won't you?"

I glanced over at Jack, who was still busy with the girls. He was now contributing to their drawings, adding constellations to Sparrow's night sky, showing her how to connect the individual stars into shapes.

"I should probably be getting back to the city."

"Nonsense." She turned to face me, her wide smile blinding. "You have to stay another night. I haven't finished reading your book. And we have so much to talk about."

AFTER BREAKFAST, I wandered out to the backyard to call Zelda. We were supposed to have a meeting that afternoon, but I figured she'd be open to rescheduling when I told her I'd been invited to spend a second night with Jack Verity. Outside, the day was already growing hot. I walked barefoot to the centre of the lawn where I'd seen Geia entwined with Kathari the night before. Had it really happened? I still couldn't be sure. I looked around, but the grass showed no imprint of her body.

Zelda answered after a single ring. She was never far from her phone. "Agnes, how's it going over there? Film rights sold already? Screenplay in the works?"

I walked in circles around the lawn. What was I looking for? Moon dust?

"Not exactly. Working on it though. I've been invited to stay a second night."

"Oh, really?" Zelda sounded delighted. "He must really like you then."

"Well, actually—" I stopped my circling "—it was Geia's idea. She's reading the book too. She says she wants to talk to me about it when she's finished."

Zelda hooted with laughter. "Agnes, for someone who

claims to have no idea what she's doing, you sure are making things happen. I guess you're calling to cancel our lunch date today? Not a problem. Call me when you're back in the city and we'll reschedule. And keep your eyes on the prize. Who knows? Maybe Geia wants *Violets in Her Lap* to be the latest Goddess Book Club pick, or, just thinking aloud here...maybe adapting your book will be the first cinematic collaboration between Geia Stone and Jack Verity since their marriage ended. Now, that would be good press."

I took a few deep breaths before heading back inside. Was I setting up my publishing team for disappointment by letting them think a film adaptation was on the table? No one had actually said anything about film rights here. Could I really make that happen? And how long could I use that possibility as a distraction from book two?

I inhaled slowly, nose wrinkling. My sense of smell was no longer as intense as when I was a child, but I could still make out traces of the surrounding environment. Somewhere nearby, an animal had died, its body rotting in the early summer heat.

16

Geia insisted we all bike to the beach. In the garage, we retrieved six turquoise bicycles of various sizes, the kind with big, looping handlebars and baskets on the front. They were stored alongside several Vespas, a bunch of scooters, some sea kayaks, two surfboards, and an impressive array of smaller sports equipment, including countless tennis rackets.

"Do you play?" Jack asked me. "The girls and I love it."

I shook my head. Beyond running up and down Mont Royal a few times a week, physical exertion had never really been my thing.

"I don't play either, Agnes," Geia called out from the driveway, where she was lathering sunscreen on her daughters. "I don't even watch."

Jack rolled his eyes. "Geia thinks all sports are boring," he said, which I found odd. She was known for being an exercise junkie. But playing sports and working out were different, I guess.

We each grabbed a bike and set off down the driveway. The large security gate swung open as we rode off the property and Geia led the way down the street, her tanned calves flexing as she pumped the pedals at an impressive clip. Luke followed close behind, but Jack and I stuck with the girls, who couldn't quite keep up. Luckily, it wasn't far to the beach.

As we got closer, the briny smell of the ocean reached my nose in stronger and stronger waves until I felt like I was already bathing in it. We passed by more giant homes hidden behind solid fences and I wondered who might live in such places. Actors, models, musicians? Moguls, founders, tycoons? Past presidents, maybe? I squinted as we passed each house, trying to catch a glimpse of someone I might recognize.

Within seconds of our arrival, Benjamin showed up in a black SUV with a cooler of snacks and drinks, umbrellas and beach blankets, and buckets of toys for the girls. He scooted ahead of us to set up, his shiny loafers sinking in the sand as he disappeared behind the spiky green beach grasses on the bluff.

The beach itself seemed to go on forever: powdery white sand stretched into the far distance in both directions, waves creeping up the coastline in a steady, easy rhythm. It was already busy. Families played in the surf and sprawled on the sand in small clusters. The adults sat down on the blankets Benjamin had laid out for us and the girls immediately ran to the water's edge, buckets in hand.

"Thanks, Benjamin," Geia called out as he headed back to the SUV.

It was only eleven, but Luke immediately cracked open a beer. Geia, meanwhile, stripped down to her bikini and lay on her back to continue reading my book. I quickly looked away towards the water. Despite my airport stalking, I had never actually watched anyone read it before.

"Wanna go for a walk?" Jack asked, and I nodded, more than a little relieved.

We headed down the beach, walking where the sand was damp, our bare feet leaving tracks behind us. I wasn't sure what to say. So much had happened in the last two days, but last night was something else altogether. I felt like I was in a bizarro world where nothing made sense. Was I really walking down the beach with Jack Verity right now? Did Geia Stone have magical powers? Was I losing it?

"Should we talk about it?" Jack said suddenly, and I stopped in my tracks.

"Talk about what?"

He couldn't mean Geia and the moon, could he?

He took a deep breath. "Yesterday."

I stared at him blankly.

"In my bedroom?"

I exhaled. Right. Of course. He wants to talk about your humiliating crying fit, Agnes, not the possibility of his ex-wife being a supernatural being. I continued walking.

"Do we have to?" I said, as he reached for my hand. "I mean, we could, but I don't know if there's really much to say."

"Are you okay?" he asked. He sounded concerned, which only made me feel more mortified.

"Of course."

"It's okay if you're not."

"Look, I don't know what that was." I stared at the sand, searching for an explanation, but he'd already given me one. "Maybe you're right. Maybe it was just too soon."

Jack nodded. "I thought so. I don't usually rush into these things, but . . . I don't know. Maybe it was reading your book. It felt like I knew you before we even met."

I wondered if that was true. Was I really there, in my book, for all to experience? I wasn't sure how I felt about that. It hadn't been my intention to share myself with the world. I just wanted to tell stories.

"Well, I'm still getting to know *you*," I said. "There's a lot I don't know. We only met a few days ago."

He grinned. "Ask away. I'm an open book."

Some yelling caught our attention. Ahead of us, three boys tackled one another in the water.

"What were you like as a child?" I asked, nodding in the boys' direction.

Jack smiled. "Not like that. I was quiet. More subdued."

"I find that hard to believe."

He laughed, shaking his head. "Am I not subdued now? Don't tell me I've become loud and obnoxious in my old age?"

"Not obnoxious, no. Energetic maybe?"

He laughed again. "I'll take it. But no, I was much more chill as a boy. I was pretty much raised by my older sister, Imogen, because my parents each had multiple jobs and worked odd hours. She kept me calm, I think. She was the most steady person I've ever met. A rock, in every sense. My rock. She helped me with my homework every night.

She used to make the best cheese toasties. She was also the first person to introduce me to film. We watched *Alien* when I was way too young and it scared the shit out of me. But after, we talked about what made it scary, what made it good. We always talked about the films we watched. We processed them together. I think that helped me to understand them as an art form, not just entertainment."

I marvelled at how his face lit up talking about Imogen. "She sounds amazing."

"She was." Something in Jack's voice changed. He squinted, and the light I had just seen disappeared. "She died when I was sixteen."

My stomach sank. "I'm so sorry, Jack."

"It's okay. Well, it's not okay. It's stupid, actually. Stupid and unfair. The steadiest, most responsible person I've ever known made one small mistake and now she's gone forever."

"Mistake?"

He squinted harder, looking out at the water. "She never partied. I always tell people that because I don't want them to get the wrong idea. She was straight and narrow ninety-nine percent of the time, but it was her birthday, her twentieth, and my mum made sure she had the night off from work so that Imogen could have the night off from taking care of me. 'Go out with your mates.' I can still hear Mum saying it. 'Go have some fun.' So that's what she did. I don't know if she was drunk or what, but towards the end of the night she stepped off the pavement and was hit by a bus."

Goosebumps crept up my arms. "That's awful."

Jack nodded. "It's the kind of heartbreak you never get over. But I didn't let her death go to waste. I told myself I would work hard and make a life for myself, like Imogen always wanted for me. I cleaned up my grades and got a scholarship to film school. I moved here, to a different country. We used to dream about that together. She told me she wanted to be my date to the Oscars when I got nominated, which she was sure I would be. And she wanted me to buy a big house for the whole family, far from London, somewhere warm. It's part of the reason I want to buy my parents a new place, move them to California maybe, but I think living in the same flat Imogen grew up in helps them feel connected to her."

"That makes sense." My chest ached for him. I couldn't believe he had experienced such a profound loss when he was only sixteen. I thought my own upbringing was hard, but an overly critical mother was nothing compared to what Jack had been through.

"I'm no idiot," he said, scratching his chin. "I know, in some ways, Geia was like a substitute for Imogen. An older woman, a maternal figure."

I held my breath.

"That was good for a while," he continued. "It was what I needed at the time. But now, I want a real partner. Someone to build a life with."

I didn't know what to say to that. I had never been anyone's partner before. Girlfriend, yes, but I had worn even that label loosely. My longest relationship, Owen aside, had lasted less than eight months, and that was back in college. The thing with Owen had spanned four years, but I was never his partner. He had a wife for that. I was his mistress.

"But didn't you build a life with Geia?" I asked, chewing on my thumbnail. "You have the girls, the films."

"Sort of." He paused. His voice sounded heavy. "But it was more like Geia was driving and I was just along for the ride."

AFTER OUR DAY at the beach, we biked home and retreated to our separate rooms to shower before dinner. A part of me hoped Jack would suggest we shower together, but our earlier conversation seemed fresh in his mind. I had said it was too soon. Whether that was true or not, he was giving me my space.

For the second day in a row, I stood in the shower and rubbed Goddess™ Buff It Off Body Scrub in circles up and down my legs. Today, I rubbed harder, imagining I could make my legs grow longer, gazelle-like, more like Geia's. I washed my hair with the Goddess™ Silken-Sleek Shampoo and wondered if my hair, usually straight, would dry into her soft, perfect waves. I followed up my shower with Goddess™ Gleam Body Oil, massaging it into my arms and legs, hoping they would shine and catch the light like Geia's did. Was this what her followers believed, that if they bought her products and followed her advice, they could be just like Geia? I wondered what her fanbase would say if they knew about her pet snake and her peculiar, moonlit activities. Then again, it was well known that Geia championed controversial self-care treatments and practices, from vaginal steaming to micro-dosing magic mushrooms. In the world of wellness, was anything too strange?

Geia had given me another dress to wear to dinner, also from her Goddess™ summer capsule collection. This one was moss green, short and simple. I liked it even more than the yellow one from the night before and told her so when she handed it to me upon our arrival back at the house.

"Keep it," she said, eyes wide. "That colour looks like it was made for you."

I thanked her. I would never have guessed Geia would be so nice, so accommodating, so non-judgemental. Being raised by my mother, I had learned to keep my guard up around other women, especially older ones. But Geia wasn't like my mother at all.

Once I was dressed, I tiptoed over to Jack's room, but I could hear the shower running, so I decided to head outside to the patio by myself. Maybe if I got Geia one-on-one, I could ask her about Kathari and gently nudge the conversation towards an explanation for what I had seen.

But the only person I found outside was Luke. Another beer in one hand, his phone in the other. He was lying on one of the loungers, still wearing his sunglasses even though the sun was low, the sky a wash of pale yellows and oranges. I could smell his recent shower. He didn't look up when I sat down next to him.

"Hey," I said.

He glanced over at me. "Hey."

"What are you always doing on that thing? Crossword? Sudoku?"

He looked down at his phone and chuckled, ignoring the question.

"So, how long have you and Geia been together?"

Luke yawned, still scrolling. "A little over a year."

"Really? I've never even heard of you."

He glanced over at me again, amused, and I blushed.

"I just mean, the media usually knows all about her love life."

"Yeah, well, we like to keep our relationship private."

"I get that." I nodded.

"Do you?"

He still looked amused and I realized he thought I was talking about Jack and me, being presumptuous about a relationship that didn't even exist yet. Why was I letting this twenty-five-year-old make me feel like such an idiot? "So, what do you do for a living, Luke?"

He downed the rest of his beer.

"You're looking at it."

"You don't work?"

He took off his sunglasses and finally looked at me. His green eyes had a yellow tinge in the pale light of early evening.

"It's not what you're thinking," he said. "I just...don't work."

I supposed he was probably independently wealthy. How else would he have met Geia? They must run in the same circles.

It occurred to me then that Luke was the most recent addition to the family and may have had a similar learning curve as me: namely, getting used to a giant snake freely roaming around the house and property.

"What's the deal with Kathari?" I asked, trying to sound casual. "He's a bit, strange, no?"

Luke smiled smugly, putting his sunglasses back on. "Word of advice. If you want in with Geia, don't say a bad word about that snake."

17

I had trouble sleeping again that night. Jack slept soundly beside me, totally unaware, while I kept getting up from the bed and going to the window. But no matter how many times I looked outside, there was nothing to see. The sloping green lawn remained empty, the swimming pool still. I gazed out at the backyard and remembered Geia's body stretched out on the grass, the snake's slow, winding movement. The inexplicable burst of light. The image remained fresh in my mind. It wasn't going away. I crept back to bed, disappointed, again and again.

I must have fallen asleep at some point because I awoke to the sound of birdsong. Out of habit, I moved silently to the window once again, and to my surprise, there she was: Geia, in leggings and a sports bra, stretching on a yoga mat in the middle of the lawn. The exact same spot where she had done her moonbathing.

Without thinking, I left the bedroom and sped through Jack's quarters. I slid open the glass door to the patio and crossed the lawn. It was only when Geia turned and smiled at me, as if she somehow knew I was coming, that I realized I didn't know what I was doing. I was still in a pair of Jack's boxers and one of his T-Shirts. I wasn't even wearing a bra. I crossed my arms against my chest.

"Morning, Agnes. Did you sleep well?" Something in her voice made me think she knew I hadn't.

I shook my head. "Not really."

Geia eyed me, head tilted. "Lots on your mind?"

In that moment I was convinced that she knew what I was thinking, that she knew I'd seen her bathing in the moonlight. But how could she? She hadn't looked up at the window where I stood watching her. She had stayed firmly planted on the ground, eyes closed, body glowing. Still though. It almost felt like she was tempting me to bring it up. I fumbled, trying to find the right words, heart racing. My head ached from lack of sleep and I was growing very hot all of a sudden, even though the morning still held a chill.

"Are you all right?" Geia asked, concerned. "You don't look well."

"I don't know." I closed my eyes, rubbing my lids. Exhaustion crested in me like a wave and I felt all the wine I'd drunk the night before at dinner — Geia had made wood-fired pizza and served it with bottle after bottle of Barolo — making my insides rubbery. "I feel a bit dizzy."

"Here, come sit down."

Geia led me back across the lawn and guided me to a chair on the patio.

"Take deep breaths," she said wisely. "I'll get you a glass of water."

I inhaled the fresh air, catching whiffs of lilac and that haunting wild rose, and exhaled as slowly as possible. Each breath made me feel more solid, less like I was living a strange dream.

"Here." She thrust a glass of water into my hands. "Drink up."

I took a big gulp, but the liquid, though clear, didn't taste like water.

"What is this?"

"Water."

"It doesn't taste like—"

"You're right, it's water with a slight enhancement. Something new we're working on at Goddess. Ultra-hydrating. You should be feeling better in no time after a glass of this."

I frowned but drank the water anyway. It was vaguely sweet, a bit woodsy. It tasted the way pine trees smelled. I had to admit, within seconds of finishing the glass, I did feel better. My headache persisted, a dull ache, but I no longer felt dizzy or quite so tired.

"See?" Geia sat across from me, watching. "Magic water, right?"

I nodded. The word magic had sparked my attention. Magic water. Magic snake? Magic woman?

"Agnes, I'm so glad you woke up before the others. I wanted us to have a chance to speak one-on-one."

My pulse sped up again. "What about?"

"Well." Geia clasped her hands in her lap and smiled widely, showing her perfect teeth. "I finished your book this morning."

"Oh," I said, surprised. Did this woman never sleep?

"And I have to say, I loved it. Love may be an understatement. I'm searching for a word that's stronger than love." She looked at me. "You're a writer. Any suggestions?"

I shook my head uncertainly.

"Anyway, it was fabulous. It was unlike anything I've ever read before."

"Thank you," I said, though I wondered if she was being sincere. Maybe she was being extra nice to prove she was okay with me and Jack doing whatever it was we were doing.

"I loved it so much," Geia said, not breaking my gaze, "that I have a proposition for you."

I held my breath. My mind immediately went to the non-existent film adaptation I was supposed to be engineering. But wouldn't Jack be a part of that conversation too?

"I told you I'm going home this summer, right? To Mastika. The island where I was born."

"Yes," I said, not sure where this was going.

"Well, the reason I'm going to Mastika is to host the biggest event of my career, something I've been working towards for a very, very long time. It's called the Goddess Summit. Ten days on the island with fifty of my most devoted followers. These women are incredibly committed to their individual wellness journeys and they're ready to take their healing to the next level under my close supervision.

I've devised a life-changing self-care curriculum for them. They'll be mentored by the best of the best in a range of daily sessions meant to help them align, elevate, and expand into their highest selves, body, mind, and soul."

I waited. She sounded like the sales copy on her website, not like the fun Geia I'd come to know over the last couple of days. What did any of this have to do with me?

"We're going to be doing some challenging stuff at the Summit, Agnes. It won't be for the faint of heart. But groundbreaking innovation never is, right? If you want to move the cultural conversation forward, you have to be willing to make people a bit uncomfortable. I'm sure you've seen how the media talk about what I'm trying to do with Goddess. They think I'm insane. Or just in it for the money. Or both."

I blinked, feeling more awake. She couldn't honestly be suggesting she wasn't in it for the money. We were sitting in the backyard of her giant Hamptons summer house, for god's sake.

"Are you not?" I asked. I couldn't help myself.

"Of course not." She shook her head dismissively. "Frankly, I'm sick of the narrative that's been constructed about me and my mission. I need someone to tell my story honestly, without judgement or preconceived opinions. I need an open mind." She paused. "I need *your* mind, Agnes."

I blushed, finally breaking away from her intense eye contact. What was she saying?

"Here's what I'm proposing. You travel to Mastika to attend the Summit. You'll do the full curriculum, participating in all the sessions, getting to know my followers, and you'll write about your experience for an article in a major publication. I'm thinking *Vogue*. They've wanted to do something big on Goddess for a while."

Vogue? That sounded impossible. But so did travelling to some remote Greek island I'd never heard of to write an article about Geia.

"I need someone who's not afraid to be bold," she said, reaching for my hand.

I shook my head, laughing her off. "Then you need someone else."

Now she grabbed my other hand, holding both tightly. She leaned in close. "You are exactly what I need, Agnes. I read your book. I know your voice and your perspective. I know you see what others can't."

Goosebumps crept up my arms and she squeezed my hands tighter, her smile so wide it looked like it hurt.

PANCAKES, IT SEEMED, were reserved for weekends in the Stone-Verity household. It was now Monday morning: back to business and back to the city for me. Geia made us all green smoothies and we sat around the kitchen island once again. The girls read books quietly while Geia shared the news with Jack and Luke: I would be joining her in Mastika for the Goddess™ Summit.

Jack looked at me in surprise.

I shrugged, drinking deeply from my smoothie. "How could I say no? It's *Vogue*."

Jack frowned, though I wasn't sure why. An opportunity like this didn't come along often. I was sure Zelda, Robert, and even Jessica would be pleased. It was great exposure. And maybe I'd find an idea for book two while I was in Greece.

Geia beamed, Luke said "Mazel tov" in his usual monotone, but Jack continued to appear nonplussed. I reached for his hand under the table and though he squeezed mine in return, he looked preoccupied for the rest of breakfast.

I didn't have bags to pack, so there was no reason to stick around after we finished our smoothies. Geia was taking Goddess™ meetings in her home office, Luke was off to play a game of tennis with a young senator who lived down the street, and Jack had film editing to do. He walked me to the driveway and I felt a new distance bristle between us, like he wanted to say something but wasn't sure how.

"What is it?" I asked. "You were quiet all through breakfast."

He frowned. "Are you sure about this?"

"About what?"

"About Greece. Aren't you supposed to be focusing on your next book right now?"

I looked away, annoyed. Nearby, a gang of bumblebees dove in and out of a rhododendron bush, sipping its sweet nectar. Of course I was supposed to be working on book two—no one knew that better than me—but that was going nowhere at the moment.

"Yes," I said, slowly. "So?"

Jack rubbed one eye and I could tell he was holding back. "What is it, Jack?"

"It's just . . . Geia has a way of steering people off course.

Off their own course and onto hers. I don't want you to get swept up in all of that. Swept up in her."

I scoffed. Did he really think I was so naive?

"I know what I'm doing, Jack. I'm not one of her super-fans. Going to the Summit, writing this article, it makes sense for my career."

"I just hope you're making this choice with a clear head." He looked briefly towards the house. "I know it looks like it's all fun and games here, and I can imagine it's quite... seductive. But it's not all it's cracked up to be, you know."

I blushed, feeling anger begin to rise in my throat, hot and swift. So, not only did he think I was naive, he thought I was doing this because I had been fooled by Geia Stone's charmed life?

"Look, I'm just being smart," I said, voice high. "About my life and my career. I'm sorry you don't trust my judgement, but I have to do what I think is right."

"Okay," he said, nodding as if resigned. "I'm sorry if I overstepped."

The black town car pulled up in front of us. I moved towards it, but he pulled me back and kissed me.

"Maybe I'm just being selfish," he whispered in my ear. "But I can't wait to read your next book."

I smiled faintly but I still didn't like his tone, as if he knew better than me and I was making a mistake only he could see. As the town car headed down the driveway, I stared straight ahead. I sensed he was waving goodbye, but I didn't look out the window until we were already long gone.

PART 2

The Goddess Effect

Deep below the surface, we thrive. Unknown but essential, doing your dirty work, breathing life where there was once only death. We, the fungi of the forest, cast a spell that binds all the green together. We make it whole; we make it new.

    — *Violets in Her Lap* by Agnes Oliver

18

GODDESS™ SUMMIT — DAY 1

When my ferry departed Athens later that summer, I almost wasn't on it. No one had warned me that the port of Athens was pretty much its own city, or that I'd have to take a shuttle bus from one end of the port to the other just to find the right dock. I ran to catch the shuttle and then again to make it onto the ferry in time. I was one of the last people to board, but I made it.

I walked to the front of the boat, the wind blowing my hair in all directions. The Aegean Sea seemed to go on forever, bluer than blue, glimmering with sunlight and stretching far out of reach. Ahead of me and to the left, parched, hilly islands emerged on the horizon.

I turned when I heard loud voices speaking in English behind me. A group of three women sat together at a table on the deck. One stray glance and I knew we were headed to the same place: they were middle-aged, wearing yoga leggings, and discussing intermittent fasting. I sat down on a bench close by to eavesdrop. It didn't take long for the conversation to switch from fasting to Geia and the Summit, our shared destination.

"It says on the website she's going to be there," one of the women said.

"Yes, but does that mean we're going to see her around every day, or only at certain workshops?" another asked.

"I think it means a mix," the third spoke up. "She probably won't be around all the time, but that's the whole point of the Summit. For *her* to be able to meet *us*."

"I thought the point was to *optimize body, mind, and spirit*."

"Well, yes, but also to meet Geia. In the latest email update, she called us her *tribe*."

She. Geia. Not Geia Stone. They talked about her like they knew her. Maybe that was part of the Goddess™ effect. Geia made you feel like she was your best friend, dishing out advice on the most intimate aspects of your life, even though you had never met her.

"I heard she's really nice."

"I heard she's actually really funny. Like, she has a good sense of humour? I hope we see that side of her."

I smirked. They had no idea who they were about to meet. What would they think of the real Geia, lover of wine, potato chips, and public fornication?

One of the women yawned. Another checked her reflection in the black mirror of her phone, then fixed her hair by grabbing her ponytail in two pieces and pulling it tighter.

"At the very least, you know the food will be good."

"Oh my god, did you see the menu for tonight? All macro-biotic, organic, with options for vegan and gluten-free."

"I'm hungry now," ponytail whined.

"Oh, here. I have KIND bars. I never travel without them."

I watched as one of the women handed out granola bars to the others. From what I'd read on the Goddess™ website, tickets to the Summit were $10,000 each, excluding airfare. And still they had sold out in mere minutes. The lucky fifty who had secured spots were from all over the world. These three sounded American, but it seemed unlikely that they knew each other before today; the chances of friends getting tickets together was slim. They must have found each other on the boat, maybe back at the port, or on the flight to Greece.

It had been a little over a month since Geia invited me to the Summit. Though I'd had multiple calls with one of her assistants to arrange my travel plans — evidently, Benjamin was just one lifeline among many — I still couldn't believe I was really on my way.

Mastika. A tiny speck of an island located on the eastern edge of the Aegean Sea. There was very little written about it. I had tried to look it up online, but found only a few mentions of the island, all of them vague. All I knew for sure was that Geia had been born there. There was also, apparently, a sweet liqueur called mastika, made from the resin of trees that grew on the island.

I wondered what it would be like to see Geia again, and in such different circumstances. I had thought about her constantly since my weekend in the Hamptons, still consumed by what I had seen through the window. After a few glasses of wine one night back at my apartment in Montreal, I read up on pagan rituals involving the moon, but nothing resembled what I had seen that night. My best defense was to convince myself I had dreamt it all up, but when I closed my eyes and remembered that scene, it was vivid. It was real. What did that mean though? I figured the Summit would offer an opportunity to observe her again. I would pay closer attention this time, watching for anything odd or unusual.

THE BOAT REACHED Mastika midafternoon. The island was smaller and greener than the other islands we had seen on our journey, with a ridge of high mountains running its length. The port was a single dock in a tiny village: a swathe of white and blue buildings curving up a grassy hillside. From the dock, one restaurant was visible on the water-front, at which a handful of men sat drinking together at an outdoor table. They watched us disembark from the boat, no change in their solemn expressions.

The few Greeks aboard the ferry scattered immediately and disappeared into the village, while the rest of us were left standing together on the boardwalk, one obvious group of women from elsewhere. There were twelve of us in total. We knew there was supposed to be a bus picking us up, but the road in front of the port was empty, save for a few cars and a moped.

The women seemed unnerved by the staring men. I heard someone mutter "creepy" to their neighbour. Most of the women turned their backs on the town, facing the water instead. I considered suggesting we get a drink across the way, but someone else beat me to it.

"Looks like the bus is late," a woman with a sleek platinum bob said. "Anyone wanna grab a drink?"

A few of the women turned and eagerly agreed; others came along begrudgingly. Maybe they didn't want to be tipsy when meeting Geia, though I doubted she would be part of our welcome committee. I assumed we would only see her occasionally, at special events, likely from a safe — for her — distance.

We crossed the street and grabbed a couple of tables near the group of men. I smiled and said hello to them. They nodded in response but said nothing. Soon, a young server appeared. She was stunning, no other word for it. She had a gorgeous olive complexion, clear blue eyes, and legs that seemed to go on forever. She looked like Geia. Were they related? Maybe she was a cousin or something.

The server spoke only a little English. I asked what she had to drink and she offered two options: beer or mastika.

"Oh, you make that here, right?"

She nodded. "From trees." She pointed to a tuft of bushy green trees, thin trunks and heavy tops, in a nearby courtyard.

"I'll have that."

"Bottle?" she asked, eyebrows raised, looking at the group of women. Her eyebrows were perfect, dark and arched and full, just how everyone wanted their eyebrows to look these days.

"Sure," said the woman next to me, the one who had suggested we grab a drink.

The stunning server disappeared to get our drinks. I glanced over at the group of men and noticed they too were beautiful. Dark, striking features, the same great skin. I had no idea how old they were. From far away, I had assumed they were middle-aged or older because of their nondescript clothing and their quiet demeanour, but now I wasn't so sure. They looked oddly ageless. They could be thirty-five or sixty, or any age in between.

Geia, the server, these men. I imagined the island was like that place in Japan where people live longer than anywhere else in the world, only here, you didn't live forever, you just looked forever young. The fresh air preserved your youthful physicality, or maybe it was the sea, clear and blue, revitalizing.

The server returned with a bottle of mastika. She poured each of us a small glass. I took a sip and was surprised to find it was sweet and woodsy. It tasted like pine, like the tincture Geia had added to my water back in the Hamptons. Magic water, she'd called it.

"I'm Ellen." The woman with the platinum bob offered me her hand.

"Agnes."

We shook.

"Good idea." I gestured to the table, the drink. "I needed this."

Ellen shrugged. "I've heard Greek transportation is notoriously late. Who knows how long we'll be waiting?"

Another woman spoke up from across the table — auburn ringlets, suspiciously full lips. "Honestly, I expected better. We're paying top-dollar for this trip. I thought it would be better organized."

A few of the others nodded, but how could they possibly complain about this? I gazed out at the bright blue water, my new obsession. Earlier in the day, it had been an incredible turquoise. Now, as the sky turned light and hazy, it looked almost sapphire. I sipped my mastika. It was sweet but not cloying. I felt immediately refreshed, with more energy than I'd had since leaving Montreal two days ago.

Several women lowered their voices to complain some more amongst themselves, not touching the mastika, and I glanced pointedly at Ellen, who grinned at me behind chic tortoiseshell sunglasses. Despite the long day of travel, her hot-pink lipstick was immaculate. She slipped off her sandals and rested her feet on a free chair, crossing her legs.

"What do you do?" she asked.

I hesitated. I wasn't sure I wanted the Summit participants to know I would be chronicling the event for *Vogue*, at least not yet. It might change how they acted around me and I wanted to be able to write honestly about the personalities and voices that made up this thing. I decided to tell her part of the truth, that I was an author who wrote fiction. That wouldn't raise any immediate suspicions.

"Cool," Ellen said brightly. Then, the necessary follow-up: "Would I know anything you've written?"

"Oh, probably not. My first book just came out."

"That's amazing. Congratulations. What's it called?"

"*Violets in Her Lap*."

"Oh my god! I bought your book last month. I haven't got around to reading it yet but now I have actual motivation. I've met the author."

I smiled. "What about you? What do you do?"

"I'm in film." Ellen poured more mastika into her glass and topped up mine. "Production mostly."

"Now that's cool."

She shrugged. "It's mostly a lot of work, a real hustle. That's how I know Geia, actually. I got my start in Hollywood working on *The Opposites* films."

"You know Geia?" auburn ringlets chimed in.

Ellen nodded. "Yeah, I've known her for years. I know Jack better though. Jack Verity. Her ex-husband?"

My chest lifted a little when I heard Jack's name. We continued to text over the last month, but I had become less enthusiastic about the whole thing after our exchange in the driveway, and I think he sensed that. At first, he talked about coming to visit me in Montreal before I left for Greece, but we never settled on a good weekend and eventually the idea fizzled out. After the book tour, I was happy to be home in my apartment, alone again. I still wasn't getting any writing done, but now I had the space and time to do it when the inspiration struck. Hearing his name now, and knowing Ellen knew him too, made me miss him suddenly.

The other women looked at Ellen with awe. A connection with Geia. Someone who actually knew her. One degree of separation.

"What's she like?" auburn ringlets asked, all wide-eyed.

Ellen looked at the water. Quiet waves gently rocked a few small fishing boats tied to the nearby seawall.

"She's exactly as she seems online. Only better."

19

The shuttle bus arrived soon after. Ellen and I paid the bill, downing the last dregs of mastika from our glasses, while the other women gathered their things and boarded the bus. There was some mastika left in the bottle and Ellen suggested I take it.

"Better you than me," she said. "I might drink it all in one go. It's delicious."

I grinned and stuffed the bottle in my backpack. I liked her.

"They don't seem very fun," I said to Ellen, nodding at the women clustered around the bus. It was silly, but I wanted to secure our bond. We were different than the others; we could be friends here. But she only smiled, close-lipped, swinging her purse over her shoulder and pulling her suitcase behind her. I immediately regretted saying anything. Nice one, Agnes. You've already outed yourself as a gatecrasher, criticizing the other women like that.

I gestured goodbye to the local men as we departed. They nodded again, saying nothing, but I could feel their eyes on us as we hurried over to the bus.

The shuttle driver, another smooth-skinned local, confirmed my name from a list on his clipboard. I boarded the bus and found a window seat near the front. Ellen was already seated elsewhere, rifling through her bag. As the bus departed, I watched the small village fall away while the other women chatted happily behind me. Soon the concentration of white and blue buildings dwindled, making way for long stretches of white sand along the shoreline and lush orchards of olives and lemons, peaches and apricots. We passed fields teeming with vibrant flowers and others marked by leafy rows of vegetables. As we drove over a small bridge, I heard a few women gasp in awe. I turned my head to see a gorgeous slice of waterfall on the opposite side of the road, splashing down the side of a mountain into a clear blue lagoon.

I wondered if my mother knew about this place. Destinations one might call "paradise on earth" were the kind she preferred for family vacations when I was a child. Remote, exotic, deeply relaxing. When my mother took time off work, which was rare, the four of us would travel to far-flung locales, tropical or Mediterranean, because these settings demanded slowing down and spending time outside. They forced her to relax. Those trips felt like dreams. A week, sometimes two, with the family together. Beach days. Dinners. It was the closest my parents ever came to being happy, the only time I ever saw them hold hands or kiss. I remembered trying very hard to be as quiet as possible on those trips. If I said the wrong thing or brought too much attention to myself, everything could go south fast. On vacation, I imagined I could turn invisible. That would keep the peace. Sometimes, I'd disappear on long walks down the beach, out of sight. An hour gone and no one seemed to notice. Whenever I returned, my parents and Max always seemed to be laughing together. A funny moment I wasn't a part of.

The bus suddenly went dark. We were driving through a tunnel carved into the wet rock of a mountain. The women around me fell silent. It was dramatic: the lack of light, the change from seeing so much to seeing nothing at all. But then we were out the other side, sunlight flooding our views again. More green, more white sand, more otherworldly blue water.

We passed by a lone donkey standing in a pasture, who looked up at us as we drove by. Maybe it was my fancy, but it seemed more lively than other donkeys. Less forlorn, his coat shiny. No reason not to be happy in paradise.

When the bus turned off the main road, I spotted a flock of white buildings and tents nestled together by a long crescent beach in the distance. Geia had told me the Summit would be held at a luxury hotel she'd bought and restored a few years back. We would be the only guests there for the next ten days.

The bus rolled down the long driveway. We passed an orchard, a vegetable garden, and a small vineyard. The whole property was abloom with colour: rows of bushy olive trees and tufts of brilliant wildflowers, few of which I recognized, a sea of purple, yellow, pink, and green.

At the end of the driveway, the bus pulled to a stop in a cobblestone courtyard. The hotel was four storeys high with two distinct wings flanking the coastline. The building was made of that iconic whitewashed limestone, with windows and doors trimmed in bright blue. Fuchsia bougainvillea crawled up the corners of the building and potted lemon trees, ripe with fruit, stood throughout the courtyard.

We disembarked from the bus and wandered towards the entrance as a group. Everyone was quiet, taking in our new surroundings. I was overcome by the scent of the wild-flowers: their sweetness, their herbaceous undertones.

Through double glass doors on the far side of the court-yard, we entered an airy white lobby with tall ceilings and more potted lemon trees. Everything felt minimalist and clean, just like Geia's living room in the Hamptons had. Five hotel staff, wearing identical sleeveless white dresses that reached mid-calf, greeted us with cucumber-spiked water and serene smiles. They were also gorgeous, as if they too could be related to Geia and our server back at the bar.

I wondered about their dresses. Linen, on closer inspec-tion, and unusual for a staff uniform. White dirtied so easily. Maybe they were designed to keep the staff cool in the summer heat?

We checked in and were given our room key cards. The staff member who gave me my key also handed me a piece of paper. I opened it and saw it was a map of the hotel complex, which was even larger than I'd thought. She told me to get settled and then head *here*, pointing to an unmarked loca-tion on the southern side of the property, behind a large garden. She lowered her voice to tell me Geia wanted to welcome me. I thanked her and made my way upstairs, stomach fluttering.

I had a lovely corner room on the third floor with an amazing view of the ocean. I felt like I was on a cruise ship—everywhere I looked, blue, blue, blue, and down below me, a terrace green with plants, a patio, and a swimming pool.

I was sweaty from the day of travel; I showered and changed into a fresh sundress. I spritzed myself with Goddess™ Dew, a cleansing face spray I had taken from Geia's home in the Hamptons. I smelled like a fucking spring meadow. I looked in the mirror, applied a little mascara, and realized I was primping to look good for Jack's ex-wife. That's weird, Agnes. Who are you trying to win over here?

I checked my phone. A few emails had come in, but nothing from Jack or Zelda. As I suspected, Zelda had been thrilled about the *Vogue* piece, but she had also insisted I remain focused on book two. My October deadline was looming, and despite my best efforts, there was no talk of another extension.

The Summit was supposed to include a digital detox. Starting tomorrow, we weren't allowed to use our phones. I wasn't sure how that would actually work, if it would be like an honour system or whatever, but regardless, it would be hard for me to communicate with Zelda or Jack for the next ten days.

I followed the map to Geia's unmarked quarters as instructed. From the lobby, I walked through a door opposite the one we'd entered earlier. This led to a sprawling lawn and one of the large white tents I'd seen from the bus.

I could hear activity inside: people setting up for one of the Summit workshops, maybe. I took a stone path to the right of the tent, passed through a lush, tranquil garden, and there it was: a two-storey villa, white and blue, with more of that beautiful bougainvillea.

I hesitated before knocking on the door. I recognized that familiar insecure feeling I'd had at Orchard House and in the Hamptons. Stomach snakes. Just do it, Agnes. Don't be an idiot.

I exhaled and knocked, and another staff member in a white dress answered the door. She led me quietly through the house to the back patio, surrounded by a dense hedge and a small plunge pool. Geia sat in a lounge chair, her long, tanned legs stretched out and crossed, her feet bare.

"Geia," the staff member announced. "Agnes is here."

She turned and smiled.

"Finally! Please, drinks are in order. We're celebrating."

20

The staff member brought us a bottle of mastika that tasted even better than the stuff we'd had in town. This bottle was more intensely woodsy, with a cleaner aftertaste. I didn't usually like sweet drinks, but I could drink a lot of this.

"Cheers," Geia said, clinking her glass against mine. "I'm so glad you're here, Agnes."

She was wearing a pale floral jumpsuit, sleeveless, with high-cut shorts. Not something many forty-five-year-olds could pull off.

I sat on a lounge chair next to her, my legs stretched out, not nearly as long as hers. There was no view of the water from here, but I could see how the hedge, which surrounded the patio, was essential, especially now that I had met a few of the Summit participants. No prying eyes or photos without consent here. A bit of seclusion.

It was shady and cool. I rested my head against the lounge chair, feeling the dull ache of two days of travel, and glanced sideways at Geia. She looked beautiful, her skin tanned and glowing, but not in any magical way. There was no indication of the strangeness I had witnessed, or *thought* I had witnessed, that night in the Hamptons. We were just two women hanging out, sipping our drinks, watching the leaves of an olive tree rustle in the faint breeze.

"So tell me, how was Athens?" Geia asked. "You had one night there, right?"

"Half a day and one night." Geia's assistant had arranged it that way. "It was a whirlwind. I managed to squeeze in a trip to the Acropolis."

"And what did you think?"

"Amazing. So much history."

"How were the crowds?"

"Oh, awful. I waited in line for over two hours to get in and then the place was teeming with tourists."

Geia watched me for a moment. "Is it really so awful that people are still interested in history? It makes me think maybe humanity isn't doomed after all."

I smiled, embarrassed. I hadn't thought of it that way.

"Have you spent much time in Athens?" I asked.

Geia set her glass on her bare thigh, holding on to the stem.

"Of course. Greece has always been very oriented towards its centre. If you want to get anywhere in Greece, you have to start in Athens. I prefer the islands though." She gestured around with her glass. "This is home."

I told her the island seemed incredible so far.

"I'm so glad you like it. I hope the others do too. Any read on that? How are our fearless attendees enjoying themselves so far?"

I thought back to the group of women I'd met in town, their complaining, their breathless excitement to meet Geia. 'Fearless' wasn't a word that immediately came to mind.

"People were pretty impressed by that waterfall on the drive here from the port."

Geia beamed. "I asked the driver to go the long way so you could see it."

As she spoke, I reached a finger up to my right temple and pressed on the skin. My head had started to ache; a dull, throbbing pain behind the eyes. Probably from a lack of sleep or dehydration, side-effects of travel.

"Headache?" Geia asked.

"Mm."

"May I?"

She held out her hands towards me and I must have looked confused. She explained that she knew a bit about head massage and tension mitigation.

"Sure." It was a strange offer, but this was Geia Stone after all.

She got me to sit with my back to her and immediately began moving her hands around my scalp. It didn't feel like a massage. More like someone messing up my hair. If it wasn't so weird, I might have laughed. Instead, I stared straight ahead at the corner of a patio stone, trying to take in what was happening. Geia Stone was touching my head. I was in the middle of nowhere, on an island no one had ever heard of, and one of the most famous people in the world was giving me a scalp massage. Her hands felt warm and soothing. I tried to focus on that, but I was worried that my hair was greasy.

"You have amazing hair," she said, as if reading my mind. "Is this your natural colour?"

I nodded and she continued to move her hands all over my head for another minute or so. Then she rested her palms on either side of my skull, her fingers covering my eyes and forehead. Right, okay. This was even odder, but I wasn't going to protest. What would I say exactly? Stop?

The pain of my headache seemed to be getting worse. It was now close to a migraine. Bright, unbearably intense. I felt mildly nauseous, like I might throw up on her clean, perfect patio stones. And then, just like that, the headache was gone. No trace of pain at all.

Geia removed her hands, as if sensing her work was done.

I turned to look at her.

"That was amazing." I reached up to touch my temples, but my head felt completely fine. "You really know what you're doing."

She shrugged, smiling. "I'm glad it helped. Keep drinking this stuff." She held up her glass of mastika. "It will help too."

"I thought it tasted familiar. Is this what you gave me in the Hamptons?"

Geia nodded. "It's similar, but the tincture I added to your water in the Hamptons is a highly purified version of what we're drinking now, with no alcohol. The Greeks have been making mastika for centuries using sap from the mastika trees. People like it because it tastes so fucking good, but actually, it has incredible restorative properties. Hydration. Detoxification. Complete re-balancing of important digestive enzymes. The list goes on. It's a wonder ingredient. Hence why we're testing that drink I served you. I think the world's going to go crazy for it, once they get on board."

I watched as her eyes brightened while she spoke.

"You really love this stuff, don't you?" I asked. "The whole wellness thing."

She tilted her head to the side. "Guilty."

I thought about my article. I should be using every private minute I had with Geia as an opportunity for an interview. "Can I ask, when did it start, your interest in wellness?"

Geia chuckled. "Well, interest probably isn't the right word. Wellness is my passion, my mission, my life's purpose. It's been that way for as long as I can remember." She paused, thinking. "Jack told me you liked our films. *The Opposites*. Is that true?"

I told her it was.

"Well, what I'm doing with Goddess is deeply connected to what we explored in *The Opposites*. People thought those films were ground-breaking works of feminist art because their core message was care. Care for one's self, care for others. With Goddess, my hope is to spread that message even further. *The Opposites* series was critically acclaimed, and just as I expected, the riddles I wrote into the screen-plays piqued the interest of fans and ensured their invest-ment in the story. But our audience was limited. So I made a change. I built a larger audience for myself by playing the Hollywood game for a while, doing big commercial films until I became a household name. Then I retired from acting to do what I've always wanted. Help people. That's how I see Goddess, as a helping resource. And because I'm famous, people have allowed me to help them. To guide them, really, towards an ethic of self-care."

I remembered what Geia had said in the Hamptons, how Goddess™ wasn't about the money. Why then not make the "help," as she called it, freely available? Like a not-for-profit or something? I asked her as much and she nodded as if she had known this question was coming.

"Goddess was first imagined as an information resource, like an online magazine," she said. "So, content primarily. Free content, available online. But I quickly realized that while some people want to consume information, almost everyone wants to consume *things*. You know, products and clothing and gadgets. People want to buy *stuff*. Learning has become a passive gesture, but purchasing something? That's active. And if that was the best way for me to reach more people, I was okay with that. I know people question that choice, but I really don't care. I would rather help as many people as possible to get healthy, to change their lives. That's how we developed the blended model we have on the website now: complete integration of free content and e-commerce."

"And you were right," I said. "I mean, you must have millions of followers."

Geia nodded, looking proud. "Isn't it wonderful?" She finished the last of her mastika and leaned back in the lounger. "My plan is for this Summit to be the first of many. With *The Opposites*, I wasn't reaching enough people. Now, with Goddess, I'm reaching more than I could have ever imagined. But I still want to improve how I'm reaching them. I've learned that information and products can only go so far, given the infinite distractions of our time. Technology, social media, burnout culture. These women need in-person, face-to-face guidance in an isolated environment. They need to separate from their regular lives and find time to commit fully to their development, to each other's development. That's the goal behind the Goddess Summit. Plus, you know, I have a few surprises in store."

She fell quiet and I noticed movement in the bushes behind the olive tree. Her message was more intentional than I had expected. Her journey so far, the Summit — Geia came across as genuinely committed to her cause, though I found it hard to accept she wasn't after money too. Wasn't everyone? Even me, with my writing. I wanted to tell stories, but I also wanted financial success. Then again, I had managed to get an almost-unheard-of book advance and it hadn't changed anything; I still felt like I didn't know what I was doing.

"Holy shit!" I yelled.

Mastika splashed out of my glass and Geia laughed as a large green snake emerged from the leaves and began slinking towards us.

Kathari.

The snake wound himself into a circle at the bottom of Geia's lounger, paying me no mind. He was even bigger than I remembered. Green like the garden. I had the keen sense that he had been listening to us talk. How had Geia even gotten this thing all the way to Greece?

I watched as she reached down a hand to stroke Kathari. That night in the Hamptons returned to me once again. I considered just asking her for an explanation. But how would I phrase that, exactly?

I glanced at her face. *Tell me what you were doing that night.*

"Agnes, I have to say, I'm so happy you're here and we can talk like this. It would be very easy for you to feel uncomfortable around me because of my history with Jack. But it doesn't need to be that way, does it? We can choose to set societal expectations of awkwardness and discomfort aside. We can have our own relationship, outside of Jack."

I smiled. "I'd like that."

"So, how's it going anyway, with Jack? He's falling for you. You know that, right? I hope you're not going to break his heart."

I looked down at Kathari, unsure how to respond. With his eyes closed, he looked so peaceful and still, like he could be made of stone.

"I don't know," I said finally. "We text, but where can it go, really? I'm supposed to be writing my second book. I don't have time for a relationship right now."

Geia smirked. "Really? That's your excuse? Speaking from experience, I've found being in a relationship with Jack Verity very creatively stimulating."

I ignored the pangs of jealousy stabbing in my gut. "It's different for me. The only reason I was able to write the first book was because I cut men out of my life completely. I had to end a relationship before I could even write a word, or a good word at least."

She watched me, silent, wanting me to go on.

I shook my head. "It's a long story."

"I'm in no rush."

I hesitated. Was I really going to tell Geia Stone about Owen? My palms were already sweaty. I downed the last bit of mastika from my glass. "Well, when I finished college, I was dead set on writing a novel, and I made a series of choices to finally make that possible. I rented a studio apartment. I got a café job with flexible hours. And I cut anyone out of my life who didn't support my dream. But within a month of starting life as a writer, whatever that means, I met someone. Owen. We fell in love fast and it was an all-consuming kind of thing."

Geia topped up my glass, sensing I needed it. I had a good buzz now, which helped the words come easier. At least I was getting detoxified and re-balanced at the same time.

"Owen was married," I blurted out. "And I knew it. He didn't hide it from me. He always wore his wedding ring, and still, I dove right in."

I waited for Geia to show disapproval, but her face remained calm. "Go on," she said.

"I think probably the fact that he was married made it even more enthralling. I was always waiting for him. Would he text? Would he come over? Our time was stolen, snatches here and there, and I was in total limbo. Not eating enough, drinking too much. Definitely not writing. That was the worst part. I felt like such a failure on multiple levels."

"How long did it last?" Geia asked.

"Four years."

"What? Agnes, you poor thing."

"Oh, don't pity me. It was my own doing."

"Still."

I shrugged.

"How did it end?" she asked.

"It's funny. Ending it was the easiest part, strangely. I just needed the right push." I shook my head. "He was constantly saying he would leave his wife and I was stupid enough to believe him. But then one day, when I had the afternoon off work, I went to the park by my apartment to read and there he was, having a picnic with his wife. It was unusual for them to be in that park because they didn't live nearby. I still wonder about that. Was he tempting fate, bringing his wife and his lover so close together? Anyway, there they were. I stopped dead when I spotted them." I paused. I could still see them both so clearly. "She looked different in person than she did online. She was less pretty than her photos, not as sophisticated, but more beautiful at the same time. I used to check her Instagram obsessively. I guess it's easy to write someone off when all you ever see is their selfies. But that day, there she was in front of me, not just a feed of pictures, but *a real person*. She had this sweet, dimpled smile that she never shared in any of her posts, and her hair was kind of messy." I shook my head again. "She was making him laugh. Telling a joke or teasing him, maybe. I don't think I ever made him laugh, not once. Our love was never happy or playful. It was twisted, illicit. Self-destructive. I saw them together that day and it was all I needed. I realized the only thing that made me feel as joyful as they looked was writing. I turned on my heel and ran back to my apartment. I deleted his number and I opened a fresh Word doc on my computer. I started writing *Violets in Her Lap* that day."

"That's fucking incredible," Geia said. She looked genuinely impressed. "You took a really shitty situation and you turned it into an opportunity."

"I guess so. It felt more like I was finally pressing play after being on pause for so long."

"I like that. Here's to pressing play." Geia clinked her glass against mine. "That being said, I don't think you need to be alone to do what you love, Agnes. The right person can nurture you on your creative journey."

I thought about this. It sounded nice in theory, but I was scared to lose myself again, like I had with Owen. Most days back then, I existed in a fog, totally out of touch with my own needs and desires, let alone my creative impulses. Owen was my everything. I didn't just put writing on pause for him. I put myself on pause too.

"Geia?" The staff member appeared in the doorway. "It's getting to that time."

"Duty calls," Geia said with a small sigh. "See you at dinner?"

She stood and Kathari awoke, slithering off into the bushes. The staff member showed me to the door. I walked back to my room through the garden, feeling tipsy, wondering if it really could be different with Jack. If *I* could be different.

21

That night we dined on the beach. Ten round tables of five were set up on the long half-moon of white sand in front of the hotel. As we took our seats, the sky erupted around us in variations of pink and orange, a huge red sun sinking into the horizon. Similar to Jack's birthday party, dinner felt like a wedding, with elegant place settings and gorgeous floral arrangements. Only the best for Geia's followers.

Each place was set with a name card. On the table, there was a larger card explaining that the women we sat with tonight would be our "pod" for the rest of the Summit. This meant that we would dine together every night, and would attend the various sessions and workshops of the Summit as a group.

It is my hope you will forge powerful, lifelong friendships here, the card said. *Lean on each other. Support each other. Don't be afraid to be vulnerable. To start, why not introduce yourselves? Share your name, your age, your occupation, and something you hope to work on at the Summit with your pod members.*

The card was signed by Geia.

The woman sitting next to me read it aloud to the table. She was small but muscular, tanned, with a sleeve of tattoos winding up her right arm. Her dark hair was tied back in a long braid.

"Fun," she said in a British accent. "I like activities. I'm Skye, thirty-six. I run a yoga studio in London. I'm hoping to continue the work of learning to love and accept myself while we're here, both spiritually and physically. I'm eager to arm myself with new tools to make that possible."

We all nodded politely in response. I couldn't believe people actually talked like this in real life. Another woman said, "I love that," and Skye beamed.

The woman on Skye's left was about to introduce herself when a staff member tapped her on the shoulder before she had a chance. A few words were spoken in a low voice, and the woman was led away to another table. Ellen appeared and took the empty seat, flashing a smile at me.

The one person I had met and liked, assigned to my pod. I wondered if Geia had something to do with that. But how could she know?

Ellen introduced herself to the group. She told us she was thirty-nine and was here to continue the work of learning to live a more intentional and balanced life.

The other members of our pod were Pearl, seventy-two, a writer of romance novels with shoulder-length grey hair, aqua blue fingernails, and no specific hopes for the Summit, other than to be exposed to as much as possible; and Leslie, forty-four, a lawyer with honey-coloured hair slicked back in a tight bun, who said that more than anything she just needed a break from her life and family, and what better place to commit fully to self-care than the Goddess™ Summit?

I introduced myself as an author once again—no one at the table had read my book—and explained I was a newbie to the wellness scene, so I was hoping for a crash course on the subject. It wasn't a lie, but it didn't sound quite as Goddessy as what the others had said. I waited for someone to call me out, but no one did. They were all supportive and encouraging, nodding along as I talked as if they understood completely.

I took a sip of my wine and exhaled. Not bad, Agnes. You haven't scared them off yet.

Geia waited until everyone had settled in to make her entrance. She appeared alone, walking from the hotel down to the beach, waving and smiling as she got closer. She had changed since our visit in her garden. She now wore the same white linen dress as the hotel staff: sleeveless, a modest neckline, long enough that it fell to her mid-calf. Her dark hair was loose and wavy. Her feet were still bare.

The crowd, chatty just moments before, fell silent at her arrival. I noticed a lot of mouths open in astonishment, even a couple of women tearing up. For most, this was the first time they were laying eyes on Geia in the flesh. She was no longer just an image on their screens; she was a real person, and they were about to dine with her.

"Hi, everyone!" Geia beamed, waving at the group.

The women applauded, a few cheering lightly as Geia made her away across the beach. When she took her seat at the head table, the women returned to their chatter. Skye remarked, "Oh my god, I love her dress!"

At the head table, Geia chatted with a group of women who didn't look like Summit participants. They were too easy with her, too comfortable. Laughing like old friends. I nodded in their direction and asked Ellen if she knew who they were.

"They're our mentors for the week. They'll be leading all the workshops."

I looked closer; a few of them did seem vaguely familiar. I must have seen their photos on the event website when I was researching the Summit. Other things I had learned in my research: the ten-day event would consist of a series of workshops on topics including astrology, energy healing, something called "holotropic breathwork," and clean makeup. Each pod would work through the full series of workshops on a different schedule, but everyone would come together on the last day for a day-long intensive session led by Geia herself. This final session had piqued my interest because the description was so vague, with few concrete details. I knew Geia was passionate about wellness, but what exactly could she teach us that would take an entire day? As much as she was considered a guru, she didn't have any actual New Age credentials.

My pod chatted about the journey to Mastika, their first impressions of the hotel and our rooms, and the quality of the cold white wine we were now drinking. Leslie reminded me of the women Ellen and I had met earlier at the bar in town: the grumblers and complainers. She took at least ten minutes to tell a story about an argument she'd had with a flight attendant on the way to Athens. Something about a crying baby and a seat change; to be honest, I tuned most of it out. Skye, meanwhile, seemed surprisingly anxious despite her tough exterior. She tore at her fingernails while she told us how this was the first time she'd left her yoga studio in the care of someone else. She'd left one of her senior instructors detailed lists of all daily operations, but she still feared he'd tank the business while she was away. Pearl was the most relaxed of the group. She kept our wine glasses topped up and explained she was here at the Summit between two other trips: she'd just spent three weeks in Sicily and next she was headed to Istanbul. "Travel keeps me young," she said with a laugh, drinking deeply from her wine glass.

Soon, our first course appeared: a salad of crunchy green vegetables, many of them unfamiliar to me — presumably local — topped with a piece of plump, shiny feta as big as my palm. I was starving. I could eat five of these. I dove into my salad and realized too late that no one else was eating. I followed their gazes to Geia, who was standing up, holding her wine glass aloft. Conversation faded around us as the sun finally sank below the surface of the sea behind her. It was all very cinematic. I munched the rest of my mouthful as quietly as possible and set down my fork. Ellen glanced over at me and chuckled.

"Hi, everyone," Geia said to the crowd. "Wow. This is amazing. Seeing you all here in a place that means so much to me." She paused, looking from table to table. "I know we're all hungry, so I won't keep you from your food, but I wanted to welcome you all to the first ever Goddess Summit."

The group erupted with excited applause.

"This marks the fulfillment of a lifelong dream for me. Wellness has always been my passion. When I started Goddess, I had no idea there were so many of you out there just like me. But I'm so glad we found each other!"

More applause. At my table, Pearl let out a loud hoot.

"And now, fifty of you have travelled all the way to this beautiful island to spend ten days with me and a few of my good friends. We hope the days to come will be restorative, healing, awakening, and inspiring. We hope you'll be able to tune into yourselves in new ways, and we hope, most of all, that you will remain *energetically open* to the different experiences we've worked so hard to create for you."

No applause this time; instead, rapt silence. They were all hanging on her every word. I noticed Geia sounded different talking to this crowd. Her voice was lower and gentler, devoid of the brazenness I'd grown accustomed to.

"In Greek," Geia continued, "instead of 'cheers' we say *ya mas*, which means 'to our health.' I can't think of a more appropriate toast to start the Goddess Summit. I invite you to raise your glasses and repeat after me. *Ya mas!*"

I joined the crowd as we repeated the phrase, our voices ringing in the quiet of the evening. Everyone clapped again.

Now, we could eat. The others began discussing the schedule for the week while I scarfed down the rest of my salad.

"I'm excited about tomorrow morning's session," Skye said. "Movement Hour? Sounds incredible."

Pearl spoke up: "I'm not embarrassed to say I'm most looking forward to our session on self-pleasure later this week. The Mechanics of Masturbation with Lydia Gilmore. We're so lucky. She's been teaching women how to get off since the early eighties."

I laughed loudly, but I was the only one. The rest nodded as if this was all very normal. I looked down at my empty plate, still hungry.

"I can't believe she's right there," Leslie said, looking towards Geia. "I've loved her for years, and now I could literally touch her if I wanted to." Leslie glanced at each of us, hastily adding, "Of course, I would never."

We all looked towards the head table. Geia was leaning forward, chatting intimately with a brunette woman across from her. For a brief moment, I wished I was that woman, that Geia was focused on me alone.

AFTER DINNER, I excused myself from the table. The others were still chatting about their lives back home, but I was tired, ready for quiet time. I wandered back to the hotel under a gleaming full moon. I thought again of Geia, glowing like an ember beneath its glare back in the Hamptons. I continued to search that memory for a possible explanation: a light source I hadn't noticed that might have caused that kind of radiance, for instance. But what could have created that?

Back at the hotel, my room was peaceful and cool, a breeze off the water blowing through the open windows. I unbuttoned the front of my sundress, my pajamas calling to me, and saw that I'd missed a FaceTime call close to an hour ago.

Jack.

The Wi-Fi must be better inside the hotel than out on the grounds. I sat down on the bed and sent him a message: *Sorry I missed your call. I'm in my room now. Better connection.*

Beginning tomorrow morning, we wouldn't be able to communicate because of the digital detox, and after my conversation with Geia, I realized I didn't just want to text Jack goodbye. I wanted to see him, to speak with him. Maybe I had overreacted about what he had said in the driveway. I was probably being too sensitive. Owen always used to say I was thin-skinned.

I stayed seated on the bed, waiting. I turned up my ringer so I wouldn't miss his response and scrolled through Instagram, not really seeing any of the images as they slipped away under the flick of my thumb. With a shiver, I thought about what Geia had said: "He's falling for you. You know that, right?"

I opened my email and saw there was a new message from Zelda. Subject line: Book 2 progress?

Hi Agnes,
I'm just wondering if you can give me an update on how the book is coming along. I know you're on assignment in Greece right now, but it's important to keep the book top of mind. Can you let me know your latest word count? Or at least, give me some idea of the premise? Jessica was in touch and she wants to make sure you're on track. She's suggesting you send along the first few chapters so she knows what to expect from this book. Any bone I can throw her would be most

welcome...Eagle Eye sees all!!
Enjoy the sun!
Zelda

My heart sank. The first few chapters? I didn't even have the first few words. I racked my brain for a premise I could send to Zelda. I knew they were all hoping — and expecting — I would write something as unusual as *Violets in Her Lap*. It could have human characters this time, but it still needed to push the envelope of contemporary adult fiction. Apparently, that was my brand. For a moment, I thought of writing about what I had seen in the Hamptons, but no, that wouldn't work. I didn't understand what I had seen that night. How could I put it into words?

I typed a hasty reply saying the connection was bad on the island, and though I was happy to send my latest pages, the upload kept failing. I ignored her question about a premise entirely. My stomach was tight with guilt and my head foggy from all the mastika and wine. I'd just have to get my act together, starting tomorrow. Time to focus, Agnes. Time to get to work.

Jack would like to FaceTime...

I let my phone ring three times before I answered. When Jack appeared on the screen, I looked at myself before I really looked at him: the tiny rectangle in the bottom corner. I fixed my hair, which looked flat.

"Agnes!" Jack was grinning in that way I liked. "You don't have to do that, you know. Message before you call. You can call me any time."

I smiled. Another behavioural hangover from my time with Owen. I could never just call him in case his wife was there. The few times I had, he'd scolded me for playing with fire, and not in a sexy way. Apparently, I was too needy. His words.

"I wanted to see you," Jack continued. "Your digital detox starts tomorrow, right?"

I nodded. My sundress was still unbuttoned at the top, exposing my bra. I wondered if he noticed.

"All the women here are freaking out. Ten days, no social media."

Jack laughed. It would only be late afternoon in the Hamptons, where I knew he was, but he looked like he was in a dark room. Editing, probably.

"Ten days is nothing." he said. "I could use ten months away from this thing."

"Are you alone?" I asked.

He nodded.

"Working?"

"Kind of. Not really getting anywhere today. That's why I called you."

I felt a familiar ache. I wanted to take Geia's advice and give this a try. I wanted to fix what I had ruined in the Hamptons with my crying and overreacting. Owen and I often had phone sex when we couldn't be together. Maybe that was an option now? I lay back on the bed. My dress gaped open even further.

"How is it so far?" he asked, not catching on.

"What?"

"The Summit."

I sat up a little. Why was he asking about Geia right now? "Oh, it's fine. I had a drink with her before dinner."

"Geia?"

"Yes."

"What did you talk about?"

"Just, you know, the idea behind the Goddess Summit." I buttoned the top of my dress, annoyed. We clearly weren't on the same page.

Jack nodded, but he seemed to notice my irritation. "Look, Agnes, I've sensed you pulling away these last couple of weeks. If you're over this, you can just tell me. I'll understand."

Was he kidding? He was the one who seemed over this. I was offering myself up here and he wasn't showing the least bit of interest.

"I'm not over it," I said. "I just have a lot on my plate right now."

"Have you started working on your book?"

"Yes," I lied. "And I have the article to write. It's a lot of pressure. It's hard to make time for anything else." That too was a lie. I'd done everything *but* write the last few weeks. I'd gone for long runs, binge-watched two seasons of *Buffy the Vampire Slayer*, and completely re-organized my bookshelves.

"I get that. I'm happy to hear you're writing though. And not just the article. The article is whatever. That's Geia's thing. You need to be writing for you right now. That's the only way you'll find your way to back to what you love."

My face burned. He was doing it again. Acting like he

knew better than me, and like Geia was using me. But before I could respond, he continued: "I know you don't like me talking like this, but look, I care about you, Agnes. And I've been there. Geia is...a force. She's amazing but she's also a bulldozer. If she has her mind set on something, she will run roughshod over anyone who gets in her way. Like the Goddess Summit. She's obsessed with its success. She says she wants an honest article from you, but I'm not sure that's true. I just don't want you to get hurt."

I rubbed my eyes with my free hand. Why was he stuck on this? Why didn't he trust my judgement?

"Look, I'm getting tired. I understand you're just trying to look out for me, but I can take care of myself."

I'd been doing so my whole life.

He nodded. "Just watch your back, okay?"

I gave him a look. "Watch my back? Jack, we're talking about the mother of your children."

"I know," Jack said, his voice hesitant. "It's hard to explain. I've known her for so long. And you're talking to an example of her collateral damage. I got so wrapped up in her, in her ideas, that I lost myself. I don't want that to happen to you."

That was exactly what I was trying to avoid by putting distance between him and me.

"Look, I should go."

"Okay, Agnes. But if you ever need to talk, there's a café in town owned by a guy I know from my time on Mastika. It's called Koukoutski. Tell him you know me. He'll let you use his phone."

Why was he being so dramatic? It wasn't like they were

going to confiscate our phones. And even if they did, I could still find a way to get online if I really needed to.

We said an awkward goodbye. It only occurred to me later, as I lay in bed trying to fall asleep, that Jack might be feeling jealous of all the time I was spending with Geia. I'd gone out of my way to travel thousands of miles for her, after I'd pretty much ignored his suggestion of a visit to Montreal. But that was ridiculous. My decision to come here had been purely professional.

22

The morning sun woke me, its bright warmth on my face. I'd left the windows and curtains open so I could listen to the waves crashing against the shore from my bed. I had slept well, better than I had any night since *Violets in Her Lap* had come out.

I had a vague memory of a dream about Geia, in which she was sitting at the end of my bed, watching me sleep. I stared at the spot now, willing the dream to come back to me, but it was already hazy and fading away, the way dreams always did.

I threw back the blankets, rolled over, and chugged a glass of water. I had slept in my sundress, still buttoned at the top. I crawled out of it now, wanting out of my skin too as I relived my conversation with Jack. Could I have been any more desperate? Throwing myself at him like that. It was mortifying. And there he was, berating me for getting too wrapped up in Geia when he was so wrapped up in her himself.

Maybe ten days of no communication with the outside world was exactly what I needed. No calls or texts. Just space to be myself. I could think about what I really wanted. When Jack was right there in front of me, things felt easy and comfortable, but that was just an illusion. His life was far from uncomplicated: two kids, an ex-wife, long hours on set, no fixed address, not to mention his celebrity. We didn't even live in the same country. Could we really have a future together?

I reached for my phone and found it black. I'd left it plugged in, charging all night, but it was totally dead. Was it broken? I reached down for the European adaptor I'd brought with me, which was old and probably unreliable, but everything looked in order. I tried plugging in my laptop instead. It turned on, but there was no internet connection.

Right. The digital detox. No internet. But that didn't explain my phone not turning on. Was this what Jack meant? Did he know this was going to happen?

I heard panicked voices in the hallway. I opened my door and saw several of my third-floor neighbours holding their dead phones. One of the women speculated there'd been a storm surge that had fried all our devices, though there was no evidence of this — the weather last night had been perfectly calm. "Those European wires," she said, frowning. The other women nodded. That made sense to them, but they looked lost all the same. We'd all signed up for the detox, but this felt extreme. Now we were truly adrift on this island, untethered from the rest of the world.

I FOUND COFFEE and little granola-yogurt parfaits down-stairs in the lobby. I grabbed two parfaits and a latte and headed outside. On the patio, there were smiling women everywhere, sitting and eating breakfast in small groups, or walking up from the optional sunrise yoga class on the beach. I wolfed down the granola and coffee in a patch of shade away from the others. I wasn't quite ready to be chatty yet, and didn't want anyone to see me having a double breakfast.

I figured the other women could tell I wasn't one of them. They all seemed so smooth and shiny. Their hair was brushed. Their skin was plump. They wore large, flashy engagement rings and none of their clothing was wrinkled. My mother used to say I looked like a vagrant. Why couldn't I brush my hair? Why couldn't I find jeans without holes in the knees? Standing in my shady corner, I pretended I was invisible. A fly on the wall with an assignment from *Vogue*.

I looked at my watch and realized I had only twenty minutes before the day's first session. I finished the last of my granola and followed a group of women into a large tent, which housed the Goddess™ Market, a shopping mecca for all things Geia-approved. There were more smiling women here. It wasn't even 9 a.m. and these women were shopping.

I savoured the last of my latte and walked by a display of Goddess™ vitamins and supplements. This was a new product line for Goddess™. Pills to combat fatigue, bloating, menstrual cramps, migraines, and yeast infections. Pills to promote hair and nail growth, a bright complexion.

Next was an assortment of vibrators in a startling array of colours, shapes, and sizes. All together on the display table, they looked strange and alien. Toys for adults. Maybe we'd be using these in the self-pleasure workshop. I was not looking forward to seeing seventy-two-year-old Pearl at that one. I picked up a large purple vibrator and a Goddess™ staff member immediately appeared by my side, offering to answer any questions. She wore the same white linen dress all the staff had on yesterday. What Geia was wearing last night.

I smiled and told her I was just browsing. She nodded and fell back, giving me my space.

I put down the vibrator and moved towards the books section. Above it was a sign: GODDESS™ LIBRARY. I scanned the offerings. There were plenty of self-help books, as well as accessible non-fiction about climate change, anti-racism, technology, feminism. The Goddess™ woman was an informed woman. I made a mental note of that line for my article. On the cookbook shelf, there were titles for every alternative diet I had ever heard of, plus a bunch I hadn't. Multiple copies of Geia's cookbooks were there as well.

I saw a shelf labelled ELEVATED BEACH READS. Amongst the Emma Straub and Celeste Ng, I spotted *Violets in Her Lap* — that familiar green, leafy cover with my name in white block letters, the tiny, bright red bird — and felt the usual stomach wobbles. I picked up the only copy, turned it over, and then retrieved a pen from my backpack, thinking I might sign it. I opened the book, balancing it on my hip, but then felt stupid, worried someone might see me doing it.

What are you doing, signing that? Who even are you?

I could explain of course, if someone actually asked me what I was doing, but I didn't want the hassle or the attention. I put the pen away and hid my book underneath the latest offering from Sally Rooney. I moved on.

Most of the women in the tent seemed to be gathered in the clothing section. GEIA'S CLOSET, the sign read. I went over and discovered a table of overpriced plain white T-shirts, a few racks of high-waisted linen trousers, and many racks of the same sleeveless white dresses Geia and the Goddess™ staff had been wearing. The women were mostly going for the dresses; when Geia wore something, the whole world wanted it.

I squeezed my way closer and managed to grab a dress. It was pretty unremarkable. Plain, borderline boxy, and definitely overpriced. I examined the tag. Produced by Goddess™ of course. The tag had a black-and-white picture of Geia wearing the dress and a short quotation: "My secret is a good uniform. Appear ready to do the work."

I put the dress back and another woman immediately grabbed it from the rack.

"Sorry," she said, though she didn't sound it. "That's my size."

I retreated. They were going to clean the place out of those dresses on the first morning. I really didn't get it, the whole influencer thing—*she wore it, so I want it*—especially in this context, where you could see you were buying the same thing as everyone else.

"Agnes!"

I turned and saw Ellen standing in line, waiting to pay for her own white dress. She waved me over.

"How'd you sleep?" Ellen asked. Today, she wore cherry-red lipstick. Now that I was close, I saw that she was actually holding *two* of the dresses.

"Great. Took me a little while to get to sleep, but then I pretty much blacked out."

"Me too. And I don't even feel jet-lagged. It's, like, ten thirty at night in L.A. right now. I should feel like I'm getting ready for bed."

"Must be the Mastika air," I said.

I stood with her in line while she paid for her dresses and we chatted about our phones not working. Ellen had a theory that Geia's IT team had worked some magic overnight, disabling our phones with some special code. That didn't add up to me, but I said nothing because I didn't want to make Ellen feel stupid or seem stupid myself.

Ellen then had to run up to her room to stash her purchases before Movement Hour. I waited for her downstairs in the lobby, where breakfast had already been cleared away. Summit participants headed out to their respective sessions. They looked excited, ready for self-improvement in whatever form they were about to get it.

"Ready?" Ellen asked, breezing down the main staircase. She had already changed into her white dress.

"That was quick," I said.

"What do you think?"

"Looks good."

"It's so comfortable. I never want to take it off."

A SMALL GROUP was spread out on the beach, facing the water: our pod and two others combined. Waves lapped against the beach's perfect white crescent. I spotted Skye and Leslie near the front of the group. Pearl gave us a smile when she saw Ellen and me approaching. Our mentor, Zoë Boz, stood facing the women.

I found a spot on the far side of the group and slipped off my sandals, as the others had done, so my bare feet could enjoy the warm sand. Ellen made her way closer to the front.

"This is everything we already know," the mentor was telling us, the sky a vivid blue behind her. "This is what we were able to do effortlessly as children. Today, we remember how to move."

Zoë wore a linen tunic that complemented the white linen dresses worn by Ellen and a few of the other women. Zoë told us to close our eyes and place two fingers to our pulse.

"Listen to the beat of your heart. Feel your inner rhythm."

I didn't know who Zoë was until I'd read the Summit program, but I knew her work. She had been the choreographer for *The Opposites*: the imagination behind Geia's famous dance scene in the first film, in which Geia's character, who has special healing powers, dances to increase her ability to understand the ailments of others. The dance itself was controversial, and often cited as one of the reasons the films didn't develop a mainstream following beyond their niche, cult audience: it was too weird and visceral. In the film, Geia jerked her body in violent gestures, making weird faces, convulsing. This was interspersed with softer motions: the swoop of an arm, the lift of a leg. When audiences first saw the dance, they didn't know how to react. It was confusing, unlike anything viewers had seen before. But some were wooed by it. The strangeness was beguiling. Fans learned the choreography and posted videos of their performances. Some claimed the dance offered a gateway to bliss and euphoria—that it could actually heal.

I wasn't that kind of fan. I never learned the dance. But when I saw Zoë listed on the Summit program, I was intrigued about meeting someone involved in Jack and Geia's films. Movement Hour would also be excellent fodder for my article. The weirder, the better.

"Listen," Zoë said again. "Feel."

I could feel it. The steady flutter at my wrist. Soft and familiar.

Growing up, my mother thought this kind of stuff was a joke. Mindfulness and the like. On one of our family vacations, I remember my father saying he had met an amazing yoga teacher at the pool of our resort. She was teaching an evening class that night and he was planning to go.

My mother immediately attacked the idea. "Why on earth would you do that?"

"Something different." My father shrugged.

She sighed heavily, as if the very notion of a yoga class exhausted her. "Will they be teaching you to self-actualize as well? We all know you could use help in that department."

My father didn't end up going to the class. Who would, after that? The next day at breakfast, a pretty woman in yoga pants approached our table.

"Noah," she said to my father, "we missed you last night."

He apologized. Something had come up.

"Maybe see you tonight?"

"Maybe," he said, but we all knew he wouldn't be attending yoga classes anytime soon. My mother glared at the instructor as she walked away.

Zoë told us to open our eyes. It was time to warm up. She didn't turn on music but she began to move anyway, encouraging us to mimic her. We swept our arms above our heads, making large circles originating from our shoulders. She added a bend in the legs, which created momentum in my body, a forceful bounce.

I felt ridiculous. These movements didn't come naturally to me and I suspected that was pretty obvious. In college, the girls in my dorm liked to go out to bars to dance. "Let's go dancing!" they'd say, like it was a tonic for everything wrong with their lives. And I would go, because I wanted to be included, but I always ended up feeling like an idiot. I was too conscious of my body, too controlled. "Dance like no one's watching." I'd seen that fridge magnet. It wasn't an option for someone like me. Dancing meant feeling watched and judged.

Zoë switched up the movement. Now we needed to shake. Everything. Our feet, our hands, our arms, our legs, our heads, our hair, our chests.

"Just shake," Zoë said. "Shake up all those parts of you, the tiny muscles, the ligaments, the fascia, that usually lie dormant. Wake them up, shake them from their deep slumber!"

She looked wild, but I would have looked the bigger idiot if I just stood there. I glanced at Leslie and Skye. They were really going for it. I shook as I was told. I wondered how we all looked from far away. I imagined the hotel staff watching us from the big windows that looked out onto the beach, shaking their heads at the crazy rich women seeking answers in the strangest ways.

Next, we stretched. We reached above our heads and then bent at the hips into a forward fold, swinging our arms. Zoë told us to stick out our tongues and make an *ahhh* sound.

The others did, but I kept my mouth shut.

"Again," she said.

I stuck out my tongue but didn't make the sound.

"Okay, roll up."

When I came to stand, I felt a bit dizzy. All the blood rushing from my head.

Zoë sighed deeply. "I always feel better after a good hang, don't you? Now that we're warmed up, we're *really* going to start to move. Spread out. Make sure there's a good amount of space between you and your neighbour."

I took a few steps back so I was less close to the others around me.

"This exercise is about giving voice to feeling, good and bad, through movement. I'm going to say some words," Zoë told us. "One word at a time. I want you to move however that word makes you feel. Some of the words are going to be uncomfortable, maybe even triggering, but I encourage you to move *through* those feelings. *Accept* fear. *Accept* discomfort. And *process* the negativity by moving your body. Try not to think. Just move. Great healing can be achieved if we allow our bodies to express what's buried deep inside."

Oh, god. Digging up buried feelings was the last thing I wanted to do.

"Okay," Zoë said. "First word: Turtle."

Really?

I was happy to see I wasn't the only one not immediately reacting. We all just stood there. One woman looked

196

like she was about to bend down, maybe crawl, but thought better of it.

"Turtle," Zoë said again, her voice even. "Don't think. Just move."

Slowly, the group began to move. A few women, including Leslie, crouched on their hands and knees, crawling slowly, backs hunched like a shell. But that wasn't right. That was a logical, literal interpretation of the word. We were supposed to move how the word felt. How on earth did the word *turtle* feel?

I wrapped my arms tightly around my torso, giving myself a hug. I rocked side to side. The woman in front of me was turning in a circle. Watching her made me dizzy.

Zoë walked by me and I expected her to commend my interpretation. Turtle as guarded, secure. But she said nothing. She just weaved around me and continued through the crowd, watching us all, silent.

"Okay. Next word: Pavement."

Pavement? Was she kidding?

My first thought was to lie down flat on the beach, make myself part of the ground, but that was what the crawling turtle women were doing. What is pavement? How does it feel?

A few women were moving, but the rest of us were stumped. I found Pearl's eyes. She winked.

"You're thinking too much," Zoë said. "And that's okay. This is all very new. But try not to think as best you can. Turn off your mind. Listen to your heartbeat."

I started to sway my hips, side to side. This wasn't how pavement felt, but it was something.

"Blood," Zoë said, and for some reason, blood made me think of my second book. Jessica would be out for blood if I didn't start writing it soon.

The jumping woman in front of me began marching on the spot. Soon, I could hear her sniffling. Was she crying? She was turned away from me so I couldn't see her face. Zoë walked over and stood in front of her, staring intently. The woman kept jumping and her sniffles turned into sobs. Zoë continued staring at her for what felt like a full minute.

"Milk," Zoë said.

"Eagle."

"Shame."

I thought of my mother. How she could shame anyone with just a roll of her eyes or a shake of her head, or by looking so deeply concerned by your actions that you began to doubt yourself and your own sanity. My poor father. There was nothing wrong with wanting to try yoga, not really. And there was nothing wrong with a little girl wanting to write weird fairy stories. Why had we let her control us like that?

I raised my arms above my head and swayed them side to side. This wasn't how shame made me feel, but it was how I wished I had felt when my mother tried to shame me: like I didn't care, like I was free.

23

Lunch was leafy salads and sparkling water. Everyone gathered to eat on the large patio at the back of the hotel, overlooking the rugged cliffs and the sea below. Salad in hand, I skirted by the tables of women and tucked myself around the corner where no one could see me. I knew my pod would wave me over and invite me to sit with them, but I just needed a few minutes alone.

I sat cross-legged on the ground with my back against the wall of the hotel and picked at my salad with a compostable wooden fork. I wondered if Movement Hour was just the beginning. Would it get weirder than that, and if so, how weird? What exactly would Geia's self-care curriculum require of me?

I pulled out my notebook to jot down my thoughts about the first session, but the only word that came to mind was *shame*, and I couldn't write that. I was here to document an event, not share my personal story. Maybe I should start with Geia. She was the originator of this whole thing.

Geia Stone has always been distinctly unrelatable, I wrote. *Her beauty, her wealth, her perfection. Often criticized by the media for being out of touch, she's one of those celebrities who magically never has an off day. Fortunate for her, Geia Stone's followers don't mind unrelatable.*

I looked out at the sea. Was any of that true? Now that I knew Geia, did I still see her as so unrelatable? I thought back to the Hamptons: the five-course meal she made for Jack's birthday; the way she'd been off picking strawberries in the sun when we arrived; how her clothes never seemed to wrinkle; how her hair seemed to be made of actual silk. So yes, she was perfect and definitely not relatable, but she was also more than that. Much of what I liked about her didn't really fit with her brand: the drinking, the cursing, the wicked sense of humour. I wondered how I could get that across on the page.

And then of course there was the darker side of her. There was Luke, the much younger—honestly incomprehensible and surely off-brand—boyfriend. And the snake. Her bizarre moonlight ritual. I was pretty sure she wouldn't want me writing about any of that in my article. Was this what Jack was getting at last night on the phone? Maybe he was trying to warn me to tread carefully because he knew Geia had secrets other people wouldn't understand. Like the ability to soak up the light of the moon with her trusty snake companion. Or whatever that was.

I realized I had written *trusty snake companion* in my notebook and promptly crossed it out. Get it together, Agnes.

OUR AFTERNOON SESSION was on astrological compatibilities: romantic, platonic, familial. We met in a private, shady corner of the garden, near a bubbling fountain. Seated on stone benches, our pod and another, we were introduced to our mentor, Julia, a blond woman who talked ecstatically with her hands. All around us, the smells of the local flowers were intoxicating. Their blossoms were huge, in colours I'd never seen before, and their layered scents made me feel sleepy almost immediately.

I fought to keep my eyes open, crossing and re-crossing my legs, while Julia explained that our relationships could be better understood by examining our astrological birth charts along with those of our lovers, friends, and family members.

"This isn't a case of 'Do Taurus and Leo make a love match?' Our sun signs are just one part of a very complicated equation," she said earnestly.

I knew what she was referring to. All those websites where you could read the pros and cons of different signs getting together; I was embarrassed to admit there was a time I had secretly pored over those sites in desperation, looking for the one that might finally hold the key, the piece of information I needed to better understand Owen. To make him leave his wife and stay with me. But they all said the same thing. We weren't a match but we also weren't not a match. We would clash, yes, but we could also make it work, if we tried. No real insight on how of course.

"Your sun sign, the sign you likely identify with, is important, but it's not everything," Julia said, tucking her hair behind her ears. "Your rising sign, your moon sign, and most importantly for love, your Venus sign, all have a role to play in how you connect with others. What I do for my clients back home is I look at their birth chart and then I look at the birth chart of the individual they want to learn more about. Together we probe where and how these two people will inevitably activate each other, and where and how they could stifle each other."

Now, that was interesting. Activation versus suffocation. Any relationship I had ever been in had felt stifling, but also, in some ways, activating. Owen definitely did both. He could make me feel like I couldn't breathe, like I was boxed in, unable to move, every step a misstep — Why was I always crying? Why couldn't I be stronger, more patient, less dramatic? But he could also make me feel like I was flying. Mostly in the bedroom.

Did Jack stifle me? All that talk about protecting myself from Geia had rubbed me the wrong way, but I had to admit he seemed to be trying to light something up in me. He cared about my writing. He wanted me to be fulfilled creatively. Plus, maybe he knew something about Geia the rest of us didn't.

There you go again, Agnes. Why do you have to be so defensive all the time? Maybe Jack was actually trying to help you.

Julia handed out pieces of paper to the group. Ahead of the Summit, we had been asked to submit the date, time, and location of our birth. She had used this information to map our birth charts. Looking down at my own, I saw she had highlighted what she thought was important for me to know moving forward in my relationships.

You tend to seek out romantic partners who will replicate

a familial dynamic, she had written. But wasn't that true of everyone? Didn't we all have daddy or mommy issues?

You are most often motivated by fear.

I shifted my seat on the bench. That one was a little more personal. I reread the line and then glanced at Pearl's sheet to see if it said anything similar.

You constantly seek adventure and may struggle to find a partner with the same hunger for new experiences, I read over her shoulder. She looked at me, catching my eye, and I quickly looked away.

On my chart, Julia had drawn an arrow from the word fear to the bottom of the page. Here, she had written *Failure is not the worst thing.*

I watched Julia. While we all reviewed our charts, she was gazing at a hummingbird, watching it drink from a spiky pink flower. Where had this part come from? It didn't seem to be connected to any particular area of my chart. I wanted to ask, but I didn't want to draw attention to myself.

Of course I didn't like to fail. I already knew that about myself. Still, I didn't like how she had written it so plain and clear at the bottom of the page, as if it summed up my very being. It reminded me of something my father once told me about my mother. This was back when he used to visit me in Montreal, while I was still in school. He'd come for a long weekend and we'd eat at a French bistro he loved, famous for its steak frites. One night at dinner, I asked him how he and my mother first met.

"You don't know?" he asked, pouring us more red wine.

I shook my head. The mythology of their relationship wasn't talked about in our family. It had always been a mystery to me how they ended up together.

"She was a server in a restaurant near the college where I was doing my doctorate. It wasn't a fancy place, not like this." He gestured around with his wine glass. "It was Polish, actually. They had the best perogies, so cheap, and they were open late. I used to go there after working in the library, and she was a vision. Beautiful, hard working. She was the only server for the whole restaurant and she dashed between tables like a dancer."

That sounded like her. I knew that my father came from money and that my mother was the first person in her family to pursue higher education. Her parents owned a small convenience store. They never had much. I knew she worked two jobs while she was in school. She had to pay for everything herself. I always thought part of the reason she and Dad didn't get along was that she resented him for having it so easy. He was one of those men who seemed to coast through life. His parents supported him through all three of his degrees. He got a good job quickly. People flocked to him and wanted to be around him.

"We fell in love fast," he continued, cutting off a piece of steak. "I was in another relationship at the time, so I had to get out of that first. But then, yeah, we moved in together, the whole thing. I worked on my dissertation and she finished her journalism degree. And then she was hitting the pavement every day looking for a job. There was this sense that anything was possible."

"And then you got a job," I said, "at the college."

"Yes. And we bought the house and she got pregnant with Max."

"When did she start working at the newspaper?"

"Not for a few years. After Max was born. But as soon as she was hired, she was all in. She became totally committed to her work. You were a surprise," he added. "But a happy one."

I wondered if that was true. It sounded like my mother had finally got her dream job and then I came along, messing everything up. I had always felt like a mistake. I was so much younger than my brother. They hadn't seen me coming.

"Happy for *you*," I said.

"No, happy for the both of us. But you know your mother. Work will always be her first love."

"Was that hard for you?" I asked. "Coming second?"

"I think you mean third. Max was second."

We shared a knowing smile.

"Yeah, it was hard. I didn't see it going that way when we first got together."

I took a deep gulp of wine. "Why didn't you break up sooner? You both seemed so miserable."

"You know me, ever the romantic," he shrugged. "I loved her, despite everything. And I think for her, it was about not wanting to fail. If she admitted things weren't working, she would also have to admit the role she played in that. Your mother doesn't like to lose, as you know."

I nodded, re-folding my napkin on my lap. I remember I felt a twinge of pity for her in that moment. I knew it had taken a lot for her to finally leave him.

I hadn't thought about that conversation in years, but it came back to me now, vivid, complete. It was strange to think my mother was ever motivated by a fear of failure, that we could have similar fears. We were so different. If Julia read my mom's birth chart, would she write the same thing at the bottom of the page? *Failure is not the worst thing.*

But if not failure, then what?

Julia asked the group if anyone had had a reading of their birth chart before. I looked around as everyone raised a hand except for me and Pearl. Julia nodded wisely.

"Some people find the experience very life-affirming," she said, speaking to Pearl and me directly. "Others find it burdensome. Keep in mind, your chart is not your fate, it is a path you will be inclined to take, but that doesn't mean you have to. You have a choice."

Pearl and I both nodded to indicate we understood. I then folded my chart once, twice, three times over. I kept folding until it was small enough to fit in my pocket, small enough to forget about.

24

Dinner was once again held on the beach. We all found our way to the same tables we'd sat at the night before, though I noticed there was no head table tonight. Perhaps Geia and the mentors were dining privately.

I sat next to Ellen, who promptly poured me a glass of mastika. Each table had its own bottle, along with a bottle of white wine on ice. For all the talk of health and balance, the women at the Summit could certainly drink. Skye and Leslie were already seated, comparing their astrological charts, and Pearl joined us shortly after, looking refreshed from a late afternoon swim.

"Oh, look." Skye reached for a card in the middle of our table. "Another message from Geia."

"Let me see." Leslie leaned in close to read over Skye's shoulder. She looked like she was resisting the urge to grab the card out of Skye's hands.

"It's a prompt," Skye said, excited. "She wants us to

share *the origins of our respective wellness journeys* with each other. Fun! Who wants to go first?"

I looked at each of my pod members in turn. Did anyone besides Skye think that sounded like fun?

"I'll go first," Leslie said, smoothing her napkin and sitting up straighter in her chair. "I think I told you I'm a lawyer, right? Well, you know lawyers. Work is everything. Long hours. An endless caseload. That's been my life since my midtwenties. And then, ten years ago, I decided to add kids to the mix. My wife always wanted a big family, and I wanted to make her happy. We now have three girls."

She paused, letting that sink in. "Three. Who has three kids anymore? No one. Two is more than enough. Don't tell anyone I said so, but we should have stopped at two. My youngest is a total terror. I think she spent too long in the womb or something. Anyway, now not only do I work my ass off all day, I also have to juggle ballet and soccer and theatre and music class. When I'm not working, I'm driving my kids to their next activity, and when I'm not driving, I'm making snacks. The need for snacks in our house never ends. It's insane."

Leslie took a deep breath and I realized I was holding my own, listening to her talk.

"I was losing it . . . lashing out at everyone in my life, my wife especially. Then a girlfriend gave me a new moisturizer for my birthday. It was from the Goddess anti-aging line. Something about rubbing that glorious stuff on my face each night made me feel a little better. Within a month, I had bought the whole line of products, and now I use them religiously. Every night, I lock myself in the bathroom for twenty minutes of me time. I take a bath, I do a face mask, and then I apply the retinol, the serum, the moisturizer, the eye cream. It's my heaven. And it's saved my marriage."

I wondered if a moisturizer could really be so life-changing. But then, it wasn't really about the moisturizer, was it? It was about Leslie carving out a little time for herself. The skincare regimen was just an excuse.

"That's amazing," Skye said, her eyes wide with admiration.

Ellen nodded in agreement as a server presented our first course of the evening: a chilled lemon and leek soup.

"My story is similar," Ellen offered, diving into her soup. "I used to be a total mess. Addicted to my job, working too hard and too long every day. That meant I wasn't getting any sleep. I was exhausted all the time, not exercising, and I was totally reliant on uppers to get through the day."

It was hard for me to imagine breezy, cool Ellen strung out like that. She seemed so at peace with herself. The woman exuded an I-don't-give-a-fuck calm.

"I was a nervous wreck, and frankly, a real bitch. No one I worked with could ever do anything right, so I just ended up doing it all myself. I chased away every man I ever loved, and I pretty much ignored my family for a decade. And then, one day, I just broke." Ellen shook her head. The pain of the memory showed on her face. "I blacked out in an elevator on my way to a very important meeting with this big-time director, and I ended up in the hospital. They told me I was sleep-deprived and severely dehydrated. I stayed there for close to a month. My heart rate was all over the place."

"Wow," Leslie said, touching her napkin to the corners of her mouth.

Ellen nodded. "It was messed up. Anyway, I knew Geia from when we'd worked together, and she must have heard about my episode through the grapevine. She sent a basket of Goddess swag to my hospital room, including a book about sleep that changed my life. It's like she knew that sleep was my problem. I don't know how. Maybe she saw those habits when we worked together, but sometimes I think she might be psychic or something. She has this deep intuition about people."

Geia, psychic? I hadn't considered that. Could that be connected to the moonbathing?

"I read the book and never looked back," Ellen continued, her usual bright self again. "I started exercising, cooking at home, drawing boundaries around the different parts of my life. And sleeping, finally. I make sure to get nine hours every night. After I finished the book, the Goddess website became my daily go-to reference. I'm not sure what I would do without it."

"I'm glad you're okay," I said, offering her what I hoped was a supportive smile. I wished she hadn't had to go through that. It sounded awful.

Ellen shrugged. "Me too. I'm better than okay though, and I thank Geia for that."

Leslie and Skye nodded as if there was indeed a lot to thank Geia for.

Skye then told us about her eating disorder, which started in high school and continued into her twenties. It was the reason she first turned to wellness. As she spoke, she switched from tearing at her nails to biting them to thinking better of it and tucking her hands under her legs.

"I saw an interview with Geia online," Skye said. "She was talking about intentional eating and listening to our bodies. I went on the Goddess site to find out more and it was my first step in the right direction. It took years of therapy and work, but I wouldn't be here if it wasn't for Geia. She's the reason I got into yoga. The reason I have a career and my own studio."

Skye looked away, tears brimming. She unearthed her hands to wipe at her cheeks, laughing. "Sorry. I'm just so grateful to have a good life after so many years of pain."

Leslie put an arm around her shoulders and Skye leaned into her embrace. I wondered what that felt like. I had never had a friend who I could lean on like that. But watching Leslie comfort Skye, I realized that probably said more about me than about any friend. Leslie had offered her arm, but Skye had accepted it without hesitation.

"What about you, Pearl?" I asked. She was the one I was most curious about. From what I'd seen so far, she didn't fit the description of a typical Goddess™ follower.

Pearl smiled and ran a hand through her silver hair, still damp from her swim. "Well, ladies, it all started when I left my husband after forty-four years of marriage."

She paused for dramatic effect and I realized how much she was growing on me. She was sassy, and not just for her age. The four of us looked at her in surprise and wonder.

"He was dead weight." Pearl shrugged. "I wanted to travel and see the world, and all he wanted to do was sit in front of the television. So, I gave him an ultimatum. Come with me to Rome or say goodbye to me forever. He chose the television and I had a fabulous Italian holiday."

We all laughed and Pearl told us about how her time in Rome inspired her first romance novel, a runaway hit about love and food called *Cacio e Pepe*. All of her books were about travel, with titles like *The Weekender* and *Love at the Louvre*. They were all national bestsellers. Pearl said writing about new places was a great excuse to see the world.

"For research," she chuckled.

Travelling was how she spent most of her days now. If her grandkids wanted to see her, she told them to meet her in various locales around the globe.

"The thing is," Pearl said, "I didn't even have a passport when I left my husband. I'd come across the travel section on the Goddess website. There were all these articles about these wonderful places I had never even dreamt of visiting. I decided I didn't have enough time left in my life to waste another minute."

Pearl told us she had always wanted to write but it wasn't until she began travelling that she found her inspiration. She credited Geia for leading her down the right path. "I'll go anywhere Geia tells me to go." Pearl laughed. "Rome. Kyoto. Mastika. That woman knows how to live a good life and that's my number-one priority these days."

A server cleared away our dishes and I smiled at Pearl across the table. It was quite a thing to take charge of your life like that. Especially at her age. It struck me that each of these women credited Geia and the Goddess™ website with turning their lives around.

The second course arrived—a vegan spanakopita made

with "herbs from the mountain" — and now the four looked at me. I was the only one who hadn't shared, but I wasn't on a wellness journey. I took a swig from my glass of mastika.

"I guess you could say my wellness journey is just beginning," I said slowly. I didn't want to lie to them, but I wasn't quite ready to share the real reason I was here. "I don't have a big story like the rest of you. I mean, I told you last night, I'm new to this stuff."

I glanced at Ellen, who was watching me with expectant eyes.

"I guess my life is kind of a mess right now," I said, surprising myself. Where did that come from? "It has been for a while, really," I admitted. "I'm supposed to be writing my second book and it's not going well."

"What's it about?" Leslie asked.

Pearl placed a hand on Leslie's forearm. "We don't ask those questions of writers, love," she said, winking at me. "Sometimes you don't know what a book's about until it's finished."

I smiled, grateful. "I'm also kind of seeing this guy. It's complicated. He comes with a lot of baggage. An ex-wife, two kids. And we live in different cities... different countries, in fact. It seems like it would be a lot of work to make it anything real. Work that I just don't have time for these days."

The words had slipped out so easily, I barely knew what I was saying. Why was I telling them about Jack?

"Is he good to you?" Ellen asked thoughtfully. "This new guy?"

I hesitated for only a moment. "Yes, he is very good to me. Maybe too good." Again, the words seemed to pour out of me. Had I had too much to drink already? It wouldn't be the first time. I felt my cheeks burn and nudged my glass of mastika away with a finger.

"Then it's worth the work, Agnes," Ellen said. "It's always worth the work when they're good. So few are, you know?"

I nodded and smiled but didn't say anything else. The conversation quickly shifted to relationships, and while Skye told us about the yoga teacher at her studio who she was sleeping with—the same one she'd left in charge—I stayed silent, relieved we were no longer talking about me, and unnerved by how much I had said without meaning to.

25

GODDESS™ SUMMIT — DAY 3

When I awoke the next morning, I was certain I had dreamed of Geia again. I'd had the same vision as the previous night: Geia sitting at the end of my bed, watching me silently. But this time, she held something small and shiny in one hand, gleaming in the darkness. Catching the moonlight perhaps. I didn't know what any of it meant. I didn't usually have recurring dreams, especially not two nights in a row.

I got out of bed and went to the window. It was still early; I could see the sunrise yoga crew just gathering on the beach. It amazed me how the hotel staff managed to clear away any sign of dinner before we woke up each morning. The sand was freshly raked, smooth and ready for the day's activities.

With a start, I realized I didn't remember the end of dinner. We'd all shared our wellness origin stories, then the others had done a deep dive into their respective romantic histories — but what had happened after that? I couldn't even recall walking back to my room. I looked down at the T-shirt I'd worn to bed, unable to remember putting it on. I must have drunk more than I thought, but I didn't have a hangover. Was that the benefit of drinking mastika?

I got ready for the day, resolved to drink less tonight. All that blabbering about my mess of a life. No one needs to hear that, Agnes. Even if they say they want to.

OUR FIRST SESSION that day was Parenting Your Inner Child. When I arrived, I saw immediately it was a larger session, with four pods participating. We met in a conference room with glass doors looking onto the patio and pool. The mentor, Celeste, encouraged us to gather around four tables at the front of the room.

"This isn't the homiest setting," she said. "So let's try and make it feel less . . . corporate. Get close, everyone."

Celeste's long wavy hair was completely grey, but her heart-shaped face looked young. With large blue eyes, she surveyed the room as we took our seats. She smiled, close-lipped, exuding patience. I noticed a bag next to her on the floor but couldn't see what was inside.

My pod took the table on the far right side of the room. I sat down next to Ellen, who wore fuchsia lipstick this morning. I leaned in to ask her what had happened at the end of dinner last night — was I totally out of it? — but Celeste started talking and Leslie shushed us with a pointed look.

"Well, well, well. Here we are." Celeste beamed, looking around the room. She let her eyes rest on each of us in turn. She reminded me of a kindergarten teacher: her patient tone, her bag of surprises. "Today, ladies, is all about fun." Celeste reached into her bag and began placing paper and crayons on each table. "Today, we're going to draw. Nothing in particular to start, just whatever comes to mind as I'm speaking. I'll talk and you'll draw. Simple as that. Sound good?"

I glanced at each of my pod members. Only Pearl looked vaguely unsure about these directions, but when she caught my eye, she shrugged.

We all reached for paper from the middle of the table. I was already imagining including an image of my finished drawing in the *Vogue* article. People loved visuals and this was just too good. Parent your inner child by making time to draw with crayons. Readers would love it.

"Start with your favourite colour," Celeste said, her voice cheerful. "All kids have favourite colours. When we're children, we announce our favourite colour proudly, as an identifier. But as adults, we tend to move away from this kind of behaviour, even though our preferences for the simplest aspects of life remain unconsciously strong. Your favourite colour might be different now than it was when you were a kid. I want you to admit, today, what your favourite colour is, and use that crayon first."

Skye didn't hesitate to reach for a bright-pink crayon, which surprised me. Pink didn't fit with her outer toughness. But that was assigning too much significance to the activity. It was just a colour. We all gravitated towards certain colours; it didn't necessarily mean anything.

The rest of us followed Skye's lead, grabbing crayons from the middle of the table, but I hesitated with my hand over a sky blue. Did I like blue or did I just wear a lot of it? If I was including an image of this drawing in my article, I wanted to choose wisely.

Pearl caught my eye again. "It's not as easy as it sounds," she whispered, and Ellen nodded in agreement.

I reached for a dark-green crayon instead. If I had to choose a favourite colour, this would be it.

"You may start drawing," Celeste continued. "Draw whatever you want. Shapes, forms, or just scribbles. Don't think too deeply about it. Tap into the freedom you felt drawing as a child, when you had no judges."

No judges? I couldn't honestly say that was ever the case for me as a kid. Again, I hesitated, holding my crayon above the paper. What did I want to draw? Beside me, Leslie was putting orange stars everywhere on her piece of paper. On my other side, Ellen was sketching purple clouds. Pearl was creating a red border on the edge of her sheet, and Skye seemed to be drawing an animal of some sort in hot pink.

I exhaled and started drawing trees with my green crayon. That made the most sense.

"When we are children, the people in our lives are supposed to take care of us," Celeste said in a sing-song voice as we drew. "We may be cared for by our biological parents, adopted parents, siblings, aunts and uncles, grand-parents — our family. But family is not always as caring as one would hope."

I almost laughed. No, Celeste, definitely not.

"Often, we seek care and love outside of our families,"

she continued. "I want you to think of someone beyond the borders of your family unit who played a role in your care when you were a child. It could be a teacher, a friend, a neighbour. Someone who took a special interest in you and made you feel protected or nurtured in some way."

I continued to put trees on my paper, all different sizes, some with spiky needles and others with petal-like leaves. The only person who came to mind was the mother of a high-school friend. Sam's mom, Lisa. She was unusually kind to me, certainly more than my own mother ever was.

"The thing about these outside caregivers," Celeste said, circling the tables where we were hunched over our drawings, "is that they often see us very differently than our actual family members. There's a distance there, an objectivity, and as a result, a freedom. They see us as we are when they meet us, not who we were when we were younger. Not who we are in our family unit, but alone and individual. There's a profound power in that," Celeste explained. "For many of us, we likely felt most understood when these outside figures were seeing us, separate from the dynamics of our families. Who comes to mind for you? Think about that person. Imagine their face."

I tried to picture Lisa. I met her when I was sixteen, when I started to spend more nights at Sam's house than my own. Max was gone by that point, away at college, and my mother still travelled regularly for work, while my father taught night classes. I didn't ask questions about why they were never home.

If I was home in the evening, I was usually by myself. Alone, the dark got to me. The security lights would flash on, and I'd look out the windows, searching for the source.

I started sleeping at Sam's partway through my junior year. Sam was one of those friends that you bond with in high school and then immediately lose touch with after graduation, as soon as staying connected becomes inconvenient. She liked to party. So did I. She was always texting kids who were older than us, finding parties for us to go to and people to buy us booze. We called ourselves "social-fucking-butterflies."

Coming back to Sam's house after a party was amazing. The kitchen was a treasure trove of good snacks. Frozen pizzas, chips, all the makings for nachos. That was thanks to Lisa, who kept the cupboards lovingly stocked. Lisa was a dream. Sweet, easy to talk to, a fantastic cook. I loved being at their house for dinner. Her vegetarian shepherd's pie was my favourite. My own mother didn't cook—I'd only seen her open the fridge to retrieve pieces of fruit—and while my dad did okay at the stovetop, as soon as Max and I were old enough, dinner became a fend-for-yourself situation.

Celese continued, "With their face in mind, ask yourself: What do they make you want to draw? You can now use other colours if you wish. Draw something that you associate with this person."

What did Lisa make me want to draw? I remembered how, for the first month I started staying at their house, I slept with Sam in her bed, but eventually Lisa suggested I take the spare room, which had once belonged to Sam's older sister. I didn't actually move in, but I kept some clothes and books there. I tried to imagine what my life would be like if I'd had Lisa for a mother instead my own. She was a reader too. We exchanged books all the time, and discussed our mutual love for Angela Carter and Shirley Jackson. Lisa would make a pot of tea after dinner and we'd sit together in the living room, just the two of us, talking or reading. It felt so normal and warm. If Sam felt left out, she didn't let on. They had a wood stove. Lisa taught me how to build a fire, when to add a new log.

That's what I would draw. The wood stove. The fire. The warmth and love it seemed to represent. I reached for oranges and reds and yellows, beginning to sketch flames on a new sheet of paper.

We had a wood stove at our house too, but we rarely used it. No one could ever be bothered to order wood or take the time to build a fire, especially in the later years. When I was staying at Sam's, home felt like an abandoned war zone by contrast. My mother and I weren't arguing as much, but that's because we rarely saw each other. My parents too seemed to have given up the fight. I remember wondering if either of them had someone new in their lives. It would have been very easy. There was no accountability. They were basically free.

"Think about how this person parented you, in whatever form that took," Celeste said, her voice carrying across the room. "Look at what you've drawn. Think about how that person made you feel."

I looked at what I had drawn. It wasn't menacing, like you might expect from a fire. It looked like comfort, like home.

"As we move through our adult lives, it's important for us be our own parents. You may still have parents in your life, but it's you who must act as the outside caregiver now. I want you to remember what you've drawn today, and think about how you can cultivate those feelings in your life. It's up to you to be your own source of care. If you don't do it, who will?"

AFTER A SHORT, practical session on Total Body Exfoliation with a woman named Ronny, who was more enthusiastic about dry brushing than most people are about anything in their lives, my pod had the rest of the day off. I found a lounger by the pool and pulled out a notebook to jot down more of my thoughts on the Summit. From accessing buried feelings during movement hour, to understanding ourselves and our relationships through astrology, to learning to nurture our adult selves today in Celeste's drawing exercise, Geia's self-care curriculum seemed to be about returning to childhood via the body, both to unpack any trauma we may have experienced and to tap into the lack of inhibition we felt as children. That was all well and good, but what about those of us who never really got to feel like children *because* of our trauma? My memories of childhood were marked by anxiety and disappointment, not freedom and silliness.

"Agnes, how are you?" Geia stood at the end of my lounger.

"Good." I smiled, a little surprised. I hadn't seen her coming. "I was just making some notes."

"For the article?"

I nodded, shading my eyes with my hand. The sun shone bright behind her.

"Excellent! You look very focused. I shouldn't interrupt."

"No," I said. "Please, do."

Geia sat at the end of my chair, folding one leg neatly under the other. She was wearing another one of the white dresses, as more and more of the women at the Summit were doing. In three days, it had become the unofficial uniform. Pearl and I were two of the few hold-outs.

"Are you getting good material for your article? From what I understand, you have a pod of very interesting women to hang with while you're here."

I wondered if she knew the configurations of all the pods or just mine. "I do. Pearl is hilarious and Ellen and I clicked from the start."

I noticed a few women in the pool looking in our direction. So far, Geia had been largely absent from the Summit, aside from dinner on the first night. They were probably wondering why she was talking to me of all people. I wasn't even wearing the uniform.

"I knew you and Ellen would hit it off. We go way back. That's why I moved her into your pod at the last minute."

So, that *was* her doing.

"You have a good intuition about people," I said, partly to see how she would respond. "Ellen thinks you might be psychic."

Geia laughed cheerfully. "Isn't that nice? I've always prided myself on being a good reader, of books, of situations, of people. It's all the same, isn't it? You just have to pay attention. You just have to care. To read between the lines, as they say. You probably understand that better than anyone."

I hesitated. What did she mean? I suddenly remembered what she said when she first invited me to come here. "I know you see what others can't." That conversation had been strangely hazy in my mind — maybe because I was feeling off that morning — but it came back to me now. Had she been telling me she knew what I had witnessed in the window that night?

"How so?" I asked.

"Well, you're a writer. Aren't good writers also, by necessity, good readers?"

I smiled. Right. So that's what she had meant back in the Hamptons. She was only trying to give me — and my writing — a compliment.

"Sure," I said, nodding. "Of course."

Geia sighed deeply, looking at the sea. "Oh my god. What a fucking perfect day. Sometimes I wonder why I ever left this place. Have you gone for a swim in the sea yet? The water is incredible."

"No. Not yet."

"Well, you'll have to! Take your pod. There's a secret beach just west of here. Follow the footpath on the other side of the vineyard. That's the best place for swimming on the whole island. But don't tell the others." She looked towards the women in the pool. "It won't be a secret if the whole Summit knows about it."

I assured her I wouldn't tell, and then Geia said she had to get back to work. She headed back towards the hotel, and the women in the pool watched her go with obvious fascination. I wondered what it felt like to be so observed. At least being a writer provided me with some anonymity.

Jack was the only person who'd ever recognized me from my book jacket.

My stomach twisted into knots. I felt more and more ashamed of how my conversation with Jack had gone the other night. I really hadn't been fair to him. He was only encouraging me to keep on track with my writing. I just hated the possibility that he thought I didn't know what I was doing. I felt that way most of the time; I didn't need other people seeing that side of me too. It only made my inadequacies seem more real.

With Jack in mind, I turned to a fresh page in my notebook. Book two. I needed to give it some attention. Come up with an idea, Agnes, and the rest will follow. It seemed to be the hardest part, settling on the premise for a story, but really, every part of writing seemed like the hardest part while you were doing it: brainstorming, outlining, writing, revising, editing. All of it was difficult. But it also used to be the thing that made me feel most alive.

How did I do this last time, with *Violets in Her Lap*? I looked back to my childhood and remembered my unexplainable experiences in the forest. That became my starting point. Since then, the only other unexplainable experience I'd had was watching Geia that night in the Hamptons. My chest lifted. Maybe none of it was real, maybe it was my mind's way of creating stories for me to tell. That seemed the most rational explanation. I felt significantly lighter at the thought. Maybe there was no big mystery about Geia, after all. You really do have a wild imagination, Agnes.

I began to write down what I'd seen from the window. I described Geia swimming laps in the pool, the shock of seeing Kathari curled up in a dark coil on the pool's edge. I wrote of Geia's elegant walk to the centre of the lawn, how she lay down under the stars, and how the snake soon followed. I painted a picture of how they looked together, intertwined, each of them glowing with the light of the moon. And then of course, the big flash of light. I wrote about how it seemed to erupt from Geia's own body, sending radiant waves in all directions.

But this wasn't a book idea. This was just a scene. I reread what I'd written, hoping it might inspire some sense of who this character was, this glowing woman, and how she turned out this way, but nothing came to mind.

26

GODDESS™ SUMMIT — DAY 4

I had been dreading this day since I first read the schedule. After a morning of infrared therapy, followed by a paleo cooking class in the hotel's outdoor kitchen, it was my pod's turn with Lydia Gilmore, masturbation guru. Thankfully, it was a closed session: Lydia mentored only one pod at a time, but I still wasn't looking forward to it.

I came down to breakfast with a tight stomach. Today there was chia pudding and fresh fruit on offer. I picked out an orange, grabbed a coffee, and found a seat on one of the lobby sofas. Women breezed down the staircase towards the buffet. Everyone looked happy and relaxed. Leslie waved at me as she poured herself a coffee. She didn't seem at all nervous about the afternoon session. Then, suddenly, I heard a loud, anxious voice.

I turned towards the front desk. One of the women

seemed upset, which was all the more disruptive given the calm atmosphere. She was gesturing wildly at the staff member on duty.

"I just don't understand. Why can't I remember?" the woman said, her voice raised in panic.

I didn't know her name, but I had seen her around. She was very tall, with artfully tousled brown hair and those curtain bangs few women can actually pull off.

"First you need to take a breath," the staff member said calmly.

"Take a breath? I need an explanation!"

Now everyone was watching. The staff member remained calm. She stepped out from behind the desk.

"Please, miss. Why don't you come with me?" She gestured towards a closed door, just off the lobby, marked STAFF ONLY.

The tall woman hesitated.

"I'm sure *Geia* would be happy to help you," the staff member said.

"Geia?" the woman asked, lowering her voice to a normal volume. She nodded and followed the staff member through the doorway. Within seconds, the lobby returned to its usual quiet chatter. I glanced back at Leslie, who rolled her eyes at the outburst.

THE SELF-PLEASURE SESSION was held in a cozy, low-lit room down a long hallway off the lobby. Pearl nodded at me as I entered. I gave her a small wave in return and headed for the far side of the room, away from both Pearl and Leslie, who were already seated together. Skye and Ellen arrived soon after. None of us spoke. It was all a bit awkward.

The floor was covered in plush rugs topped with jewel-toned pillows. I sat on a pillow, feeling a little shaky. When I agreed to attend the Summit, I hadn't even considered what the curriculum would entail. This was exactly the kind of workshop *Vogue* would want me to write about in detail. The content was provocative and demanded vulnerability. But that meant it would require a lot from me.

When Lydia arrived, she asked us to sit in a circle. She was older than I was expecting, a contemporary of Pearl's. She looked like a hip grandmother. The skin on her face was deeply lined, and she was short and quite stocky. She wore the white linen tunic, what I now knew was the mentor uniform.

We moved to form a circle. I didn't want to sit too close to anyone, but the circle demanded it. I found a place between Ellen and Leslie.

"Hi," Lydia said, beaming at the group. "How are you?"

At first, there was silence. I wasn't sure if she wanted us to reply in unison or individually. Pearl said she was good and that seemed to suffice.

"Good," Lydia said. "I'm glad you're good. Me? I'm just okay. I've been thinking a lot about my daughter since I arrived here. She would love this place. She recently had a miscarriage. She's having a hard time."

What were we supposed to say to that? Everyone was quiet, but Lydia didn't seem to need us to respond.

She continued. "I'm feeling better now, sitting here with all of you. I'm glad you're here. That you want to learn more about yourselves. While it won't be easy, what we do here today, I can promise it will be worth it. We're going to start very simply. I'd like to go around the circle and for each of you to introduce yourselves. Tell me your name and something about your sexual life. It can be anything, as long as it's true. How does that sound?"

Again, Pearl responded for the rest of us. "Good," she said, nodding confidently.

"I'll start." Lydia shifted on her pillow and rubbed her palms together. "My name is Lydia and I haven't had sex with anyone but myself in seventeen years."

She let that sink in for a moment. The room was very quiet. I guess that tidbit shouldn't have been a total surprise, given the content of the session, but really, no one else? I wanted to ask if that was by choice.

Lydia turned to Pearl. "Okay. Your turn."

Pearl too shifted a little in her seat, adjusting her limbs, re-crossing her legs. "My name is Pearl." She scanned the circle and looked at each of us. "I often feel like I was born too soon. Like the world wasn't ready for me. Men my age think I'm too *out there*. That what I like, sexually, what makes me feel good, is wrong. I think if I had been born later, I would have been more accepted."

I was surprised to see Pearl tear up a little. She was usually quite stoic in our sessions. She shook her head and I felt bad about being standoffish when I entered the room. That was about me, not her.

"No, it's fine," she said, when Leslie placed a hand on her shoulder.

"Thank you, Pearl," Lydia said. "That's a difficult

position to be in. We all sympathize with you and your struggle."

Next, Leslie told us she had always hated kissing but she suffered through it for the sake of her partner. Ellen then tearfully shared that she had no sex drive these days. It had been over two years since she had felt like she wanted to have sex, with herself or anyone else.

Skye changed the tone slightly, saying she had a deep fear of intimacy, something she'd been working on in therapy for the last thirteen years. It translated into her feeling she didn't deserve love. She thought it was likely connected to her eating disorder.

And then I was up. Shit. I had meant to plan what I was going to say, but I had gotten so wrapped up in everyone else's stories and trying to figure how I could write about this for *Vogue* while protecting these women's privacy. Now, everyone was looking at me.

"Hi," I said. "I'm Agnes. I, uh . . ."

I *what*? I was drawing a blank.

"Sorry." I shook my head.

"It's okay," Lydia told me. "This is a safe space."

"Right," I nodded, though I had never understood the whole "safe space" thing. Saying a space is safe doesn't make it so. But the others had shared uncomfortable truths about themselves. I owed them something honest in return.

"The last time I tried to have sex was on the phone. Phone sex, you know? But it didn't go well. The guy didn't catch on. I was humiliated. I don't know if he doesn't see me that way anymore or if I was just being too sensitive. I basically hung up on him. Not my best moment."

They all looked at me. Where was my show of sympathy and support? I felt the need to continue. I avoided everyone's eyes.

"And the time before that, with the same guy, I cried when we tried to have sex. I don't know. I think something about him scares me. Not in an aggressive way. He's just different than any guy I've been with before. I worry I won't live up to his expectations. That I'm not good enough or something." I sighed. I was on a roll now. "I also worry I'm not cut out for men in general. When I'm with a man, I become obsessed, and they tend to take over my life. There's no space for me and my thoughts. It's been a long time since I've had a relationship. I'm afraid to go there again, with this guy especially."

Lydia nodded in understanding, saying something about making space for our emotions within the sexual act. I exhaled quietly, shaken by my own confession, which had seemed to pour out of me. Word vomit, again. What was with me lately? The other night and then today. It was like I couldn't stop myself once I got going.

I was relieved when Lydia announced she would next give us a tour of the vulva. I snapped my attention back to the circle. Focus, Agnes. This is gold for the article. We watched as Lydia stood to remove her underwear and then hiked up her tunic, sitting back on the floor with her legs spread wide open. We could see everything. Her pubic hair was bushy and partly white. Her skin below was almost purple. I was surprised by how normal this felt. Looking at someone else's body, their genitals; there was nothing sexual about it. Maybe this was what it was like for doctors.

A kind of detachment. I stared at the folds of her skin, the way they led to an inner darkness.

Lydia explained that the clitoris was much larger and more complex than it appeared. She pointed out the external clitoral glans — what many people call the clitoris — and described how it connected to the internal clitoral body, which was suspended from the pubic bone. She also identified the outer and inner lips of the vulva, the vaginal opening, and the beginning of the vaginal canal, probing herself with her fingers while she spoke. Another misconception: she explained that what most people thought of as the vagina was actually the vulva. She told us that every vulva looked different, and just as we should embrace the ways each of our bodies have a unique shape and character, we should embrace the distinctiveness of our vulvas.

Next, Lydia invited us to remove our own clothing. We had been warned about this before the session: mandatory nakedness. She encouraged us to spread out and lie on our backs. I retreated to my previous position, close to the wall. I slipped my shirt over my head and squirmed out of my cut-offs as quickly as possible. I then promptly lay down, determined not to look at anyone and hoping nobody looked at me.

Lydia distributed mirrors. Then she invited us to take off our underwear and examine ourselves, identifying the parts of our vulvas she'd just shown us.

I held the mirror in one hand and slipped my underwear off with the other. I looked in the mirror. There I was; all the parts of me. Now they had proper names. I sat up slightly, staring at my reflection, and found each part as instructed, naming them in my mind. Inner, outer. The clitoral glans. The vaginal opening. Okay, done. I lay back down, still holding the mirror in one hand. My heart was racing.

Lydia put on some music: loud drums and chanting. "Think of a name for your vulva and say it out loud."

The first name that popped into my head was Maude—no idea why—but that sounded old-fashioned and matronly, kind of like Agnes. Growing up, I'd always hated my name. Apparently, it was the only name both my parents could agree on: serious-sounding enough for my mother, with Greek origins to satisfy my academic father. Over the years I had grown used to my old-fashioned name, but I certainly didn't want an old-fashioned vulva.

The other women started calling out their names: "Ocean," "Lilac," "Red," "Spark."

"Goddess," I said, and then immediately regretted it. My face burned, staring up at the ceiling. What a cliché.

Next, Lydia instructed us how to pleasure ourselves: "With two fingers, stroke the left side of your glans from up to down in a slow, steady motion. As arousal starts to build, switch to a clockwise circular motion."

Why clockwise? Did it really matter?

I sighed, starting to sweat. Everything about this was making me uncomfortable. I felt very exposed. I started to think about how all five of our vaginas—sorry, *vulvas*—were breathing the same air. That was probably true whatever room you were in, but with nothing on, it felt much more real.

I tried to stroke myself as Lydia had instructed, but it

only made me think about Jack, about crying in front of him, about the other night on the phone.

Lydia turned up the music. She urged us to "let go." I continued to touch myself but felt nothing. There was too much going on. All these women, the music, the thoughts in my head. The room was boiling. I couldn't let go.

"Try going slower," Lydia said, her voice close.

My eyes flashed open and I pulled my hand back from where I was touching myself. She was standing over me, watching. Her eyes were big and round. She looked like an owl, peering down at me.

"Start slow and when you get a good rhythm and begin to feel something, increase your speed."

I nodded and she moved on.

Okay. Find a rhythm, Agnes. My heart was still racing. I started slow, as Lydia had instructed. I closed my eyes and breathed deeply. I thought about Zoë in the movement class, telling us to tune in.

Tune in, Agnes!

I could hear my pulse in my ears.

I had just started to feel something when Leslie began moaning very loudly. What the hell? Uptight Leslie was already coming? I resisted the urge to look sideways, but the damage was done. I had lost my rhythm.

Okay. Try again. I reached down but I wasn't wet at all. No wonder this didn't feel good. I let my hand fall away. I was worried Lydia was going to come back and tell me what I was doing wrong, but I just needed a minute. I closed my eyes. The drums and the chanting mixed with the moans of my fellow participants was just not working for me. This all felt very primal. I guess I didn't like that vibe in the bedroom.

Lydia approached again and asked if I would like her to help me. For the sake of the article, I said yes, but I was close to tears. I don't think I'd ever felt so uncomfortable. She saw that and told me to sit up. She crouched down next to me and gave me a hug. It was very strange to be naked and hugged by someone I'd just met.

"It's okay," she said kindly, seeming more like a grandmother than ever. "What do you think is going on?"

I shook my head, starting to cry. "I don't know."

I was mortified. I couldn't believe I was this emotional. It was like being in Jack's room all over again. What is wrong with you, Agnes?

"Take a breath, my dear. Take a few. Deep, big ones."

I listened to Lydia, slowing down my breath, attempting to calm myself.

"You can stop," she said. "If you want. And you can leave. Or you can try again. But this time, before you even touch yourself, I want you to think about what makes you feel most awake sexually. What gets you going?"

I continued to take deep breaths, contemplating what to do. Leaving the room sounded most appealing, but I knew the others would see me go. They'd wonder what was wrong with me, why I couldn't pleasure myself like the rest of them. And, knowing my pod, they'd want to talk about it over dinner.

"Okay," I said, wiping the tears from my cheeks. "I'll stay."

"Good. You made the right choice," Lydia said, still crouching next to me. "Tell me, what does get you going?"

I hesitated. I should have an answer for this. But I wasn't sure, really. I told her so.

Lydia nodded. "Okay. Well, when was the last time you felt sexual?"

I thought back to the attempted phone sex with Jack. But did I feel sexual then, or did I just want to feel wanted? Like how Owen used to make me feel.

"I think I feel most sexual when I feel wanted by someone else," I told Lydia in a whisper.

"Right, okay. That's a big part of sex for most people. Feeling desired." She hiked up the sleeves of her tunic and for a horrifying few seconds I thought she was going to touch me. Thankfully, she kept her hands to herself. "Let's try again. I want you to lie back and close your eyes. I want you to think of the last person who made you feel truly wanted."

I lay back on the pillow and wasn't sure who to picture. Not Jack. Things had been too complicated in that department so far, which was maybe my fault. But not Owen, either. Owen only made me feel wanted sometimes, I realized. Most of the time, I was left wondering if I would ever be enough for him.

I opened my eyes.

Lydia was still next to me, one hand on my arm.

"I don't know that I ever have," I said, sitting up, voice breaking. "Felt truly wanted, I mean."

Lydia nodded wisely, gave me another hug, and told me to try to relax for the rest of the session. I nodded and rested my head back on the cushion. Tears fell from the corners of my eyes, streaming past my temples and into my hair.

AT THE END of the session, I was the first one out of the room. My pod members lingered, slowly putting on their white dresses, smiling blissfully, satisfied. As I sped through the lobby, I heard someone calling my name. I turned. Lydia was hurrying after me.

"Agnes," she said. "Hold on a minute. I wanted to follow up with you. What we do in there—" she gestured behind her "—can be very intense. Back at my clinic, I typically work with each woman every day for at least a week. A one-off session like that? It's a lot of pressure for all involved."

I attempted a smile. She was trying to make me feel better.

"Here's the thing," she continued, "you need to ask yourself if feeling wanted is simply a turn-on, or if it's a form of validation-seeking. It's a very slippery slope. I see it in a lot of women. The problem of course is that when we use sex for validation, we become out of touch with our own desires. We exist only to be wanted by someone else, to people-please, which means we know little about what we want outside of that dynamic. Does that make sense?"

I nodded uncertainly. I didn't want to hear any of this. Couldn't she just leave me alone? The session had been traumatic enough.

"Okay." Lydia smiled, her face soft with sympathy. "If you want to talk more, let me know. I'm around. These are big issues. They take time. And you can't be expected to process them alone."

I nodded and thanked her, hoping she'd just go away. When she turned and began to walk back down the hallway, I sped through the lobby and fled outside. I found a bench in a hidden corner of the garden, next to a large apricot tree. The smell of ripe fruit, sheltered from the wind. The tears had stopped but I still wanted to cry. I felt like I could start again at any moment. What was going on with me? When I agreed to attend the Goddess™ Summit, I had no idea these sessions were designed to crack you open.

You need to ask yourself if feeling wanted is actually a turn on or if it's a form of validation-seeking, Lydia had said.

Validation-seeking. I had never thought of it that way. But yes, I had to admit, whenever Owen came over, I'd felt validated. But that's only because he had kept me in a state of uncertainty, in limbo, unsure how he really felt about me because I was only ever the woman on the side. And when I tried to initiate sex with Jack, was I just trying to cultivate some clear sign of affirmation from him, to make myself feel better about my own insecurities?

It was messed up. I was messed up. More than I'd thought.

The worst part was, it felt like Jack really did want me. But he wanted more from me than Owen ever had—he wanted me consistently, completely, not just for some quick thrill. And I wasn't used to being wanted in that way.

I stayed in the garden, mulling over my thoughts, until my brain felt like mush and my chest felt heavy from all the ways I'd pushed Jack away. Not cool, Agnes.

The sound of raised voices, headed in my direction, interrupted my spiralling. Not voices, just one voice. I recognized it immediately. Geia.

Instinctively, I hid behind the apricot tree and watched as Geia floated by on the garden path, one of her Goddess™ staff members hurrying behind her.

"Perfection isn't a goal," Geia was saying, her tone sharp, a pitch I'd never heard from her. "Perfection is the baseline. Every event needs to go off without a hitch. My followers need to know they are getting the very best. Any more slip-ups and you can book yourself a ferry home. I mean it, Stephanie."

Stephanie nodded and seemed to be taking notes on a clipboard. What was she writing? *No more slip-ups?* I wondered what she'd done wrong. Did it have something to do with the tall woman in the lobby this morning? It surprised me to hear Geia sounding so upset. Where was that coming from?

The two walked on and I waited a few moments in the foliage for them to disappear out of view. Overheard, a large black bird squawked as it flew low across the sky, shattering the silence and making me duck.

27

I waited for Geia and Stephanie to turn a corner, and then I headed back to the hotel. It seemed like there were three Geia Stones: the irreverent, fun-loving party girl; the centered, inspiring guru; and the flames-in-her-eyes don't-cross-her boss. Again, I wondered what I could — or should — write about Geia in my article. Was Jack right about her? Did she really mean it when she said she wanted my story to be an honest account?

Back at the hotel, I was ready for a cold shower and a drink. The half-finished bottle of mastika I'd taken from the bar in town was calling my name. But someone else was too. As I crossed the lobby, the woman working the front desk waved me over.

"Ms. Oliver?"

I skirted around a group of women in swimsuit cove-rups headed to the pool and approached the desk. I noticed that like all the staff, Amara — according to her name tag—looked like she could be related to Geia. She could have been a model or a movie star.

"Ms. Oliver, we have a package for you," she said.

"A package?"

Who would send me a package here? For a brief moment, I wondered if I had drunkenly ordered something online my first night and forgotten.

"It just arrived." She reached under the desk and presented me with a box wrapped in brown paper. I immediately saw Jack's name in the return address. My heart skipped.

"Thank you."

I took the box. What could this be? And when did he send it? Before or after the awful phone call? I hoped it was after. Maybe we still had a chance. Maybe I hadn't screwed everything up completely.

"It's not often we get packages from America here on the island," Amara said with a smile. "Someone went to a lot of trouble to make sure you got it during the Summit."

I nodded and she raised her eyebrows. "Someone special?"

I laughed. "Yes."

"Lucky you. Any idea what it is?"

I shook my head. "None whatsoever."

"A surprise then. Even better." She smiled again and I hurried upstairs.

When I reached my room, I sat down on the bed and ripped open the brown paper. Inside the box, the first thing I spotted was an envelope with a short handwritten note from Jack inside:

Agnes,

A few items to keep you happy (and inspired) (and well fed) while you're on the island. Consider these an olive branch of sorts. I'm sorry if I've seemed over-protective lately. In my mind, there is nothing worthier of protection than great artists and their art.

See you soon, I hope . . .

Jack

So, he did send this after our talk the other night. Now that he put it this way, I realized I really had overreacted. It was a good thing that he wanted me to work on book two. My inability to do so wasn't his fault.

I unwrapped the items inside the box. Each had a sticky note attached, explaining why he'd chosen it. There was a book on screenwriting, which he said might offer a different perspective on story construction. There were various snacks to nourish me while writing: chocolate-covered almonds, salted pistachios, dried mango. And there was a leather-bound notebook and a new pen, in case I needed a "fresh start."

It was all very thoughtful. My heart soared as I took in all the items laid out on my bed. No one had ever done anything like this for me before. Owen had never once bought me a gift, and if he had, it would never have been anything like one of these carefully chosen items that I didn't even know I needed. I had been so silly with Jack. Playing games, letting my insecurities get the better of me. I hated myself for that. I wished I could call him and thank him. I wished I could see him.

I opened the windows wide and lay back on the bed, my head propped up by pillows. I opened the book on screenwriting and began to read. Outside, I could hear the sea, and chatter on the deck below. I didn't stop reading until I realized I was late for dinner.

THAT NIGHT, GEIA and the mentors once again dined with us on the beach. I took my seat at my pod's table, avoiding eye contact. I knew they had all seen me self-destruct in our session with Lydia, and the last thing I wanted was to talk about it with the group. If anyone brought it up, I didn't know what I would do. I glanced across the beach and noticed the tall woman who was upset in the lobby that morning sitting with her pod and laughing. Apparently, she was feeling better.

A few minutes later, Geia held up her glass to give another rousing toast. As usual, she went on and on about our growth and development, our commitment to self-discovery, and her hopes for us on our wellness journeys. She then explained that part of our self-care curriculum would involve a session with Sloane Devine, a renowned practitioner of a unique form of hypnotherapy and energy healing.

"Sloane?" Geia said, inviting a woman who looked much younger than the other mentors, maybe even younger than me, to stand. She wore the white mentor tunic and her silver-blond hair was tied back in a sleek low ponytail. Sloane Devine waved at the crowd with a faint smile and sat back down.

"Sloane hosted her first session today and I was lucky enough to sit in on the experience," Geia continued. "I think everyone involved would agree that it was life-changing. I hope you'll all embody the open-minded spirit of the women who worked with Sloane today. I promise you, the pay-off will be extraordinary."

Everyone clapped and raised their glasses of wine or mastika, following Geia's lead.

"Apparently it's, like, crazy," Skye said, wide-eyed, picking at the skin on the side of her thumbnail, as the rest of us dug into our obligatory salad course. I'd consumed more salad in the last four days than I had in the last four months. "A combination of hypnosis and reiki, a total trip. Do you know Claire?" she asked the table, lowering her voice.

Ellen and Leslie nodded. Pearl and I were at a loss, but I was happy we were talking about something other than our session with Lydia.

"Which one is she?" I asked.

"The one with the curly red hair," Skye said, indicating a woman seated at a table on the other side of the beach. I recognized her, but we had never spoken. "She's nice. Anyway, apparently when it was her turn for hypnotherapy, she shared all this stuff about her brother abusing her when she was kid."

"Yikes." Ellen frowned, chasing a cherry tomato around her plate with her fork.

"But that's not even the crazy part," Skye continued. "When Sloane was working on her, Claire started levitating."

"What?" I asked. "Seriously?"

Skye shrugged. "That's what people are saying."

"Like, levitating, as in—?"

"As in hovering off the ground," Skye told us. "Or the massage table or wherever. I think she was lying down at the time."

"The rumour mill begins," Leslie said, shaking her head.

"I heard it from one of her pod members," Skye insisted. "She was lying there, hypnotized by Sloane, telling the group all this traumatic stuff about her childhood, and then she just started to float. Only a couple of inches, but it was noticeable."

Pearl laughed. "Only a couple of inches? I'd say even half an inch would be noteworthy."

"What did they do, her pod members?" Leslie asked.

"They just sat there watching. After a few minutes, she settled back on the table." Skye leaned forward. She was whispering now, even though those at the other tables couldn't hear us. "Geia was there, observing, and apparently, at the end of the session, she gave Claire a hug." Skye shivered. "It sounds amazing. I can't wait for our session with Sloane."

WE LINGERED AT the table, drinking ginger tea to finish the meal—excellent for digestion, we had learned in our cooking class—and I silently thanked them all for not bringing up my masturbation meltdown. They were pretty cool women, when it came down to it.

While Pearl poured more tea into each of our mugs, I tried to picture Claire levitating. Could that really happen? If the rumours were true, it had been witnessed by multiple people. This was different than my vision in the Hamptons. I was the only person who'd seen that, and I was starting to think I'd imagined it, just like those things in the woods when I was a child. But this was more difficult to explain away.

I glanced over at Claire's table, but she was no longer sitting with her pod. I scanned the beach for her but couldn't see her anywhere. Geia, I noticed, was also absent, no longer sitting at the head table with the mentors. I looked towards the hotel. In the distance, I could just make out two white-clad forms walking along the beach path. Geia and Claire? If so, where were they headed, and why were they together?

"I feel like a swim." Pearl sighed, setting down her cup of tea. "Anyone want to join me?" She nodded in the direction of the water.

"Now?" Leslie raised her eyebrows. "I don't have my bathing suit with me."

"Me neither," said Skye. "It's back at the hotel. But a swim sounds great."

"Well, we can't very well skinny dip in front of the whole Summit." Ellen laughed. "Or could we?"

"I know where we can swim." I sat up in my chair, remembering what Geia had said about the secret beach. "It's totally private, bathing suits optional."

IN THE NEAR DARKNESS, we found our way to the vineyard. We walked down one of the rows, giggling like we were up to no good. Above us, a spattering of stars and a dazzling moon lit our way. When we located the footpath Geia had described, we all joined hands. The breeze picked up and I felt like a teenager again, out with my girlfriends, on an adventure. Though I had never had friends I held hands with before.

The path continued for several minutes and then turned right towards the cliffs.

"Are you sure this is the way?" Leslie asked with a shiver.

I nodded. "That's what Geia said."

If Geia had said it, they were on board. She wouldn't lead them astray. We continued on the path and when we reached the cliffside, we found steps carved into the rock, leading down towards a pool of water, sheltered by a wall of jagged rocks rising out of the surf. It was less of a beach than a lagoon. A natural sea pool, still and inviting.

"Wow," Skye said, peering down the steps.

We descended towards the pool, still holding hands. Once we reached the water's edge, we all took off our clothes. Unlike in the session earlier today, I didn't hesitate. I wanted to do this. It didn't feel uncomfortable or embarrassing. It felt right.

We jumped in the pool, our shrieks echoing off the rock wall. The water was surprisingly warm; it felt like a hug, a gentle caress that made every inch of my body relax. I dove down, searching to see how deep the pool was, but couldn't find the bottom. It seemed to go on forever. When I surfaced, the others were all floating on their backs, looking up at the sky. I joined them. Above us, the stars and the moon gleamed. I laughed and no one asked me what was funny. Soon, they were all laughing too. Despite the horrible day, I couldn't remember ever feeling this good.

28

GODDESS™ SUMMIT — DAY 5

I woke myself up, shouting at an empty room. I had been dreaming of Geia again. She wore her white dress and held the same small, shiny item in her hand. I still wasn't sure what it was. This time, she had gestured to the open window, and Kathari slithered through and onto my bed. He wound himself up her torso and around her neck, tightening his hold, like he was going to choke her. I called out to stop him, but Geia shook her head at me as if this was all perfectly normal; she was in no danger. That's when I woke up, screaming.

Despite the early hour, I was wide awake, so I figured I might as well try and get some writing done. I still had hours before my first session, and the book Jack sent me had given me some ideas on how to find my way into the woman-snake-moon story. I figured it was worth a shot.

But first, I went down to the lobby to see if I could get a coffee. Amara was working the front desk again. She looked up at me as I approached and gave me the same warm smile as the day before. If she wondered why I was up, she didn't say so.

"Hey Amara, any chance I could get a coffee? I know the kitchen probably isn't open yet."

"It won't be open for another hour, but we have an espresso machine in the staff room. I can pour you one, if you'd like?"

I bowed to her in gratitude. "That would be amazing. Thank you."

Amara drifted off down the hallway, swiping a key card and disappearing behind the door that read STAFF ONLY. Her golden calves were just visible under the hem of her white dress. When she returned, she handed me a hot espresso and a piece of cake.

"Lemon," she said warmly. "My mother made it."

"You're my hero. I feel like I haven't had sugar since I arrived."

She smiled and watched me take a bite.

I widened my eyes in appreciation as I chewed. "It's so good. Please tell your mother thank you."

She nodded. "I will."

I turned to go and then stopped. "Oh, and by the way, my friend did good with that package."

Amara nodded. "Like I said, you are a lucky lady."

I headed back across the silent lobby, pleased with myself. Coffee always helped me write, and the cake was a bonus. Plus, I liked Amara. Maybe I could interview her for my article. She could offer a local perspective on the whole Goddess™ phenomenon.

When I reached the staircase, I was startled by the sound of a door opening, disrupting the quiet. I turned and saw Claire coming in through the door to the garden. She was wearing the same outfit from the night before—the white dress—and it was heavily wrinkled, as if she had slept in it.

"Morning," I said.

Claire jumped. "Oh, hi."

"Late night?"

Claire shrugged but offered nothing else.

Where was she coming from? Had she been at Geia's villa? And if so, what had they been doing together all night? I imagined them in the back garden where I had sat with Geia that first day. But what could they possibly have to talk about all night long?

I watched Claire drift up the main staircase, hurrying past me and vanishing as she reached the second floor.

OUR SESSION THAT morning was Nature Music. The mentor, Ava, was a petite woman with a mouse-brown pixie cut and very small eyes. She was nymph-like, a real-life Tinker Bell, with tiny hands and ears and a long, thin neck. As she spoke, she handed us each a towel.

"Good morning," she told the group gathered in the courtyard, our pod and one other. "It's a beautiful morning to be meeting all of you here on this gorgeous island. For the next ninety minutes, I will be your guide as we explore all that nature has to offer. First, I'd like us to take a walk. Not far, but away from the hotel, up the road a little way into the forest. We need space and quiet to gather our thoughts, and to open ourselves to what grows here on the island. Please, if you would, follow me."

We followed Ava up the long driveway. While we walked, she stayed silent, and the group followed her lead. It was hot already, the sun fierce above us. I realized I should have brought water, maybe worn a hat. Only a few in the group were dressed for a hike. I wore slide sandals, a shirt dress. Good choices, as always, Agnes.

We reached the main road and Ava turned right, the opposite direction of town. I kept expecting a car to pass by, but none came our way. It left me feeling alone, irked somehow. I realized I hadn't seen anyone besides fellow Summit members, mentors, and staff since arriving here, but that was the point I guess: isolation, retreat.

We walked for several minutes down the road until we reached the entrance to a trail. If we hadn't been with Ava, I would have missed it entirely: on the opposite side of the road, there was an opening in the greenery, the beginnings of a forest that crept up the mountainside.

"This is where we enter," Ava told us, her voice low and soothing.

We crossed the road and took the trail, trees and bushes rising around us on both sides. After we had walked only a few minutes, the forest turned dense and shady. I exhaled, relieved by the coolness. When I saw this session on the schedule, I assumed "nature music" would involve sitting in a circle in the woods while our mentor beat a bongo drum and encouraged us to reflect on our life's goals. So far, so good.

I noticed Ellen stop to slip off her sandals, going barefoot, and I decided to do the same. The ground was cool. The packed, damp earth reminded me of the trails from my childhood, though the trees here were mostly unfamiliar. I spotted more of the Mastika trees, but the rest of the vegetation was unknown to me.

Still, no one spoke. We came to a fork in the trail and Ava led us left. The path to the right seemed to head up the mountain. Eventually, we reached a small clearing. Ava stopped and turned to us.

"Please," she said, gesturing to the ground. "Sit."

We sat in a circle. Here we go. Time for the drum.

"Isn't this better?" Ava asked, sighing deeply. "We are staying at a beautiful hotel, but I find all walls to be very confining."

Skye nodded deeply as if she felt the same.

Ava rubbed her hands together. "First, we walked. We did this to escape the modern world. It still exists, over there." She gestured vaguely behind her. "But for now, we are separate from it. I want you to think of yourself that way. Separate and safe from the modern world. Technology and social media. Your families, your friends, your lovers. All of it. Within these trees, we are only creatures, a small group among many."

Pretty good, Ava. I couldn't have said it better myself.

"Now," Ava continued, "we will meditate. Before we can really listen to our plant brothers and sisters, we need to go inward, we need to find stillness." She put a palm to her chest. "Please, close your eyes. Place your hands on your knees, palms up or down, your choice. I will get you started. We will breathe in for four beats and out for four. Eventually, I will stop counting and then you can continue the meditation on your own."

Ava began counting and I did my best to follow the rhythm she prescribed.

In: one, two, three, four.

Out: four, three, two, one.

In: one, two, three, four.

Out: four, three, two, one.

I was just getting into it when she stopped counting, ten rounds in. Then, there was only quiet. The faint sounds of the others breathing. I squinted to look around. Everyone was still, their eyes closed. Ava too. I promptly closed my eyes again.

Okay, Agnes. Breathe. Go inward.

In: one, two, three, four.

Out: four, three, two, one.

I had always sucked at meditating. It was just like in Lydia's self-pleasure session; I found it nearly impossible to turn off my mind. Now, I kept seeing Claire returning to the hotel in the early morning. Her wrinkled dress, her surprise at seeing me, like she had been caught red-handed. It sent my mind spinning, coming up with possible explanations for where she'd been. I couldn't stop thinking about it.

You always do that, Agnes. You overreact and conjure up versions of events that aren't real. Owen used to say you refused to see things as they really are.

"Okay," Ava called the group back to her and we opened our eyes.

Shit. I missed the whole meditation.

"Wasn't that wonderful? It is so important not to rush into a space. To take a moment to just *be* before you embark on any kind of activity or make a request from the world around you." She paused and many of the women nodded.

I glanced over at Ellen. She looked serene.

"Now, I'd like everyone to spread out and lie down on your stomachs. Place one ear to the ground. It's time for us to listen."

I wasn't expecting this. Everyone moved into position. I found a spot, spread out my towel, and stretched out. The earth was cool against my cheek. My feet fell to either side, turned out, like a dancer.

"Did you know that all trees are connected?" Ava asked. "Beneath the earth, their roots find each other. No tree exists in isolation. They are an invisible community, always communicating."

I held my breath. Memories of the dust I'd seen as a child came back to me. I'd understood it to be a way for the trees to speak to each other.

"Trees, once believed to be isolated beings," Ava continued, "are actually social in nature. Interdependent. Trees communicate through their root systems. They alert each other to disease, insect attacks, and drought. Their communication takes the form of a kind of pulse, an electrical signal, believed to make a clicking sound imperceptible to the human ear."

My pulse hammered. I had read about the communication system Ava was describing. It was different than what I had experienced, but it suggested that trees really could talk to each other. I had seen the dust. Did that mean I could hear the trees too?

"Below the earth," she continued, "there is constant activity. The natural world is moving and reacting, moment by moment. I'm going to stop talking now. I want you to close your eyes and tune in to what lies beneath. No questions, no getting up. Give yourself over to the experience. Be a good listener."

I couldn't see Ava from where I was lying, but I could feel and hear her drop to the ground. She was listening too.

I switched ears, turning so the other side of my face touched the ground. I didn't hear anything. Ava had said the clicking of roots was imperceptible to humans. I guess we were just supposed to try to hear something? Or imagine we could? As I lay there with my ear to the ground and my eyes closed, I pictured bugs crawling amongst a complex root system just beneath my body. I imagined the trees around us sending messages to each other about the silly humans trying to hear their chatter. I imagined the clicking sound to be like knuckles cracking, a reverberation travelling through the darkness. All the while, my heart raced. If trees could talk to each other through their roots, who was to say they couldn't also communicate by releasing spores into the atmosphere? Why hadn't I thought of this before?

After several minutes, Ava got us to sit up again and talk about how we felt. A few people said they felt sad, like they had reconnected with an estranged friend after too long apart. They felt they had wasted so much time, disconnected from nature. Others said that lying on the ground made them feel, I kid you not, "grounded."

"Ava," I said, wringing my hands in my lap. I felt Ellen's eyes on me. I never spoke in session unless called upon. "Do trees communicate in any other ways that you know of?"

Ava blinked in my direction. "Such as?" she said.

"Well, you talk about this electrical signal, um, this clicking sound." I swallowed. I had kept the dust a secret for so long, but I had to know if I'd made it up. "What about other forms of language? Like, say, scent-based?"

"Scent-based?" another woman in the circle spoke up. "What does that even mean?"

But Ava nodded wisely, as if something had suddenly fallen into place. "You're familiar with the theory of pheromones?"

I shook my head uncertainly.

"Research suggests that plants, and trees specifically, purposefully emit pheromones to influence their environment. To deter a pest, for instance, they might emit a substance that makes their leaves seem less attractive. Some people think of that process as a form of communication. So, yes, scent-based communication is precisely right."

My pulse pounded. That was what I had witnessed as a child. How I had always understood it, even if it I wasn't sure it was real.

"These pheromones," I said. "Are they visible, something we can see?"

Ava shook her head. "No. Much like the clicking signal beneath the earth, these substances are imperceptible to human senses, though nature devotees like myself believe that even if we can't hear or see or smell the mark that trees make on the world, it still touches us. We still experience it."

My mind reeled. So, I hadn't imagined the dust. It wasn't just a projection that would one day lead to a novel. It was real. And for some reason, I could perceive it when no one else could. But what did that mean about my more recent vision? Of Geia and her snake in the moonlight?

29

We had the afternoon off, so I decided to go into town, to the café owned by Jack's friend. I wanted to talk to Jack, to thank him for the care package, and to ask him about Geia. Something weird was going on. And he knew her better than anyone.

When I mentioned my afternoon expedition to Pearl — leaving out the specifics of why I needed to get online of course — she said she'd like to join me.

"I'm dying to check to my email," she whispered, so the others wouldn't hear. "I sent my editor my latest book just before the detox started. I'm desperate to know what she thinks."

There was a hotel shuttle bus for those who wanted to go into town, so we approached the front desk to arrange a ride.

"Amara!" I said, surprised to see her again. "Do you ever stop working?" By my estimate, she'd been staffing the desk for two days straight, including the early morning shift.

She looked up from the computer and frowned. "Sorry?"

"I just mean, I hope they let you go home and sleep at some point. You deserve a break."

She smiled politely but looked like she had no idea what I was talking about. My eyes went to her name tag. "Dimitra." That was odd. This woman looked exactly like Amara.

"Oh." I blushed, my stomach dropping. "I'm sorry. I got you mixed up with someone else."

Dimitra said it wasn't a problem. Why did everyone on this island look identical?

The shuttle was already out taking a group on a tour of the island, but Dimitra said her boyfriend, Ezio, could take us into town. In regular times, when the island was full of tourists, he was like a second shuttle for the hotel.

Tall and broad, with a full head of dark curls, Ezio was gorgeous. His car, however, was not. It was an old, boxy thing with a dented bumper. When he emerged from inside it, Pearl gasped.

"It's too perfect," she whispered. "Beautiful man. Ugly car. He's going to be the love interest in my next novel."

Ezio drove fast into town, the island speeding by us. I was sweating and feeling nervous about calling Jack. I clasped my hands together in my lap and squeezed.

The town was quiet and sunny, just as it had been the day of our arrival. Ezio indicated he would wait for us, gesturing to the beach by the pier. I asked him for directions to Koukoutski and he told us the way in heavily accented English.

Pearl and I wandered through the maze of streets, seeing no one. It felt like a ghost town.

"Did he say left or right at the fountain?" I asked Pearl. I was glad she was with me. The quiet of the town was giving me the creeps.

"I think he said left."

We walked down another street lined with shops and restaurants, all of them closed. Was it a holiday or something? You'd think July would be the height of tourist season. Where was everyone?

"There it is," Pearl pointed.

Just ahead on the corner, we saw a café. It was tiny and narrow, a few tables outside, plenty of flowerpots around the entrance. A hanging sign read KOUKOUTSKI.

My chest fell. It looked closed. The doors were shut and there was no one sitting at the outdoor tables. But then a man appeared around the side of the building, holding a watering can.

"Excuse me," I said, approaching him. "Is the café closed?"

He looked down at me. Like everyone else, he was incredibly handsome. Dark hair, strong chin, though definitely older than Ezio. He wore a white linen shirt and navy-blue shorts.

"It's *mesimeri*," he said. "Quiet time. Siesta. Everything's closed."

"I'm a friend of Jack Verity's. He said maybe you could help us?"

The man's face brightened at the sound of Jack's name.

OTIS SET ME up with his laptop at a table in the corner of the empty café. He made Pearl and me coffee, and they sat outside chatting while I made my call. Otis already had Jack on his FaceTime—apparently, they talked every couple of months—so I clicked on Jack's name, exhaling slowly.

It rang only twice. Jack's face appeared on screen. He was sitting outside, sunlight and greenery behind him.

"Agnes." His face broke into a big smile. "What a nice surprise."

"Jack." I smiled too. It was so good to see him.

"I see you took my advice. How's Otis?"

"He's great. He's out front charming my friend right now. She's seventy-two."

Jack chuckled. "Isn't he the best?"

"He is." Sounds of the pool, laughter. "Where are you right now?

"Still in the Hamptons. The girls are trying to out-belly-flop each other."

"Cute." I looked down at my lap and back up at the screen. "Listen, Jack, I wanted to thank you for the care package. It was so thoughtful."

"No worries. It was fun to put together."

I bit my lip. "I also wanted to apologize. I know I've been acting weird lately."

Jack's face turned serious. He waited for me to go on. I hadn't planned any of this but I knew exactly what I wanted to say.

"I have this thing, because of my mom I think, and maybe my ex too—I'm completely allergic to criticism. Or at least, what I perceive as criticism."

I knew in my gut it was true. In our astrology session, Celeste had said I would tend to seek out romantic relationships that repeated a familial dynamic. My mom had always been hypercritical of me, and after I had cut her out of my life, I'd found someone new who was just as disparaging. Owen had used a different approach—more belittling, more gaslighting—but it had the same effect. They both had a way of making me feel constantly fearful, like I was always on the verge of messing up.

I pressed on. "When you were questioning my decision to come here, I overreacted. I saw it as judgement, as you not trusting me."

"But that wasn't it at all," Jack said.

"I know that now. But it's hard for me to recognize it in the moment. I think everyone is doubting me all the time because my mother always doubted me as a child. And now I doubt myself. I see now that you were only looking out for me. Encouraging me to write for *me*, not for anyone else."

He nodded. "That's really all I meant by it."

"So, can you forgive me?"

He laughed lightly. "Of course, Agnes. I already have."

"Good." I exhaled. My whole body felt lighter.

"So, how's the Summit going?" he asked. "You look different."

"Do I?"

"You look good, refreshed."

I smiled. "Jack, I need to talk to you about something."

"What is it?"

"It's about Geia."

263

He got up to move away from the pool and his splashing daughters. "What about her?"

I hesitated. What was the best strategy here? I couldn't come right out and ask him about everything I'd seen: the night of the moon, all the weirdness on the island.

"She was born here, right?"

Jack nodded.

"Does she still have family on the island?"

"No, I don't think so."

That struck me as odd. "No one?"

"Why do you ask?"

"I thought I might like to interview her family. For the article."

Jack frowned. "I'm sorry I can't be more helpful. I've never actually met her family."

That was even more odd. "Never? Why's that?"

He paused. "They're estranged."

"Ah, okay. Well, is there anyone you think I should talk to on Mastika? Maybe one of her staff?"

"Agnes, what kind of article are you writing? I told you to be careful. Geia's going to expect a glowing review of her Goddess Summit. Nothing less."

The word *glowing* made me pause. I couldn't ask him, could I?

"Jack, in the Hamptons, I saw something...weird."

His frown persisted. "What did you see?"

"Geia. She was out on the lawn, late at night. She was with Kathari. It was a full moon." I exhaled slowly.

Just do it, Agnes. You can trust Jack.

"It was like she and the snake, they were...glowing.

264

Like the moon was making them glow or something? Is that possible?"

"Maybe you were dreaming," Jack said, looking away.

I shook my head. "I wasn't."

Jack looked at me and I could tell he was holding back. There was something he wasn't saying.

"Jack, if you know something..."

"I don't... I can't."

"I feel like I'm going crazy over here. Please."

He sighed heavily. "Agnes, I can't help you. Not really. But, well, maybe I can help you find clarity for yourself."

"What does that mean?"

He paused. "There's a special hike on Mastika. To the top of the mountain. I think you need to do that hike."

I frowned. "What are you talking about?"

"Just trust me, okay? I think maybe you'll find the answers you're looking for there."

30

GODDESS™ SUMMIT — DAY 6

I woke before sunrise and dressed in the dark. I donned the workout clothes I hadn't touched since arriving and put on my running shoes. I moved swiftly downstairs and through the lobby, glancing only briefly at the front desk. Neither Amara nor Dimitra were working yet. Outside in the court-yard, Ellen was waiting for me.

"Ready?" I asked.

She yawned and nodded in response.

We didn't need directions; we knew the way. When Ava had taken us on our nature walk, we passed a fork in the trail. Today we would take the path on the right, up the mountain.

As we walked away from the hotel, the light around us began to lift, the first bit of yellow bleeding into blues and greens on the horizon. It was still cool. Goosebumps bloomed all over me. I was glad I had thought to ask Ellen to join me on the hike. I didn't know what I was going to find, but I felt better having a friend with me.

"Are you nervous about hypnotherapy?" I asked Ellen, our footsteps crunching on the gravel.

Last night at dinner, there had been more rumours about the day's session with Sloane Devine. More whispers of levitation, this time about a woman named Maya. I got Skye to point out Maya to me; she was sitting with her pod nearby. I had seen her around the hotel. She was tall and she always wore colourful headscarves tied around her braids. It differentiated her from the mob of white dresses.

"Kind of." Ellen took a sip from her water bottle. "But excited too. If it's as life-changing as everyone says it is, I'm down."

"What do you make of all this levitation stuff?"

She moved her head from side to side. "I don't know. Sloane's method isn't just hypnosis, apparently. I'm told it also involves energy healing. I've never done reiki, but I've seen videos of the practice. People's bodies often contort in weird ways. Maybe that's what people are seeing."

I considered that. It was as good an explanation as any.

I had kept a close eye on Maya throughout dinner. During dessert, Geia approached her table to whisper something in her ear. The other women in the pod gaped as Geia and Maya left the beach together, just like Geia and Claire the night before. I didn't know what Geia was doing with these women, but it had to be connected to whatever was happening in hypnotherapy. It was like they were being selected for something.

The main road was empty save for a couple on a moped,

driving too fast around a sharp corner. The woman clutched the man from behind. Neither of them wore helmets. When they passed, the woman looked at me with terrified eyes. For a moment, her fear felt contagious. But then I remembered Jack had sent me on this adventure. He wouldn't lead me anywhere dangerous.

We located the start of the trail and when we reached the fork, we took the path on the right. We climbed steadily for an hour. We passed countless mastika trees, recognizable by their thin, crooked trunks and bushy tops. They smelled like the liqueur: sweet pine and spruce. When we saw a natural spring on the mountainside, Ellen finished the last of her water and refilled her bottle, offering me a drink. Cold and clean, it felt like ice going down my throat.

"So, be honest," Ellen said, as we continued on our way. "You're not just a writer here to sort out your life, are you?"

I looked at her. "What do you mean?"

"I'm on to you, Agnes Oliver. Let me guess. You're here undercover to expose the dirty underbelly of Geia Stone's wellness cult?"

I raised my eyebrows.

"Warm?" she asked.

"Room temperature." I guessed now was as good a time as any to spill the beans. Ellen wouldn't care that I was writing an article, especially when Geia herself had asked me to.

"It was Geia's idea. I'm writing a piece for *Vogue* about the Summit. Though it's less an undercover exposé and more an honest discussion of what Geia's trying to do with Goddess."

Ellen's face lit up. "*Vogue?* That's big time, Agnes. Congratulations."

"Thanks."

"You don't sound very excited."

I sighed. "I have no idea what I'm doing these days. I'm supposed to be working on my second novel, but then this article came along, and it's just, like, I don't even remember how to write anymore. Literally, I have no good ideas."

Ellen smiled sympathetically. "I'm sure that's not true."

"I thought, after publishing my first book, it would get easier. I thought I would finally feel like a writer. But I don't, at all. How can I be on the *New York Times* bestseller list and still feel like a total fraud?"

Ellen stepped carefully, navigating a narrow patch of the trail. The path was getting more rugged as we climbed higher up the mountain.

"Success is funny, Agnes. In my experience, it's a moving target. When I was first starting out in Hollywood, I had all these clear goals in mind, but as soon as I achieved them, I set my sights on even higher goals. I was never satisfied. Never. Until, you know, my breakdown. Now, I take a minute every time I accomplish something to celebrate my victory. I honour myself and all the hard work I've put into my success."

"But what does that look like?" Her point about success being a never-ending story rang true for me. The big book deal, the tour, all the reviews; none of it was enough. I had no idea how to truly celebrate my accomplishments.

"It doesn't have to be complicated," Ellen said. "And it can be different every time. Sometimes, I take myself out to lunch. Sometimes, I buy myself a gift, something special and extravagant, to mark the occasion. The key is that it's just about me, no one else. Me and my work, my achievement. I think success should be a private relationship, between just you and your work. Or, in your case, you and your writing."

I liked what she was saying—all those bookstore readings had made me feel like my success rested in the hands of other people—but I wasn't sure a solo lunch or a new purse would really do the trick.

"Maybe you haven't properly honoured the success of *Violets in Her Lap*," Ellen continued, ducking under a branch. "Maybe that's why you're not able to write."

"I just don't know how to honour it properly."

Ellen smiled. "Well, no better place to meditate on that than here at the Summit."

The sun peeked over the side of the mountain. The sky was now a brilliant orange. We stopped briefly to watch the sun take flight, floating above the surface of the earth.

As we got closer to the crest of the mountain, the vegetation changed, becoming sparser. The last stretch was yellow rock, dry and dusty, with a few hardy bushes. It reminded me of Athens: the rugged outcrop of the Acropolis.

When we finally reached the top, I breathed deeply, taking in the view. We could see almost the entire island. Green everywhere. The clump of buildings in town. The hotel. A few farms and not much else. The forever sea.

Ellen sat on a rock and drank the last of her water. "I needed that hike. It feels like ages since I've had a good workout."

"Mm." I nodded, distracted.

I wasn't sure what I was looking for. Jack had told me to hike the mountain, but nothing here explained anything about Geia or what I'd seen in the Hamptons. I looked around. The summit was rocky, mostly flat. On the other side from where we came, I noticed another footpath leading down the mountain.

"Where are you going?" Ellen asked, as I started to wind my way down the path.

"Just exploring," I called.

A few metres down, hidden behind a clump of bush, was a rock that seemed to have a doorway in it. My chest fluttered. Could this be what Jack wanted me to find? I had to bend down to cross the threshold, but once inside, I was in a cave about twice as tall as me and four times as long and wide. The first rays of the sun illuminated the entrance, offering just enough light to see by.

"Hey," Ellen said, appearing behind me. "What is this?"

"I don't know."

We ventured deeper inside and my eyes soon adjusted to the semi-dark. The cave was empty, nothing really to see. I turned to go, disappointed, but Ellen gestured towards the back of the cave.

"Look," she said.

My stomach dropped. There was a statue carved into the rock face, small enough that it wasn't immediately noticeable. I walked towards it. The sculpture was of a hand holding a cup, encircled by a snake. Was this what Jack had wanted me to see? But what did it mean? Aside from the snake, there was something familiar about the cup, but I couldn't put my finger on where I'd seen it before.

"Ew," Ellen said in disgust. "What *is* that?"

I shifted my gaze from the sculpture to look at the ground where she was pointing. A pile of dirty rags had been left directly below the statue. Most looked old and faded, but the one on top looked more recent. It was stained bright red—the scrap of a T-shirt. I nudged it with my shoe. Ellen squealed. Beneath the red fabric, a clump of hair. Long and dark. It looked human.

31

When Ellen and I returned from our early-morning hike, we rushed to get ready for the day's first workshop, which was on breathwork. I then skipped lunch so I could go back to my room and write about what we had seen on the mountain. I didn't know what it meant, or how it connected to Geia, but it must have been important if Jack had led me there. I drew a quick sketch of the sculpture so it would be fresh in my mind. The cup felt so familiar to me, but I still couldn't place it. Where had I seen it before?

That afternoon, all Summit attendees were invited to a clean-beauty demonstration, co-led by Geia herself. The demo was held in a large tent next to the Goddess™ Market. The space was packed, and I was late; I found a wooden pole to lean against at the back of the tent. I scanned the crowd, looking for my pod members. I saw a lot of white. Everyone was wearing the white dress now, except me and a few others. Even Pearl had caved.

I tried to get a better look at the stage. From back here, it would be hard to see the actual makeup application. The stage backdrop was a lush green wall of woven flowers and leafy vines. The word GODDESS floated in the middle in white. It reminded me of my book cover. There were two chairs set up, plus a small table with — I squinted — what looked like a mirror and an assortment of Goddess™ makeup products. I only recognized it as Goddess™ because of the familiar blush-pink packaging.

The crowd chattered in quiet excitement. Soon, a Goddess™ staff member walked onto the stage and the crowd grew quiet. She wore a microphone headset, and with her white dress, she looked like some kind of spiritual guru.

"Good afternoon," she said, as all eyes were on her. "Welcome to Clean Beauty 101. I'm thrilled to introduce our guest and mentor for today's workshop, renowned makeup creative Chanel Hadley."

Applause from the crowd, which I joined half-heartedly. I hated when people used the word *creative* as a noun.

"Chanel started her career over twenty years ago, working as a makeup artist at the Clinique beauty counter at Saks Fifth Avenue. It was here that she met famed fashion designer Diane Von Furstenberg. After Chanel touched up the designer's makeup, she hired her on the spot as a makeup artist for her 1998 fall/winter runway show. Chanel went on to do runway makeup for countless other iconic designers and brands, including Oscar de la Renta, Yves Saint Laurent, and, appropriately, Chanel. She's also worked with celebrities including Julia Roberts, Naomi Watts, Julianne Moore, and last but not least, our leader, Geia Stone."

Our leader? That was a bit much.

"Today, Chanel is joined by Geia, her long-time friend and collaborator, for a short makeup demonstration, followed by a Q&A. Please join me in welcoming them both to the stage now."

The crowd broke into loud applause as the two women walked on stage, holding hands. It struck me that Geia should have been introduced first, and her esteemed guest second, the whole order-of-importance thing. I didn't recognize Chanel from the head table at dinner. The two women sat down on the chairs onstage. Both wore microphone headsets. Chanel wore a pair of thick-framed glasses on top of her head.

"I'm so glad you're here!" Geia beamed at Chanel.

"I'm so glad to be here!"

"How was your trip?" Geia looked at the audience. "Chanel just arrived last night."

Chanel laughed. "You don't make it easy, do you? I feel like I'm at the end of the world."

The crowd laughed too.

"You know me. I don't shy away from difficult."

"It's true," Chanel told the audience. "Geia always goes the extra distance to make something special. In this case, literally."

The audience tittered again.

Chanel rearranged the Goddess™ makeup on the table in front of them, getting organized, and the two women talked briefly about their friendship. I was surprised to learn they had met when Geia hired Chanel to do her makeup for *The Opposites*.

"We go way back," Geia explained. "Jack and I were still figuring out how to actually make a movie. We had this tiny budget, with little money for makeup and wardrobe, but I managed to convince Chanel to come on board by sending her a copy of the script."

Chanel nodded. "It's true. I fell in love with the story. I'd never read anything like it. I knew I had to be involved."

"And then later, when we decided to launch a clean beauty line at Goddess, I knew we had to get Chanel. She acted as a consultant for all product development in this line."

They moved on to the makeup demo. Chanel picked up one of the pink jars, took off the lid, and dipped a small brush into it. She then donned her large glasses and Geia tilted her chin up so Chanel had full access to the contours of her face.

"Geia has never liked to wear a lot of makeup," Chanel explained. She had a very soft, soothing way of talking. I wondered if that came from having to be so close to people all the time, right up in their faces. "So, if she has an event, we go minimal but still polished."

"I've been known to remove lipstick when Chanel puts it on me."

Chanel laughed. "It's true. I avoid lipstick or anything too bold on Geia now. I've learned my lesson."

Chanel applied something to Geia's cheeks. The stage was too far away for me to tell what it was. Blush, maybe?

"The thing with Geia is, she's the most naturally beautiful woman in the world, so she really needs no embellishments. Instead, it's all about subtle enhancements."

Chanel continued to work on Geia's face, using brushes

to blend products that I couldn't identify. She blended much longer than I would have thought reasonable. Beyond thirty seconds, were the brushes even doing anything?

While Chanel blended, she and Geia chatted about the makeup line. They had wanted to create a collection of high-quality, high-performance, totally clean products that could all work together. Nothing was overly colourful. It was all about a natural look—the Goddess™ look.

After Chanel finished Geia's makeup—as far as I could tell, she looked unchanged, but again, I wasn't very close to the stage—there was an audience Q&A. The questions were what you'd expect at any makeup class.

"How do I know which red lipstick is right for me?"

"Should I stop wearing highlighter at a certain age?"

"What's the best under-eye concealer?"

Chanel dutifully answered the questions. While she spoke, I noticed Geia starting to look bored, then annoyed, then almost angry. Her usual glowing smile vanished; her mouth became a thin line. Finally, after a question about mastering contour, she intervened.

"Hold on a minute, Chanel," she said, turning to look at the crowd. Her tone was cross, her voice raised. "This is the world's leading developer of clean makeup, people." She grabbed a few products off the table and held them up, shaking her head. She sounded just like she did when I overheard her scolding Stephanie in the garden. "This stuff is non-toxic, vegan, organic, and it actually works! What is wrong with you people? Don't you have any questions about *that*?"

A few women with their hands up lowered them. I saw some frowns in the audience. Then, ten or so hands shot up.

"Yes?" Geia said, pointing to a woman near the front, her eyebrows raised.

"What toxic ingredients should I be looking out for in my makeup?"

Then, "What is the environmental impact of using unnatural beauty products?"

Then, "If I've been using non-clean makeup since I was fourteen, is it too late to benefit from switching to natural makeup now?"

It was like the audience suddenly remembered where they were, and why they were here. Time to put on your clean, green wellness hat and prove you care about yourself and the world around you. Immediately, Geia brightened. She weighed in on their questions alongside Chanel and was proud her students were acing this particular test.

THAT EVENING AT dinner, I noticed Ellen wasn't sporting her signature flashy lipstick, but her cheeks glowed rosy with a light shimmer. After the clean makeup session, she had rushed to the Goddess™ Market, where she promptly bought every product in the makeup line—even those she already owned. "It never hurts to have doubles," she said. I wondered if she had removed her bright lip colour because Geia had said she never wore lipstick. The thought made my chest heavy.

Geia started the meal with a special toast, her tone more saccharine than normal, almost as if she was making up for her earlier show of displeasure. She told us how wonderful it had been to watch us all grow and thrive during the last six days. She hoped the remaining days of the Goddess™

Summit would be even more illuminating for our souls, our minds, and our bodies. She hoped the "diverse modalities" of the sessions yet to come would continue to touch us and open up new pathways of psychic and spiritual well-being for each of us.

Geia then introduced a woman named Eleni, who was sitting to her right. Eleni stood. The top of her head barely reached Geia's shoulders.

"Eleni is a dear friend of mine," Geia said. "She was born on this island and has never left. This place is all she knows and all she ever wants to know."

Eleni gazed calmly at the crowd. Her face was hard to read. She wasn't smiling, but she looked at ease. I wondered what she thought of us.

"Eleni is eighty-two years old," Geia said, beaming.

Audible gasps from the assembled diners. How could that be? I would have guessed fifty-five, maybe, but only because of how Geia spoke about her, like she was a wise family friend, someone Geia looked up to, and was therefore older.

"I know what you're thinking," Geia said. "She looks great!"

A few people laughed; Eleni didn't. I realized then that Eleni likely didn't speak English and couldn't understand what Geia was saying, hence her serene obliviousness.

"Eleni is a symbol of everything Goddess represents. She lives a life of intention. She eats only whole, unprocessed foods. She swims in the ocean every day. She sleeps at least nine hours a night. She meditates. And, most impressively, she carves out time and space for herself every single day, despite having six children and eleven grandchildren. In all ways, she manifests balance."

Geia paused, and though there was a moment's hesitation, the crowd quickly realized its role and began to clap.

Eleni smiled at the applause.

"Do you see what living well can do?" Geia asked. "Do you see what following my counsel can give you? Goddess was inspired by women like Eleni who choose their health and wellness above all else. Only when we do that can we be good partners, friends, mothers, citizens."

I glanced around discreetly to see how this speech was landing. Most of the women looked enthralled, just as they had at the makeup demo. Evidently, Geia's earlier scolding hadn't scared anyone off.

"I invited Eleni here to lead us in a chant," Geia continued. "Eleni is famous on the island for her singing, and tonight, she's going to teach us a song. Let's enter into a shared space of truth and intention by singing together, making all our voices one."

Geia said something to Eleni in Greek. Eleni nodded. Goddess™ staff then distributed printouts of non-English lyrics for us to read. I scanned the words and wondered what they meant.

"Eleni will sing the song once in its entirety, and then we'll all join in. We'll continue to sing until Eleni raises a hand, signalling the song is complete. In the musical tradition of the island, songs have no limits. They just have life. The leader in song decides when that life is over. It could be two minutes. It could be two hours," Geia said.

"Two hours?" I whispered to Ellen. What about dinner?

I was famished from skipping lunch. All I'd eaten since breakfast was a few handfuls of chocolate-covered almonds, courtesy of Jack's care package.

Geia nodded at Eleni, who closed her eyes and began to sing. Or rather, chant. She had a beautiful voice: low and steady. I tried to follow along using the printout. Many of the syllables were repeated four times. Then, each line was repeated twice. There was something hypnotic about the repetition. People started to nod their heads to its steady beat.

Eleni finished and opened her eyes. Then she began again. Only a few people joined in at first, so Geia waved her hands wildly to encourage us. More voices caught on, including those at my table. I glanced around. Along with me, a handful of women on the beach stayed quiet. They looked confused and unsure. I kept looking down at my printout, wishing I knew what the words meant.

The longer the group chanted, the more confident they sounded, their voices growing louder with each verse. I began to lose track of time. After a while, a few women stood up and started to sway, eyes closed, which seemed a bit much. Geia looked pleased, nodding in their direction. I glanced over at Ellen. She sang at full volume, totally committed.

The sun was down when Eleni finally raised her hand. The chanters finished the verse they were singing, which fell in the middle of the song, and then stopped.

Absolute quiet followed. Only the sound of gentle waves lapping against the shore could be heard. But there was also a sense of ringing silence, the absence of sound. I wondered if the group could be heard across the island. Was there even anyone out there, besides us?

Geia thanked Eleni on behalf of the group, and Eleni bowed in response.

DINNER WRAPPED UP quicker than usual, and we were told there would be a cocktail party on the patio, overlooking the sea. In the distance, I could see staff lighting tiki torches up by the pool and hear the faint clinking of glassware.

At cocktail time I stuck close to my pod, watching Geia carefully. She wandered through the party, a glass of wine in hand, chatting with mentors and participants. Her dark features took on a new intensity in the light of the tiki torches. She had a generous laugh; she seemed to be trying to put her fans at ease. I wondered if this was more damage control after her outburst at the clean beauty session. She was almost being too nice.

At some point in the evening, I lost track of Geia. I looked away for one second — Ellen was drunk and even I couldn't resist her outrageous stories about Hollywood after-parties — and when I glanced back, Geia was gone. I searched the crowd. I didn't see Claire or Maya either. Who else was missing? I excused myself and headed towards the lobby, taking the side door out to the garden. It was dark and eerily still. There were no tiki torches here, only a few faint solar lights lining the winding path.

When I reached Geia's villa, I saw lights on inside but no movement through the windows. Then I heard voices, laughter, coming from the back patio, where Geia and I had sat together on my first day on the island.

I crept around the side of the house, which was lined with

a tall, thick hedge. I wasn't sure what I was doing exactly. I just knew I wanted to see what Geia was up to with those women.

When I reached the back, I could see lights through the hedge. I knelt down and peered through the brush. There they were. Geia was sitting on her lounger next to Claire. Maya and another woman, whose name I thought might be Naomi, were sitting on lounge chairs nearby. I couldn't hear what they were saying, but they were all smiling and drinking mastika. At one point, Geia stood up and twirled, showing off her outfit.

Then, Claire stood up and walked towards the plunge pool. She removed her dress along with her underwear and bra. She slipped into the water, completely naked. Maya soon followed.

I looked at the others for a response. Geia watched the swimmers, unmoved, but Naomi gave Claire and Maya a mortified, put-your-clothes-back-on look. Geia then reached for her hand and Naomi looked back at her. Neither of them spoke, but their eye contact was intense. After a few moments, Naomi stood up, removed her own dress and underwear, and joined Claire and Maya in the pool. Geia lay back on the lounger, looking pleased.

What was going on here?

Geia began talking out loud. I leaned forward on my heels, my hands grasping at the foliage, trying to get close enough to hear. That's when I sensed movement to my left. My first thought was that it was one of the hotel staff. But no. This movement was not human. I turned my head and saw the large form of Kathari, slithering towards me through the grass. It took every ounce of willpower not to scream. This is it, I thought. This is how you die, Agnes. He's been after you since the first day you met him. He caught you eavesdropping on Jack's daughters and now here you are, eavesdropping again.

But Kathari only paused to look at me for a moment and then slipped through the hedge towards Geia and the others. He glided into the pool and the three swimming women didn't even seem to notice. After a minute, the pool began to glow, as if lit from within. I let go of my breath and looked back at Geia. She was staring directly at me. Even through the thick hedge, the darkness, I knew she could see me. Her lips turned up into a smile, paralyzing me for a moment. Then I stood, and ran.

PART 3

The Goddess Reveal

We appear silver in the light of the moon, pockmarked but beautiful. Tall and thin and unlike the others. We seem to shimmer, but that's just a trick of the light. Our skin is the envy of the rest, but we let it fall away in soft furls. We, the birches, are the ghosts of the forest, shivering, leafless in winter. Come spring, our green bursts forth, little hands waving in the wind, saying *come closer*.

    — *Violets in Her Lap* by Agnes Oliver

32

GODDESS™ SUMMIT — DAY 7

Back in my room, I lay in bed, and for the first time since arriving on the island, I struggled to fall asleep. I lay staring at the ceiling until the early hours of the morning. I still felt breathless. After Geia had seen me through the hedge, I sprinted back to the hotel and up to my room. I passed by women heading home after the cocktail party, but I didn't stop to talk. My mind ran circles around itself. Geia, Kathari, those women, the island. What was going on here? What had made the water glow like that, and why didn't anyone bat an eyelash as it was happening? And why was everyone naked together in Geia's pool with a snake?

As I finally drifted off, the dream image of Geia sitting on the end of my bed kept re-entering my mind. What was she holding in her hands? Only when my thoughts became muddled and irrational, sleep creeping in, did it hit me. She was holding a cup. A silver chalice. Just like the one Ellen and I had seen carved into the rock in the mountain cave.

THE NEXT MORNING I was late again, this time to catch a boat. After my restless night, I'd slept in and missed breakfast with the others. My fellow pod members were waiting for me in the hotel shuttle, some more patiently than others. Leslie tapped her watch as I hurried out the lobby doors, and Skye kept saying she hoped they wouldn't set sail without us, picking at the skin around her thumbnail.

"Of course they'll wait for us," Ellen said smoothly, easing my guilt. "We're the whole point."

Our session that morning, to be held on a sailboat, was on Accessing Intuition. When we arrived in town, we could see the sailboat, safely docked, and our mentor waving at us from the bow.

We hurried aboard and Phoebe, a tall woman with braided hair and amazing cheekbones, welcomed us with green tea and fresh fruit. Immediately, the small crew got to work and soon we were away, the wind catching our sails and sending us out to sea. The sun was fierce as usual, but it was cooler out on the water, a welcome relief. I sipped my second cup of green tea—there hadn't been time for coffee before leaving the hotel—and watched Mastika get smaller. It really was a tiny island. The mountain seemed to take up most of it.

"Don't kill me for saying this," Pearl said, sidling up next to me. "But you look tired."

"That's because I am."

"Rough night?"

I nodded. "Couldn't sleep."

Pearl munched on a peach. "When I'm working on a book, I never sleep well."

I eyed her for a moment. Could I trust her? Of all the women at the Summit, she seemed the least seduced by Geia. Maybe she could help me understand what I had seen last night.

"Pearl," I said. "Our line of work, it requires a lot of . . . invention."

"I like to call it 'making shit up,'" she said with a laugh.

I smiled. "Exactly." I paused. "Do you ever worry all the energy you invest in making shit up messes with your grip on reality?"

"Do I worry I'll start expecting some young stud to come along and sweep me off my feet because that's the kind of story I like to tell?" She eyed me, skeptical, but then her face softened. "Only sometimes."

"Sometimes I see things . . . I don't know if they're real or if I'm just imagining them before I write about them. Does that make sense?"

She frowned, eyeing me. I could tell she wasn't fully getting it.

"Can you give me an example?"

"I'm not sure." I was afraid to say out loud what I had witnessed. I had been open with Jack, and though he'd seemed like he wanted to help, I still worried that he thought I was crazy.

Pearl placed a hand on my arm. "Agnes. Whatever it is you're seeing, whether it's real or not, think of it as part of the process. You are both a seer and a teller. You take in the world and you make it into something original through your writing. That's the job. Don't fear the strange things you see. Lean into them and try to figure out what story they're telling you." She smiled. "Our imaginations are our gift, right?"

I nodded. Pearl was right, despite what my mother had always said. I shouldn't turn away from these visions, even if they didn't make sense or they scared me. I should seek to understand them. Only then could I be sure if they were real, and if they were, what was really going on with Geia.

"Thanks, Pearl. I needed that."

"Any time, my dear. Us writers need to stick together."

I nodded as she squeezed my arm.

Just then, Phoebe called us to the front of the boat. She'd spread blankets on the deck and now encouraged us to lie down on them. We did as she instructed, and it struck me that much of this wellness stuff took place on the ground. But I was used to it now. I rested my arms at my sides with my palms up, feeling the sun on my face and limbs. The boat rocked gently in the deep sea.

"Why a boat?" Phoebe asked, stepping quietly around us. "Why the journey away from the island?" She paused, and above us, a flag flapped loudly in the wind. "We journey away from the island because we seek to journey closer to the self. Many believe the sea is a space of complete freedom. Here, on the water, you are untethered from all possessions, all investments, all relations. Here, on the water, you can simply be. The ocean is the ideal place to listen to the intuitive self."

She paused again. It was much of the same stuff we'd heard already this week. Look inward. Listen. Let yourself just be. Each session framed that act in a different way. But maybe that was the point of the Summit. It offered ample opportunity for self-reflection, in whatever context suited you best.

"The world we live in today is a chaotic place. We are all so busy, so focused on productivity. We set goals for ourselves and we want to achieve them now. We ask questions and we want answers immediately. We are often rushed to act, to think, to make a decision, and there is very little room for us to tune in to our most natural instincts first. To meditate on what feels right. That's what I want you to do today. I want you to see how it feels to give yourself space to *intuit* an answer to a question or problem in your life. This is about being patient and receptive. We have the entire morning to do this. We're not due back to port until after lunch. So, first, I want you all to think of a question. Something that's been on your mind lately. A question you don't yet have an answer to."

I opened my eyes briefly, the sky bright above me. Could I use this as an opportunity to figure out what was going on with Geia? I wasn't sure that answer really lived inside me though. It was external, a mystery I was trying to solve. Unless of course I was inventing it all. Was I wasting energy obsessing about Geia, energy that could be spent writing? The two seemed inextricably connected in my mind — Geia and book two — but I couldn't figure out how or why. Maybe I was focusing on the wrong half of the equation. If I focused on my book, would it help me to better understand Geia?

"Does everyone have their question?" I heard murmurs of assent from the others. "Good. Now, I want you to sit with your question for a while. Let it live inside you. Ask yourself: How does this question make me feel? What images does it call to mind? What memories? At this point, it's not about searching for an answer, it's about allowing the unconscious mind to grapple with the question, to better understand it."

Right. Okay, Agnes. That sounds like another meditation exercise, which, let's be honest, you suck at.

"If you're having trouble turning off the brain," Phoebe said, as if reading my mind. "Listen to the waves. Focus on their rhythm."

Sure, I could try that. Anything to solve this book problem. Though you're not supposed to think of it as a problem, Agnes. Think of it as a question that lives in your body. Better yet, *feel* it as a question that lives in your body. Shit. There I go again. Okay. Waves. Waves. I'll just listen to the waves.

Next to me, I could hear Leslie breathing heavily. The sound of the water lapping against the boat offered a steady tempo. I listened, feeling the boat rock gently back and forth. What did it mean to feel a question in your body? Had I ever done that before? I thought back to my experiences in the woods when I was a kid. I had known, deep inside, what I was seeing. The dust in the air. A part of me understood that it was a way for the trees to communicate, with each other and the other creatures in the forest. But how had I known that? Was that intuition? If it was, I was out of touch with it now. Since meeting Geia, I'd been experiencing all these strange things, but I couldn't put the pieces together to solve the puzzle. I still didn't know if what I'd seen was real. Maybe that was the problem? As Pearl said, it was about not turning away from the things I was seeing, no matter how strange. It was about looking at them dead on and figuring out what they had to offer.

I opened my eyes and closed them again. I decided to stop trying to focus on the sea and instead just let my mind drift free. I felt the warmth of the sun on my eyelids, my open palms. I felt the cool breeze rustle my hair, tickle my nose. Behind closed eyes, I saw the cup carved into the wall of the cave. The same cup that Geia held in my dreams. I realized in that moment that I had seen it somewhere else too. It wasn't just my dreams that made it familiar. Where though? Instead of racking my brain, I focused on the cup itself, its shape, its silver colour. The way it glinted in the moonlight in my dreams.

After a while, I began to drift off, the motion of the boat lulling me to sleep. Only when I had let go of the image completely did it hit me. I had seen a drawing of the cup before. I pictured it as an illustration on a white page. It wasn't surrounded by a snake like the one in the cave, but I remembered a snake being associated with the cup somehow. Inside, I stirred. I wasn't there yet, but I was getting close.

33

GODDESS™ SUMMIT — DAY 8

On the eighth day of the summit, I again woke up uncertain how I'd gotten back to my room. It was another sunny day, and though my mind felt clear, the end of last night's dinner was hazy. We had spent most of dinner talking about today's upcoming hypnotherapy session — wondering what it would be like, if Geia would be in attendance, and how our lives might be changed by it. Near the end of the meal, I watched Geia select another woman to take back to her villa. I even pointed it out to the others this time, asking them what they thought Geia did alone with these women. No one seemed bothered by it.

I slid my tongue against my teeth. They felt brushed. And I was wearing pajamas. So I must have been conscious when I returned home from the beach. I looked at the clock. It was late. I had missed breakfast again. I gobbled down the last of Jack's pistachios and dried mango and rushed to get dressed.

The hypnotherapy session was held in a bright room on the second floor of the hotel, overlooking the sea. White walls, gauzy curtains, a general sense of lightness. When I arrived, the others were already sitting on chairs arranged in a circle around a massage table. So that was where we'd lie down to expose our unconscious minds to the group.

Though Geia was only observing, she was a part of the circle too. She looked like her usual radiant self, and I could tell her presence was making my fellow pod members nervous. Leslie was talking manically about her therapist back home and Skye looked like she had lost the ability to smile: her face appeared to be made of stone. I sat down in the empty chair next to Geia. I wasn't nervous around her at all anymore, despite everything I'd witnessed — or maybe *because* of it. This woman had secrets and I was onto her... kind of. I wanted to make her feel like she didn't have the upper hand anymore. I could be mysterious too. It was her turn to be confused.

"Agnes, hello," she said, her voice low and placid. I recognized it as her Goddess™ voice. "How are you?"

I wished she would just speak normally.

"Fine." I said, yawning. "But I missed breakfast this morning. Any chance we can order coffee up to the session?"

Leslie and Skye looked shocked by my familiarity with Geia. Skye subtly shook her head at me, as if to tell me to shut up.

But Geia continued to smile. "I'm sure that can be arranged." She promptly left the room, returning a few minutes later empty handed. But soon one of the Goddess™ staff appeared with a latte for me.

"Real milk," I said. "You remembered."

Geia nodded, still smiling, but there was a question behind her lips, like she was trying to figure out why I was acting peculiar.

I took a sip and sighed, satisfied. "That's better."

Sloane Devine was the last to arrive. Though we all knew who she was, she introduced herself to the group and explained how the session would work. She would hypnotize each of us in turn, and then she would offer prompts to help us explore our psyches for any trauma or pain that needed to be "exorcised." This was different than conventional hypnotherapy, which works by reprogramming the unconscious mind. Sloane emphasized that we would remember everything we had shared while under hypnosis. This wasn't about tricking us into healing; it was about accessing new chambers of our mind. In addition, she would employ reiki techniques to further amplify the exorcism, coaxing the trauma out of our bodies with her healing hands.

Right, okay. Buckle up, Agnes.

Bravely, Ellen volunteered to go first. She lay down on the table, her white dress looking like a nightgown, her face expressing calm, and closed her eyes as if to sleep, resting one hand over the other on her stomach. I glanced over at Geia. She watched the scene with a serene look.

Sloane stood on Ellen's right side and began talking to her with a soothing cadence. "Listen to my voice, Ellen. Listen to my voice. Imagine my voice is a hole. My voice is a hole, an endless dark hole. Listen to my voice, Ellen, and allow yourself to fall. You are falling down the hole, Ellen. Falling, falling, falling. You are deep in the hole now, Ellen. You are safe and warm in the darkness."

Sloane snapped her fingers and Ellen's face went blank. To start, Sloane asked Ellen a simple question: "How are you today, Ellen?"

Ellen provided an equally simple answer in a quiet, polite voice: "I'm good, thank you."

Sloane then proceeded to ask Ellen other questions about her general state of being: Was she tired? Was she energized? Was there anything she wanted right now?

Again, Ellen answered quickly and politely, no hesitation in her voice. When asked if there was anything she wanted, she replied, "French fries," and we all chuckled.

"Now," Sloane said, "I understand you suffer from insomnia."

I looked at my pod members. How could Sloane know that? Were the mentors sharing information about us? Pearl frowned, watching Sloane. Skye and Leslie seemed untroubled.

"Yes," Ellen said. "Though I'm sleeping much better these days."

"When did it start?" Sloane asked. "The insomnia."

"In high school."

"And what happened in high school that interrupted your sleep?"

In a calm, almost happy voice, Ellen told us all about her high-school bully. A girl who had it out for Ellen and used to torment her with terrifying taunts and threats. She was going to burn down Ellen's house. She was going to hurt Ellen's dog. She was going to tell the principal Ellen was having sex with a teacher. Ellen said she used to lie awake at night listening for any little sound, convinced this bully would show up at her house to hurt her and her family.

"That was when my insomnia started," Ellen said plainly, like she had always known this. "That's why I've always tried to stay busy. If I'm busy, I don't have time to be scared."

While Ellen spoke, Sloane held her hands above Ellen's body, seeming to pull on invisible strings. As she did this, Ellen's face contorted like she was in pain, but her voice remained calm.

Then, before our very eyes, Ellen's body lifted off the table a few inches and appeared to float. Ellen's face was once again expressionless, as if she were asleep. Leslie and Skye gasped. Pearl continued to frown. Sloane smiled and looked over at Geia.

Was this really happening? Was I making it up?

No, Agnes. The others see it too.

I glanced sideways at Geia. Her brow was furrowed. I wondered in that moment if it was her, and not Sloane, who was making Ellen levitate.

Then, just as quickly as it had lifted, Ellen's body settled back onto the table and Sloane snapped her fingers again. Ellen opened her eyes. I expected her to look disoriented or confused, like she'd just been woken from a deep slumber, but she simply shook her head and said, "That was amazing. What a trip."

Slowly, Ellen stood and went back to her chair.

"Who would like to go next?" Sloane asked.

Leslie followed. Then Skye. Then Pearl. All of them shared deep pain connected to roadblocks in their self-development. Despite being open with their answers, none of them levitated.

As always, I was the last to volunteer. The others smiled at me encouragingly as I got on the table. I lay down and closed my eyes. Sloane began talking to me with her weird pitch, saying my name over and over, referring to the dark hole that was her voice. In my mind, the dark hole was full of water. Warm water, like in the lagoon where we had gone night swimming.

When she snapped her fingers I suddenly felt like I was floating on the surface of the lagoon. I was still aware of the others in the room, but I felt safe and alone in the water, lighter than I had ever felt in my life. Completely weightless. It felt like nothing bad could get me in the lagoon, not even my own thoughts. I wanted to stay there forever.

Sloane asked me the same introductory questions as she'd asked the others. I surprised myself by answering them all without hesitation. It felt good not to doubt myself for once. To reply without thinking about how my words would be interpreted. When asked what I wanted, I said, "To feel like I belong."

Then she asked about the issues with my mother. I wondered again how she could know about that, but I found I didn't really care in the moment. I was so comfortable in the darkness of the water.

"It's not just my mother," I heard myself say, "it's my father too."

Sloane asked me to explain.

A memory had been bubbling to the surface of my mind lately. I had been feeling more open to letting myself remember it. I decided to tell a story.

"I was the one who spotted her first, walking up our driveway. There was a wildness in her eyes. She looked about nineteen, twenty. Twenty-one at most. She had long red hair and freckles on her arms. She wore a dark-green blouse and very tight jeans. Chunky heels, the colour of cognac. I remember thinking she looked overdressed for the woods.

"I watched her from an upstairs window. She hesitated in front of our house. What was she doing here? And how did a part of me already know the answer?

"After a moment, she marched forward and knocked loudly on the door. It was a Saturday. My mother was away for work, and my father was in his study listening to the radio and drinking his morning coffee. His weekend routine.

"She knocked again, but he had the radio up too loud to hear. My brother heard though. It was strange because we lived in the middle of nowhere and didn't get a lot of unexpected visitors. From the window, I saw the girl's face change when the door opened. Shame has a taming effect. I couldn't hear what she was saying, but I knew she was asking for my father. I heard Max calling to him through the house, then walking across the kitchen and the living room, knocking on the office door.

"'Dad, there's a girl here.'

"A girl. That's what she was. She didn't look like a woman.

"I heard the office door open and my father's footsteps. Then nothing.

"Finally, 'What are you doing here?' Then, 'Max, go to your room.'

"My father looked upset and confused. 'You can't just show up here! I have a family.'

"He stepped outside, shutting the door behind him. Their voices became muffled. He reached for her, rubbing one of her shoulders. She started to cry and he hugged her. Then gave her a swift kiss on the lips.

"Finally, she pulled away and walked back down the driveway."

I paused. The memory was so lucid it seemed to shimmer inside me. But it couldn't touch me down here in the dark.

"I wanted to tell my mother about the girl. But we didn't have the kind of relationship that allowed me to share unbearable secrets. Still, I had to try. It was important. I worked up the courage one night and mumbled through what I had seen, trying to explain that something was wrong. I had seen my father kiss someone, a girl, probably a student. She had shown up at the house wearing high heels. She knew where we lived.

"My mother shook her head at me, a withering look. 'What are you on about, Agnes?'

"She was always doing that. Writing me off. *Just Agnes's wild imagination again.* But this was different. Years later, I overheard a fight between my parents. My mother had just returned home from a work trip and was irritable. Unlike my father, she didn't have an office to hide in. She had to sit at the kitchen table, spreading out books and papers and making it very obvious to the family how important her work was. It took up space.

"I had learned to tiptoe around her when she was in the kitchen, but my father wasn't so timid. From the living room where I was watching television, I heard him open the fridge, rattle some bottles, and then crack open a beer. He slammed the fridge closed and stomped past her. His footsteps seemed to pound the kitchen floor. I imagined her looking up at him, annoyed.

"'We need to talk about this,' she said, lowering her voice.

"'I'm tired, Vivian. I don't know what to tell you.'

"'Do you know how humiliating this is for me? To receive an email from a colleague asking for comment on the sexual assault allegations against my husband? What the fuck have you been up to, Noah?'

"'I told you, it's not true.'

"'Silence. Then, 'I don't believe you.'

"'That's not my problem,' my father said. 'You can believe whatever you want, but the truth is the truth. I barely know that girl. I mean, I know her, she was in my class, but it was just a schoolgirl crush gone wrong. That sort of thing happens all the time. She wanted my attention. I didn't give her enough. And now she's retaliating.'

"'Women don't falsely accuse their teachers of sexual assault because of schoolgirl crushes. I'm talking statistically here. Do you understand that, Noah? Women don't lie about this sort of thing.'

"More silence from my father.

"'What did you do, Noah? What did you do to that girl?'"

I paused again, remembering what happened next. Or rather, what didn't happen.

"Somehow, the allegation was never made public. Did the girl get cold feet? If she had spoken up, would other women have come forward? In any case, after that fight in the kitchen, my parents' relationship deteriorated quickly. They divorced; they sold the house. For a long time after this, I kept expecting my mother to come to me and apologize. She should have listened to me all those years ago when I told her about the girl who wore high heels to the woods. But there was only silence.

"My father never talked about it either. Of course he didn't. He just went on being his usual charismatic self. Blaming my mother, calling her loony. He got an apartment close to the university and my mother moved to a city in another state.

"'She's unhinged, Agnes,' he told me once. 'You know this. She's always been awful to both of us.'

"Why did I side with him? Because he was nicer to me? Or because she didn't believe me when I tried to tell her about the girl? I knew what he was doing was wrong. But she didn't trust me enough to listen to what I was saying. I was only trying to help her."

"Why did your mother not believe you, Agnes?" Sloane asked.

I told her what my father had said to me years before.

"My mother stayed with him because she didn't want to admit defeat. Leaving him would mean she had failed, that she had chosen the wrong man. And believing me would mean acknowledging that failure out loud.

"My father had walked into her restaurant and charmed the hell out of her. My mother, who was so focused on making her dreams come true, so hard-working, got side-tracked by a handsome man who promised her passion and romance. I know this is what happened because it happened to me too. I fell in love with a man who was nothing more than an exciting, painful digression, a man who offered me a path away from myself."

Owen. The fairy tale that was actually a nightmare.

"Do you think that love is always a digression?" Sloane asked me.

"No. I met someone recently, someone different than the other men in my life. He senses the real me hiding away and wants more of that me. I think I could be happy with him. I think it would be safe to be my absolute self with him. But I'm scared to let him in."

Deep down, I'd known this about Jack all along, though I hadn't fully realized it until now.

Sloane then asked me, "Agnes, do you believe your mother loved you?"

"Yes," I said, surprising myself. "But she doesn't know how to love in a way that lets other people thrive. My father was so out of her control. She knew only how to love her children by controlling them. My brother was easy because he was like her, he complied, but I was the girl who liked to tell stories and dream. She knew what dreaming got you: A cheating husband. A man who abused his students. A performer. She didn't want that for me. She wanted me to stay on the right track, to avoid life's messy digressions. That's why she was so hard on me."

Sloane asked me more questions about this, but I found myself repeating the same sentiment.

"My mother was only trying to protect me from repeating her mistakes. But that kind of thinking is misguided. Controlling people isn't a way to help them."

I had tried to control people too, I now understood. I did this by only showing them parts of myself, the parts I thought they'd like. That way, I reasoned, they couldn't criticize or judge me, like my mother had done. But in trying to control others, I had been controlling myself as well. I hid. I cowered. I was so afraid that people wouldn't like me, I hadn't even tried to like myself.

When Sloane snapped her fingers and my eyes opened, I saw a circle of friends. Ellen, Skye, Pearl, and Leslie, even Sloane and Geia, their faces drawn in soft lines of sympathy and understanding. I felt the hot sting of tears on my cheeks. I was overwhelmed by everything I had just said aloud, everything I had always known but hadn't understood.

When I returned to my chair, Ellen leaned over to put an arm around my shoulders. I fell into her embrace, resting my head on her shoulder, letting my tears drip down her bare arm.

34

"We know so much," I said, staring at my salad.

It was lunchtime. My pod sat on the patio overlooking the sea, none of us talking much. The session with Sloane reverberated between us. I had finally accepted that my mother didn't hate me. Maybe she even liked me? I had also learned something more important. Even if she or anyone else didn't like me, that was okay. I didn't exist to be liked. It was a cliché, but I finally got it: I needed to like me first. Other people could choose to like me or not. That wasn't really my concern, was it?

"I mean, we know so much, but we don't know it. It's there, somewhere inside us, but we can't access it." I was grasping for words again, but I didn't feel self-conscious anymore. I knew I could say anything to these women and they'd keep listening. They wouldn't judge me.

"Maybe, in regular life, we only access that knowledge when we really need it," Pearl suggested.

"Or when we've done the work to earn it," Ellen added.

I thought about "the work." It was a phrase often used by Geia and the mentors, but what did it mean, really? Was the work therapy, talking to a professional, allowing them to help you process the knowledge buried deep inside you? Or was the work life itself? Living each day, failing, learning a little, failing again, learning more. The latter was a slower process, but it was a way forward, nonetheless. Not something to fear.

I am still learning, I thought to myself. And I wouldn't want it any other way.

I looked at Ellen and wondered what other knowledge she contained. Today, I felt like I had started to know myself in a way I never had before. I'd had a conversation with my psyche. What a thought! Maybe that was what these women were trying to do here; maybe that's what wellness was all about. Not an attempt to better yourself—whatever that meant—but an attempt to know yourself better. It was admirable, really.

Pearl suggested we order some French fries. "Ellen's idea," she said.

They weren't part of the lunch spread, but surely the hotel could whip some up. We deserved it, after everything we'd been through that morning. Everyone agreed, and when they arrived, we ate them hot and fast, no regrets, licking the salt from our fingers.

BECAUSE OF THE intensity of the hypnotherapy session, our pod had nothing else scheduled that afternoon. Ellen and

I decided to go on another hike. She had heard there were some good trails along the cliffs, near where we had gone swimming. We headed west through the vineyard. Ellen wore an oversized sun hat that reminded me of the one Geia had worn in the Hamptons.

My mind still buzzed with the revelations of my hypnotherapy session. I felt a new sympathy for my mother, for all she'd put up with from my father.

"So, when do I get to hear more about this mystery man you mentioned in hypnotherapy?" Ellen asked, interrupting my thoughts. She flashed a grin.

I laughed. "What do you want to know?"

"Who is he?"

We turned onto the footpath that led towards the cliffs.

"You know him, actually."

"I do?"

"It's Jack."

It took a moment for her to understand. "Jack Verity? No way! How did that happen?"

"We met on a flight to New York about a month ago. He's the one who introduced me to Geia. She read my book and then asked me to come here and write about the Goddess Summit."

"You met Jack on a plane?"

I nodded.

"That's nuts."

"He said it was fate. Like the universe threw us together for some reason."

"That sounds like Jack, all right," Ellen said. "So, where do things stand with him?"

"I'm not sure. It's been...confusing. He and Geia, their lives are still so intertwined."

"I saw that breakup coming."

"You did?"

Ellen nodded. "Geia isn't really built for monogamy. Back when we were making *The Opposites*—this would have been early in their relationship—there were rumours on set that she wanted an open marriage, but Jack didn't. I once walked in on her making out with one of the actors, a woman, in her dressing room."

I thought of the women Geia had been taking back to her villa each night after dinner. What had happened after Kathari slipped into the pool, after I bolted? Had Geia joined in too?

"Ellen, do you ever think that Geia might not be as well-intentioned as she seems?"

Ellen eyed me beneath her sun hat. "What do you mean?"

"I don't know. I've been noticing some weird stuff lately here at the Summit. Like what I mentioned at dinner, how Geia keeps disappearing with a new woman each night." I paused. How much should I say? "The other night, I followed Geia back to her villa. She was there with Claire, Maya, and Naomi. They were all naked, swimming in her pool."

Ellen frowned. "So what? We went skinny dipping the other night too."

"Yeah, but this felt different. And I don't know about you, but I keep waking up in the morning, unsure how I got to my room the night before." I blushed as the words slipped out. A part of me thought that this might have less to do with Geia and more to do with my own drinking.

Ellen stopped. "Are you kidding? The same thing has been happening to me. I was too afraid to say anything in case I was making a fool of myself every night."

"You see? It's weird. And also, how did Sloane know all that personal stuff about us before our session this morning? Are the mentors talking about us behind our backs?"

"That's not so weird," Ellen said. "No one said the sessions were private. And maybe Geia just wanted us to get the most out of hypnotherapy."

"But without our consent? Something's not adding up."

Ellen fell silent. We stood at the cliff's edge and watched the waves crash against the rocks below us.

"I suppose that is a bit strange," she said after a while.

"I'm not saying she's a bad person. I just don't think this Summit is everything it seems." When I said it out loud, I realized that this was the crux of it all. Moonbathing and glowing snakes aside, something was off here. It felt like Geia had a plan for us that she wasn't sharing.

"What do you think it is?" Ellen asked.

I shook my head. "I'm still trying to figure that out."

We walked on, taking a somewhat perilous path down the cliffside. Halfway down, there was another plateau overlooking the water. We sat for a moment, the sun beating down on us, and I could tell Ellen was digesting everything I'd said.

"For the record," she said, adjusting her hat. "I love Geia. But I know better than anyone that she often has an unspoken agenda. When we worked together, I knew we weren't just creating art. She had a clear pedagogical purpose in mind. That meant every choice we made had to follow her vision exactly, even if she wasn't always upfront about what her vision was. She'd simply say no if she didn't like something. It was hard on the crew, as you can imagine. It was hard on Jack too. There was little room for his vision, for collaboration. I got the sense she'd had a very privileged upbringing. She was used to getting her way."

"Jack said she's estranged from her family."

"That's interesting." Ellen turned to look at me. "Anyway, if you need a partner in crime, I'm in. Maybe we can figure out what's going on together."

I nodded. "Thank you."

We decided to head back. I led the way, carefully stepping up the wobbly rock path. "I'm hungry," I said, as I reached the top.

Ellen laughed. "You're always hungry."

I turned, laughing too, just in time to see her fall. The rock beneath her left foot crumbled and sent her sliding down the cliff. She yelled, grasping desperately for something to hold onto. About fifteen feet down, she managed to grab hold of jagged rock on the cliffside, her feet finding a thin ledge to balance on. Below her, the waves smashed against the side of the island.

"Agnes!" she called.

"Are you hurt?" I yelled, beginning to panic. Even from here, I could see bloody scrapes on her forearms and one side of her face.

Ellen looked for a way to navigate the cliffside, but when she tried planting her left foot to pull herself up onto a wider plateau, she yelped in pain.

"I did something," she cried, "to my leg—my ankle."

I looked around for something to pull her up with, but there was nothing. We were on the far end of the complex, maybe even past the boundaries of the property. There was only earth and grass and rocks.

"Okay, I'm coming," I said.

Cautiously, I began to creep back down the cliffside, stepping on the craggy mantels of rock that jutted out from the earth. The rocks were looser than they appeared. I took a deep breath. My heart was pounding out of my chest.

I managed to get close enough to Ellen to reach out a hand to her and I guided her back up the rocks, pointing out where to step and which rocks seemed most secure. We moved slowly. She leaned on me to ease the burden on her ankle. Up close, the gashes on her face and arms looked deep. There was blood on the front of her white dress.

We reached the top and stopped to rest. I took deep breaths and encouraged her to do the same. I felt like I was going to be sick, but I didn't want her to know that. Get it together, Agnes.

"How are we going to make it back to the hotel?" Ellen asked, starting to cry.

"We'll just take it slow."

We continued on, Ellen leaning on me, breathing heavily through each step. The wind picked up and I imagined it was helping us: carried on the breeze was magic dust, created by the trees on the island, giving us strength.

When we finally made it back, the first people we saw were Geia and Chanel crossing the courtyard together.

"Geia!" I called.

She turned to look at us, her face falling. Within seconds, she was on Ellen's other side, helping me guide her into the hotel and through the lobby. She led us through the door marked STAFF ONLY, swiping a key card as we went, and down a hallway. We entered a small room with a single bed. Together, we helped Ellen lie down. She winced as I lifted her ankle onto the mattress.

"I can take it from here, Agnes," Geia said firmly, nodding towards the door.

"Doesn't she need a doctor?" I asked, wiping sweat from my brow.

"I'll make sure she receives proper medical attention. Now, you go upstairs and wash up. You've had a scare. I'll get the staff to send up a glass of mastika to calm your nerves."

Geia put an arm around my shoulders and ushered me out of the room. Before I knew it, the door was shut behind me, and I was standing in the hallway alone.

35

I walked slowly up to my room, as if moving through a dream. What had just happened? Why had Geia shut me out of the room like that? Was she calling a doctor? Would Ellen be okay?

I sat down on the bed, my hands shaking. The last hour was a complete blur. Ellen slipping down the cliff. Me scrambling down after her. The two of us limping back to the hotel in the hot sun, Ellen wincing with every step. And then Geia jumping to action.

The fall could have been much worse. My stomach twisted into knots at the thought of Ellen plunging down the cliff into the surf below.

There was a knock at the door, and as promised, one of the staff delivered me a glass of mastika on ice. I gulped it down immediately. The chill of it spread through my body, giving me goosebumps.

I DECIDED TO get ready for dinner early so I could return to the room where Geia had taken Ellen first. Surely, I'd be allowed to visit my friend to see how she was doing. I showered and dressed. When I arrived in the lobby, I saw Amara—or was it Dimitra?—walking with an armful of white towels.

"Amara!" I called, and was relieved to see she turned at the sound of my voice.

She smiled. "Oh, hello. How are you?"

"I'm okay. Have you seen my friend Ellen? She had an accident, a fall on the cliffs, and Geia was supposed to get her a doctor. She was in a room down that hallway." I pointed towards the STAFF ONLY door.

Amara's eyes grew big. "A fall? That's terrible."

"Yeah. It was bad. So, do you mind letting me in? I think I need a key card."

Amara's soft smile returned. "You don't need to worry, Ms. Oliver. If your friend is with Geia, she's in good hands. She'll be feeling better very soon, I can promise you that."

What did that mean? Ellen's ankle wasn't something a Goddess™ tincture could fix.

"I'm sure she is," I said, trying to keep my voice even. "But I'd still like to check on how she's doing. Can you let me in to see her?"

Amara shook her head lightly. "I'm afraid not. That area is off-limits to guests. Why don't you go out to the patio, and I'll send you a cold drink and a snack? It sounds like you've had quite a day."

Before I could protest, Amara hurried out of the room with the stack of towels. I stood in the lobby alone again.

What was going on here? It felt like I was being kept from seeing Ellen.

I approached the closed door and tried to open it, but it was indeed locked. I glanced towards the front desk. It was unstaffed. I crept behind it and began opening drawers, rifling through papers as I searched for a key card.

"Can I help you?" Amara asked, appearing at my side. Except, no, when I glanced at her name tag, it was Dimitra. Who was I talking to earlier?

"I'm just trying to see my friend. Geia took her and I need to make sure she's okay."

Dimitra's smile was cool. "If your friend is with Geia, there is no need to worry. Please," she gestured at the desk. "I have work to do."

Reluctantly, I backed away. I looked again at the locked door and then made my way out to the patio, feeling dazed. I sat down at an empty table. Around me, women in white dresses chatted happily about their days over pre-dinner drinks. Down on the beach, I could see staff setting up for dinner, dressing the tables with white candles and elaborate arrangements of wildflowers. Soon, a server appeared with a small bowl of plain almonds and another mastika on ice. Again, I drank quickly. I looked out at the sea and for a moment I felt like I'd been on this island, around these people, forever.

AS PEOPLE STARTED to make their way down to the beach for dinner, I decided to hang back on the patio, hoping to slip into the lobby while everyone was eating. Maybe

I could convince someone besides Amara or Dimitra to let me in that door. Surely, someone would be sympathetic. My friend was hurt. Even if she was in Geia's good hands—whatever that meant—I wanted to make sure she was okay.

But then I saw Geia walking down to the beach with a trio of mentors: Chanel, Sloane, and Lydia.

"Geia!" I called, hurrying after them on the sandy path. "Geia!"

She turned and her face was bright. "Agnes, are you feeling better?"

"I'm fine." I frowned. "How's Ellen?"

"Ellen? Oh, she's doing great. I think she's already down at your table." Geia pointed towards the beach and I saw Ellen sitting with Pearl, Leslie, and Skye. She appeared to be laughing.

"But how—" I started to ask.

"You should hurry along," Geia said. "They're already serving the first course."

A line of servers passed by us, carrying trays of salads, and everyone continued on their way down to the beach. For the second time today, I stood alone and confused. Geia was acting like nothing had happened.

I made my way to our table and sat down next to Ellen. Her face and arms showed no signs of her earlier fall.

"What happened?" I asked. "You look fine. Are you okay?"

She raised her eyebrows. "Of course I'm okay. What are you talking about?"

"The fall. Your ankle." I looked down at her feet, both

of which looked perfectly normal. "You were limping an hour ago."

"Oh, that!" Ellen laughed. "I took a tumble on our hike earlier," she explained to the others. "But we iced my ankle, and it feels much better now. I think we overreacted back there on the cliffs, Agnes. It was a just a little tumble, nothing serious."

I looked into her eyes, trying to understand. "But you were all scraped up," I said. "Your face and arms. Now, you don't have a scratch."

Ellen laughed again, and I realized it was a laugh I didn't recognize. It was louder, obnoxious somehow. I had the sense she was trying to make me feel like I was being ridiculous.

"Geia applied a new Goddess healing ointment and it seemed to do the trick." She shrugged happily. "Again, I think you and I had more of a fright than anything else. I feel fine, really, Agnes."

I searched her face for a more reasonable explanation, but she quickly changed the subject.

"So, tomorrow, our second-to-last day. I looked at the schedule and we're in for a treat. The whole day is dedicated to beauty and skincare. Facials and massages in the morning and one-on-one clean-makeup consultations with Chanel in the afternoon."

While the others chatted about what they were most looking forward to tomorrow, I sat silent, moving the salad around my plate with my fork. Why was Ellen downplaying what had happened earlier? It was traumatic and serious, and here she was, acting like it was nothing.

Throughout dinner, I tried again to ask her how she could be feeling better so quickly, but she always found a way to steer the conversation in another direction. Then, during dessert, she excused herself to go to the bathroom and never came back. Geia, I noticed, was gone too.

So, Ellen was her chosen one tonight. But Ellen and I had talked about the weird things I'd seen at Geia's villa, so at least she'd be prepared. Maybe she'd even have answers for me tomorrow.

On our way back to the hotel after dinner, I stopped Pearl on the patio, letting Leslie and Skye walk ahead.

"Pearl, you told me not to look away from the strange things I see. Well, I've been seeing a lot of strange things lately and I'm starting to think Geia doesn't have our best intentions at heart."

Pearl frowned, but I could see she was open to listening. We sat down by the pool. I proceeded to tell her everything I had seen, from the night in Hamptons until this afternoon. I had shared my concerns with Jack and Ellen, and though they tried to help, what good had it done? Jack had sent me on a hike up a mountain without providing any real answers, and Ellen seemed to have forgotten about our conversation completely. Now, she wouldn't even talk to me. But Pearl sat still, listening carefully, and didn't say a word. Then she reached out a hand and squeezed mine.

"I knew that woman couldn't be as perfect as she let on."

I asked Pearl what she thought I should do. I only had questions, no answers, but I had a hunch Geia was planning something big for the last day of the Summit. I just didn't know what.

Pearl hesitated. I could tell she was at a loss, just like me. But then she said, "What if you took a page out of Geia's book? Remember what Phoebe said on the sailboat, about letting questions live in our bodies? It seems to me the only real way to understand what Geia is up to, what all of this means, is to go about it as she would. Accessing intuition rather than reason. This isn't a puzzle, Agnes; it's a story. You just have to figure out how to tell it."

I nodded. I knew exactly what I needed to do.

We agreed that Pearl would go to our sessions tomorrow as scheduled. She would tell the others I wasn't feeling well to prevent any suspicions about my absence. And she would keep a close eye on Ellen.

"Pay attention to her laugh," I told Pearl. "It seemed somehow different at dinner."

36

When I awoke the next morning, I filled a glass with cold water and sat by the window. I opened the notebook Jack had sent me to the first page, blank and fresh, and I started writing. I wrote down everything strange I had witnessed since the Hamptons. I re-sketched the scene of Geia and Kathari, glowing under the moon, but this time I also wrote about the scents in the air that night, the wild rose and day lily that floated in on the breeze through Jack's open window. I wrote about how the night air felt on my skin, how I imagined it felt on Geia's, like a whisper. I wrote from the perspective of the moon, shining down upon these two beings, filling them up with light, giving them energy and power.

I wrote about Mastika and its inhabitants. The trees and their special drink, the perfect weather, the massive mountain with its secret cave. I wrote about the men we saw on the first day, their amazing skin, their seemingly perpetual youth, about Amara and Dimitra.

I wrote about Geia. Her beauty, her wit, her hidden temper. I wrote about her luring women back to her villa by making them levitate, ensuring they felt special and chosen.

I wrote about Sloane's voice and feeling like I existed in a dark hole filled with warm water. How happy I was there, how sure of myself. It was like being in the woods as a child, but different. In the woods, other creatures surrounded me, plant and animal. In the water, there was only me.

It was noon before I looked up from my notebook. Outside, the sun was high, making the sea glimmer. I flipped the pages to the beginning to reread all I had written, but then I thought better of it.

The words lived inside me already. I didn't need to read them again. To reread was to second-guess my own instincts.

Instead, I changed into my swimsuit, packed a towel and a bottle of water, and headed for the secret lagoon. A swim sounded just right.

THE LAGOON WAS just as warm and lovely as I remembered. I made my way down the rock steps and slipped into its depths, soothed again by its liquid embrace. Fluttering my limbs in the water, I felt every part of my body relax. Even my mind was still. This was where I was supposed to be. I knew it in my gut.

I did a few laps of the still pool and then allowed myself

to float, looking up at the cloudless sky. Beyond the rock wall that bordered the pool, waves crashed against the cliffs of the island. Their sound soon became a rhythm, something else I could sink into.

"Hello?" a voice called from somewhere in the distance.

I turned my head to find its source. I felt like I was dreaming, like maybe the voice wasn't real. But there was a woman sitting on the edge of the lagoon. She waved and smiled. I didn't recognize her from the hotel. Maybe she lived on the island?

"Hello," I replied, waving back.

"Mind if I join you?"

"Of course not," I said. "The water's beautiful."

She wore a black one-piece swimsuit, and as she stood, I saw she shared Geia's statuesque physique, though her dark hair was cut short, a pixie cut.

The woman dove elegantly into the water and emerged after a moment, sighing contentedly. We remained silent for several minutes, each of us treading water.

"This place is incredible," I said finally, looking around at the cliffs behind us.

The woman smiled. "It's one of my favourite places on the island. So peaceful, yes? And then the wild sea is right there, on the other side of those rocks."

I wondered what it would be like to swim here every day if you wanted.

"You live here? On the island?" I asked.

She nodded. "And you're with Geia, yes?"

"The Goddess Summit." I gestured in the direction of the hotel. "You know her?"

The woman nodded, her lips turning up in a small smile. "We're cousins. I've known her my whole life."

So, Geia *did* have relatives on the island.

"I didn't realize she still had family here."

"She hasn't mentioned us?" The woman laughed lightly. "Geia has many relatives on Mastika, but she's never been good at staying in touch."

I nodded. The same could be said of me. Though I had good reasons for not talking to my family. I remembered what Jack had said about Geia and her family being estranged. Maybe Geia too had a good reason.

"I'm Agnes," I said.

"Yes. Agnes Oliver, the novelist."

I opened my mouth, surprised. "How did you know?"

"This island isn't as isolated as it seems," she said, running her tanned hands through her wet hair, slicking it back.

"Have you always lived here?" I asked.

"Yes. Since the beginning. It's home. The people in my family don't turn their backs on home, except Geia of course."

I heard a note of resentment in her voice. It occurred to me that this cousin of Geia's might know something that could help me.

"She turned her back on the island? How so?"

"For us, family and place are one and the same. She rejected us long ago. We weren't enough for her. She needed more love than we could give her, so she sought it elsewhere."

I wasn't sure what to make of that.

"It's a funny place," I said, trying to sound casual. "The island. Everyone is so beautiful here. No one looks their age."

"That's the mastika. The drink. She's been serving it to you all at the Summit, hasn't she?"

Could a drink really have that effect?

"She said it has healing properties, but I didn't think—"

"You need to be careful," she interrupted, her tone turning serious. "There is mastika and then there is Geia's mastika. It is stronger, more potent. I wouldn't recommend drinking it. It has certain side effects."

"Side effects?"

"Let me ask you," she said, her eyes wide. "How is your memory these days, Agnes?"

"My memory? It's—" I was going to say fine, but I stopped myself. It wasn't fine. All those mornings waking up unsure of how the night before had ended.

Geia's cousin nodded. "See? You need to be careful."

My stomach tightened in a knot. "Are there other side effects?"

"I can't be certain." She looked off towards the rock wall for a moment, the open sea beyond. When she looked back at me, her blue-green eyes were the same shade as the water. "But from what I understand, Geia's mastika may have properties that make those who consume it more... malleable."

"Malleable?"

The cousin nodded. "You know. Compliant. Amenable. Think back, has there been anything you've done recently without really thinking about it? Just acting. Saying yes. Going for it."

I thought back to those first nights on the beach. Telling the others about my mess of a life. But also, my participation in the Summit sessions. I had done things I never thought I'd do, shared secrets and pain I'd never been able to confront before. And then of course that day in the Hamptons when Geia first invited me to Mastika. She gave me a glass of magic water, the mastika tincture, and asked me to come to Greece. I'd said yes almost without thinking. Jack had seemed surprised by my quick decision to go, to put my work on hold. And I'd convinced myself it was a good idea.

But was that the mastika or was that me? I thought I was growing here at the Summit, changing, evolving. Could it be both?

"These side effects," I said, my mind trying to catch up, "what's their purpose? Why would Geia want us to be, as you say, malleable?"

The cousin shook her head. "I've said too much already. I'm violating the code of my family even by being here, talking to you. Geia has left us behind, but we still honour her. We're still supposed to keep her secrets."

She began to swim back to the edge of the lagoon.

"Wait," I called, "there's more I need to know."

When she reached the edge, she stood, her body gleaming golden in the sunlight. She turned to smile at me. "It was nice to meet you, Agnes Oliver. Trust yourself. You'll be okay."

And with that, she climbed back up the rock staircase. Only when she was out of sight did I realize she had no shoes, no towel, no bag.

DINNER WAS FINGER FOOD, served around a bonfire on the beach. A special celebration for our last night on the island. Tomorrow, we had our final intensive session with Geia, and after that, we were due to board an evening ferry back to Athens. We were told the mentors would be leaving first thing tomorrow morning; that meant it would be us and Geia, on her own. The thought made my heart skip.

The mastika was flowing. Staff stood at the ready with bottles in hand, refilling glasses like it was water. I managed to convince Pearl not to drink — thankfully, she didn't ask questions — but had less luck with the others.

"What?" they said. "Why wouldn't we drink it? We've been drinking it all week."

I made up some excuse about the staff telling me this batch had nasty side effects, but Skye, Leslie, and Ellen only frowned, as if I was talking nonsense. I watched them gulp down Geia's special drink and resisted the urge to reach out and knock it from their hands.

"How was Ellen today?" I asked Pearl when I got her alone, the two of us lingering in the shadows on the edge of the bonfire's light.

"She seemed a bit distant. Spacey, maybe? I tried to listen to her laugh, like you said, but I didn't notice anything different about it." Pearl leaned in closer, whispering. "What did you find out? Anything?"

I shook my head. "Not really. I talked to one of Geia's cousins though. She's the one who warned me about the mastika. She said it's making us compliant. Whatever Geia has planned for tomorrow, she wants us to be submissive."

Pearl frowned. "What should we do? Try to convince people not to take part?"

I watched the other women chatting happily by the fire. They all looked radiant, more at peace than when they arrived. There was no way they'd give up their special day with Geia, no matter what we told them.

"I don't think that's an option," I said, sighing. "We'll just have to stay vigilant. We'll participate too, whatever it is, so we can be there to help the others if needed. That's the only way, right? We can't abandon them."

Pearl agreed emphatically. She nodded in Geia's direction. "Look," she said.

Geia was holding up her glass. Her final toast of the Summit.

"Tonight is our last night together," she said, beaming at the assembled women. "I hope this experience has been as amazing for you as it has for me. Getting to know you all, watching you grow. It's been a real pleasure for me."

Applause from the women.

"I have something special planned for you tomorrow. A day with me as your mentor. I can't wait for the sun to rise, but for now, I thought we should celebrate." Geia took a sip of her drink. "Mastika, made from the nectar of mastika trees, is common on many of the Greek islands. But for centuries, locals have believed the mastika trees on this island to be singular, to have unique healing properties. The drink we make from these trees is consumed as an elixir of youth and beauty. Have you noticed how gorgeous and healthy everyone is here on the island? We attribute it to this drink. Allow this medicinal libation to course through you, to cleanse and detoxify you. I promise you, tomorrow, you'll wake up feeling and looking like a better version of yourself."

Geia raised her glass high above her head. "*Ya mas!*"

"*Ya mas!*" the crowd repeated back.

Geia downed her glass in one go. Music started and she began to dance, swaying her hips. She grabbed Skye's hands, encouraging her to join in. Soon, everyone was dancing. Ellen spotted Pearl and me in the shadows and tried to drag us towards the fire, but I extracted my arms from her grasp and shook my head. She didn't insist.

Pearl and I sat in the sand. We watched the women for hours. Geia danced with different women, holding their hands, touching their hair. The ones she chose looked euphoric in her grasp. Shining with her attention.

Pearl went to bed just after midnight.

"I need my strength for tomorrow," she said.

I grew sleepy but didn't want to leave the others alone. I felt protective. Eventually, I lay down in the sand and closed my eyes as the sounds of the party faded.

37

GODDESS™ SUMMIT — DAY 10

I woke up in my bed, once again with no memory of how I got there. But how could that be? I hadn't touched a drop of mastika all night.

When I opened my eyes, the first thing I saw was a white linen dress hanging on the back of my door. The fabric swayed in the vague breeze coming through the open window. The room seemed to shift for a moment. Geia must have had someone put it there.

It was daylight already, but something about the light was different. It was darker. For the first time since arriving on the island, I saw grey clouds in the sky. I got out of bed to look out the window. The blue of the sea had turned dark as well, a reflection of its overcast ally. It looked like rain might be in the forecast. But that seemed impossible — rain on an island where the weather was always perfect.

By the time I was dressed and down in the lobby, the rain had started. I heard one of the staff mutter: "This is awkward." When she saw me watching her, she explained, "It never rains here in the summer."

I poured myself a coffee and watched the rain fall from a window in the lobby overlooking the patio. The downpour was heavy and the sea ate it up. Everything became drenched immediately. A woman ran back to the hotel from the beach, her white dress see-through and clinging to her skin.

I was one of the few who was up and ready for the day. It took a good half-hour for the others to emerge from their rooms. They were all unusually quiet. Pouring coffee, eyeing each other uncertainly. Maybe they couldn't remember how they got back to their rooms last night either.

I spotted Ellen checking out the selection of pressed juices, but she didn't make eye contact. She picked up juice after juice, reading their labels, and then walked away empty-handed. She leaned against a wall across the room, frowning.

The lobby grew steadily fuller. When Pearl arrived, she stood next to me, drinking tea. The rain continued and no one wanted to go outside. What were we waiting for? And where was Geia?

Eventually, one of the Goddess™ staff appeared from down a hallway. She smiled at us pleasantly, making her way to the staircase. She climbed up three steps so she was standing slightly above us.

"Good morning, everyone," she said, calling the group's attention her way.

The few who were crowded near the breakfast bar turned to look, clutching their juices.

"As you all know, today is your intensive session with our leader. Geia is so excited to work closely with you over the next few hours, helping to cement the profound growth and healing you've experienced these last nine days. We're just going to wait until the storm passes and then Geia will arrive, and we can get started."

The crowd murmured. I absently reached for my phone in my pocket, an old habit the digital detox hadn't broken. I would feel better if I was connected to the outside world in case something went wrong today. But that was all the more reason for me to be here. If I wasn't, these women would be totally at Geia's mercy.

The rain continued, black clouds casting unfamiliar darkness on the usually sunny island, and the group grew restless. Then it let up a little, but Geia still didn't appear. It was like we were children stuck inside on a summer day. Glum, antsy.

When the sun finally broke through and the last rain drops had fallen, a handful of women dashed to the large windows and looked out, eyes wide with expectation about what would come next.

Geia arrived a few minutes later. She slipped into the room through a side door. At first, it seemed like I was the only one to notice her. She winked at me. What was she planning?

"Hey, everyone," Geia said, barely raising her voice.

All heads in the room turned towards her. The women near the window stepped away, pulled in Geia's direction.

"Crazy storm, right? I kind of like it when it gets all dark and moody here on the island. It's super rare, but there's something quite magical about it, don't you think?"

A few women nodded, eager to align themselves with Geia.

"So, in a few minutes we're going to head outside. We have a bit of a walk ahead of us, and I see a number of you have bags with you. I recommend leaving those behind. They'll only get in the way. It looks like almost everyone is wearing the Goddess uniform." Geia looked pointedly in my direction. I hadn't put on the white dress. "Agnes, do you mind changing? The exercise I have planned for today works better if we're all starting from a blank slate, physic-ally and aesthetically. Other clothing will only distract and get in the way."

Everyone looked towards me, waiting for me to respond. Geia tilted her head to one side, smiling expectantly.

"Sure," I said, after a moment. If that's what I had to do to stay with the others, I would do it.

"Wonderful. So, let's meet back down here in ten minutes, okay? Then, we'll set off. I can't tell you how excited I am. It's going to be an amazing day!"

I EXHALED SLOWLY as I approached the group gathered in the courtyard in front of the hotel. Wearing the white dress, I felt like a stray matchstick being returned to its box. Unremarkable now that I was back in my container. One of many.

Geia told us we were going to take a coastal walk to a lagoon, and I glanced at Pearl. She must mean our secret swimming hole. This was where we'd complete a few exercises Geia had designed to "integrate" our healing. All the other women were smiling and nodding, excited. They'd go wherever she told them.

We walked the now familiar path: through the vineyard and along the cliff's edge, where Ellen had fallen. We took the single-track path that lined the grassy bluff, where I had walked yesterday. I looked over the edge and saw waves crashing white against the rocks below.

"Be careful," I said to the women near me. I remembered the look on Ellen's face as she slid down the cliffside and my stomach flipped over. "The ground isn't stable here."

The sun, returned, was fiercer than ever. I felt it on my body, reaching the skin beneath the light linen fabric of the dress. In front of me was a woman with shiny black hair, cut into a bob. Pearl was directly behind me, and Skye and Leslie were farther back somewhere. Ellen and the other women who had been invited back to Geia's villa walked at the front of our procession.

Geia of course led the way.

I wondered what we looked like. If a boat came by, they would see a line of women, all dressed in white, walking single file, like something out of a cult.

Eventually, the path on the bluffs came to an end, and ahead I saw Geia descend down the cliffside — the rock staircase.

The steps downward were steep and narrow, and the women took their time, stepping carefully. When we were all at the bottom, Geia went to the far rock wall, and we followed her, lining the lagoon with our bodies. The water was still calm, protected by its wall of jagged rock. Beyond the rocks, the waves crashed, fiercer than before. The sound roared in my ears. No one was talking.

Many in the group began to look nervous. A fear of the sea maybe, or just uncertainty about what would happen next. Many of these women were mothers; they had families at home they needed to return to in one piece. The rest looked to Geia expectantly; they'd jump if she said so.

Geia exhaled loudly enough that we could hear it on the other side of the lagoon. A big, delicious sigh. I had never seen her look more delighted. She glanced from face to face. All of us in the white dresses.

"Thank you for coming here with me," she said, her voice audible over the sounds of the surf. "I know this might be scary for some of you. But don't worry, we're here together. You don't need to be scared. You just need to trust me."

She reached behind her into a crack in the rock, and pulled out a pair of scissors. She held them up and they flashed bright, catching the sunlight. The women looked confused, glancing at each other. Immediately, my mind returned to the cave on top of the mountain, the hair trimmings, the scraps of clothing.

"For the past ten days," Geia said, lowering the scissors so she was holding them by her side, "you've been learning to let go of the outside world and look inward. You've all made me so proud. You've been doing the work, going deep and dark. Tuning in and allowing yourselves to be vulnerable. A tribe of women committed to healing. Bravo to you all." She beamed. "Now that you've done the work, you're ready for the next level of restoration and recovery."

Geia let her words sink in. No one said anything. The woman on my right began to shiver. Movement in the turquoise water caught my eye. A few of the women pointed and gasped. Out of the unknown depths, something long and dark emerged. Kathari. Somebody down the line screamed.

"What is that?" someone yelled in alarm.

"This," Geia said calmly, as the snake wound towards her in the water, "is Kathari, my oldest and dearest confidante." Geia bent down and held out a hand, palm up. Kathari licked it with his long split tongue. "We've known each other forever, haven't we, my pet?"

Geia stood up again and looked at the group. Now almost all of them seemed scared—of the narrow rock ledge, the crashing waves, and most of all, the snake. But four people looked totally untroubled by it all: Claire, Maya, Naomi, Ellen. They were all gazing at Geia like she could do no wrong, smiling like fools.

"This snake has a special power," Geia continued. "He will heal you of all that ails you. Physically, mentally, emotionally. All the trauma and baggage and inner toxins that plague your life can be eradicated by this snake. I know that sounds strange," she said calmly, "but you need to trust me."

I glanced up and down the line. Many of the participants looked unsure. Was this for real? Was it a joke?

"This is an ancient healing practice common to the island," Geia said. "The locals have done it for centuries. To reap the benefits, you need to remove all clothing and jewellery and throw it into the lagoon. Divest yourself of these last worldly possessions. Then, I'll pass around these scissors and ask that you give yourself a haircut."

336

I watched the women's faces. Expressions had changed from nervous and unsure to horrified. Our hair?

"I'm not talking a trim here. For this ritual to work, the sacrifice has to be significant. All hair needs to be cut above the ears." Geia indicated this with her hands. "Once your clothing is off and your hair is cut, you will descend into the water with Kathari. He will swim with you, and I promise you will feel the difference immediately. This snake sucks out everything bad that hides in the body, in the soul, and in the mind. You will feel reborn. You will look years younger. How does that sound?"

I almost laughed. It sounds crazy, Geia. It makes no sense at all. Not to the other women, at least. But for me, hearing these words was finally confirmation that everything I had witnessed was real. There *was* something special about that snake. But could it really do what Geia claimed?

I watched in wonder to see how this speech was going down. Geia had always been eccentric, but this was a whole new level of weird. I looked around at the faces. Most of them looked confused, some still fearful.

"Ellen," Geia said, looking at her directly. "Would you like to go first?"

Everyone was watching her. Ellen removed her rings first, two thin gold bands, and tossed them into the water. Then she removed her dress and underwear. She threw the clothing in the water too. The white linen dress looked like a ghost, floating in the still pool. Instinctively, Ellen covered herself below with one hand. Was she undressing in front of us willingly, I wondered, or was this the effect of the mastika?

Now Geia held out the scissors to her. Ellen took them dutifully and then paused, a moment of hesitation. She laughed, shivering. "Sorry," she said, looking from the scissors in her hand to Geia. "I just need a minute."

"That's okay," Geia said. "This act represents a real commitment to healing. It takes incredible strength of mind and body. Why don't the rest of us de-robe to support you in taking the next step?"

Geia immediately lifted her dress over her head and let it fall to the ground. Underneath, she was completely naked, no bra or underwear. She looked at the group, eyebrows raised. A few others followed her lead—Claire, Maya, and Naomi were the first—but the rest of us kept our dresses on. I had no intention of taking my clothes off or cutting my hair or getting anywhere near the water with that snake in it, even if Geia was promising eternal youth and beauty.

"Oh, come on," Geia said, her patience faltering. "This is nothing. This," she gestured at her body, "is natural. It's normal. I thought by now you would have realized that. Haven't you learned anything?"

Geia's eyes were narrowed, her tone had changed. She spoke the way she had at the clean beauty session when she reprimanded the group. But this time her followers bristled. To my right, shiny black hair shook her head. A few were looking towards the rock staircase, as if trying to decide whether to stay or leave.

Geia quickly realized her mistake. She tried to make up for her sharpness with her famous smile, but it was too late. I was surprised to see how fast she was losing them. Shiny black hair started to whimper. I looked at her and tried to put myself in her shoes. Geia Stone, the woman she had admired for so long, whose life she aspired to live, was suddenly behaving like a stranger, asking her to do something crazy, something she didn't want to do. That was the difference between this and all the other Goddess™ sessions. Those had been voluntary, but this...

"What if we take everything off but don't throw it in the water?" Pearl spoke up, from down the line. "I've had this necklace forever. It was my mother's."

Many nodded, clearly agreeing with her.

"This is my engagement ring," one exclaimed. "Ten carats."

"Mine is *twelve*," another piped up.

More nodded, fingering their own shiny rings.

"I understand why you're resistant," Geia said, her tone kinder than before. "But that's only because you can't see beyond the consumer culture you were born into. You need to re-program yourselves. You need to let go. It's a common weakness of mortals—blindness to your own disempowerment—but it's something you can transcend. Only when you transcend the material can you fully heal."

"Mortals?" Pearl asked.

Geia's eyes found mine. What was she trying to say?

"Okay," Geia said, sighing. "Maybe I haven't been vulnerable enough with you. I brought you all here to Mastika for a reason."

"Brought us?" Leslie's voice. Her head swung sharply in Geia's direction. "We paid to come here."

"Well, yes and no. I chose you to come here because you are my most loyal and dedicated followers. According to our analytics, you visit the Goddess site more than anyone else. You buy the most products. You're the most committed to the Goddess brand."

"What?"

"What did she say?"

"Analytics?"

"But we signed up to come here."

"Yes, but registration was only open to a select group," Geia explained, growing impatient again. "We only had so much space and I knew you'd all want to come, so I made sure that was possible."

She looked as if she expected this news to magically shift the mood. But these dedicated followers were not flattered by her manipulation of their privacy and choices.

"That's ridiculous," a woman two down from me exclaimed.

"Is that even legal?"

Geia laughed. "Please, please. I must be explaining this wrong. Let me be completely honest with you. I'm not who you think I am." She paused. What was she going to say? "My name is Hygeia. I am a goddess. The Goddess of Good Health."

Silence.

"Yes, I know that sounds impossible, but I am here to help you. You just need to trust me and do what I say. You need to take part in the ritual, and everything will be fine."

"What the fuck?" Claire said, looking from Ellen to Maya to Naomi. She had woken up.

"This woman is psychotic."

Many were laughing in disbelief, but I knew with every

fibre of my being that Geia was speaking the truth. I thought back to the book of Greek mythology my father had given me as a child. It said some gods were known to take human form. They were wise and powerful, each with unique capabilities, but they looked like the rest of us. Just more beautiful.

That's when I remembered where I had seen the cup depicted on the cave wall, the cup from my dreams. It was in that book. I had read about Hygeia, the Goddess of Good Health. The cup with the snake: it was a symbol of her power.

The way people gravitated towards Geia, the way they wanted to be near her, to touch her, to bask in her greatness. That *was* godly. But even that power had its limits.

The women who'd taken off their clothes reached for the dresses at their feet, putting them back on. Ellen looked lost. Geia, the woman she'd looked up to, was talking nonsense. She covered her bare breasts with her crossed arms, but then thought better of it. She reached back down to cover herself below. Her dress was already in the water.

"We need to get out of here," someone said.

"This is insane. Let's go."

The woman at the back of the line turned and started to climb the steps. The others followed. I looked towards Geia. She stood there, naked, watching her admirers desert her, looking completely baffled. This was not how today was supposed to go.

"Agnes?" Pearl called from the rock staircase.

"I'll catch up."

38

Once we were alone, I approached Geia. She was slipping back into her white dress, smoothing it over her chest.

"Geia," I said softly.

She shook her head. "Idiots," she muttered. "All of them."

I smiled. "What did you think would happen?"

"I thought they were strong. I thought they loved me."

She suddenly sounded very young, almost naive. I remembered what her cousin had said: that family was not enough for Geia, that she needed to find love elsewhere.

"Should we sit?" I gestured to the ledge and we both sat down, our legs dangling in the warm water. Kathari swam circles around her heels.

"So, Hygeia, huh?" I asked. "You're a goddess, like, actually?"

She nodded, then laughed a little. "I wasn't planning on telling them. I thought my word would be enough to get them in the pool, but they seemed to need an extra push. I panicked. That's the problem with you mortals. You don't know what's good for you."

"What was that about anyway? The pool and the snake? I saw you back at your villa with Ellen and others. Was this what you were doing with them?"

"What I said today was true. Kathari has the ability to heal anyone of anything. He's the source of my powers, the way I can cure people, make them feel better. He helped me heal Ellen the other day after her fall. But for total mind-body rehabilitation, they have to get in the water with him. They have to let him suck out all the bad, so they can be good. I thought choosing a few women to practice with, to get them used to the idea, would help with today's ritual. Ellen and Claire and the others, they could demonstrate that it wasn't scary. It was a good thing. But I guess having a bigger audience like that, Ellen got stage fright."

"So, this was all for us?" I asked. "You really did have our health and happiness in mind?"

"Yes," she said, but then she grinned. "But also, you know, I'm a god. I need people to worship me. That's how this works. I figured taking my influence to the next level, helping people in a whole new way, would cement my importance in their minds forever. I wanted this to be the first of many rituals. Mass healings. If this went well, I planned to turn the hotel into a clinic where people could come to me and receive treatment. I've been doing this with the locals for millennia. That's why everyone here on the island is so healthy, so beautiful. The mastika can only do so much."

"You thought the world would believe in all this?"

"They believe a face cream can counter the effects of aging. They believe gluten is an evil monster, slowly devouring them from the inside. They believe if they buy the right things, they will feel whole. Is this so much more implausible?"

I gazed at her. She was right. For centuries, the Greeks had believed their gods walked among them. We had simply traded in our old obsessions for new versions: celebrities, influencers, products claiming magical effects.

"You seemed like the perfect person to spread the word about this," Geia gestured at the lagoon. "Your book has been so popular, and it's so unusual. I figured you had a knack for sharing the extraordinary." She paused, looking defeated. "But Agnes, what did I do wrong?"

"I don't know that you did anything wrong," I said. "The world just isn't open to this kind of thing anymore."

"You are."

"Yeah, but I'm different," I said, realizing it was true. I had always been different. "Open," as Geia had said. Looking for more, seeing what wasn't there, but maybe could be.

"Do you think the world will ever be ready?" Geia asked.

"Maybe someday," I said. "But you need to realize that you *are* helping people. You might not be healing them entirely, or whatever this was supposed to be." I pointed at the water. "But these women are learning to take care of themselves because of your influence and advice. That's a good thing, Geia. You are doing a good thing. I didn't see that before, but I do now."

"You didn't think this week would change you, Agnes, but it did. You sound so sure of yourself."

I smiled and we both stared into the still pool. Kathari had disappeared, slithering deeper than our eyes could see.

"I spoke to your cousin," I said, after a moment.

Geia rolled her eyes. "Doris?"

"She didn't tell me her name."

"Short hair?"

I nodded.

"She's always butting in where she doesn't belong."

"Is she a—" I paused. It still felt so strange to say. "A goddess too?"

"She's a sea goddess. She lives in the water. You met her swimming, I assume?"

"Jack told me you're estranged from your family, and Doris made it seem like you rejected them or something. Is that true?"

Geia scoffed. "Oh, Doris. Always so dramatic. Rejection is a strong word. And if anyone's been rejected, it's me. Here's the thing, Agnes. The others, my family, they don't care about you anymore. Mortals, I mean. They don't care to be known and adored, but that's what a god is supposed to be. They're completely fine being forgotten by humanity, living in isolation. But that's not enough for me, and my family thinks I'm vain because of it. They can't believe I'm still trying to get your attention. But who am I supposed to help if not people like you? That's my purpose. Am I just supposed to sit around with my perfect cousins for all eternity? What a fucking bore."

"Does Jack know about you?" I asked. "He must."

"Oh, yeah. I had to tell him. But don't be upset he didn't share this. He's bound to secrecy. Literally. He can't say the words out loud to anyone. You won't be able to either. The others won't remember at all. I'll have to erase their memories before they return home, including Ellen and the women you saw with Kathari in my pool at the villa. Health-wise, that group will have gained a few years of life just from their short time in the water with Kathari, but they'll never know it. My family can't have a bunch of mortals running their mouths, violating their privacy."

I remembered how Jack had sent me up the mountain, how he seemed to be holding something back.

"Do you think this is the end of me?" Geia asked, her voice brittle.

"Not at all." I shook my head." You're always reinventing yourself. You'll find another way to reach them."

"I'm glad Jack met you. You're one of the best mortals I've ever come across."

I laughed. "That sounds so weird."

39

When I returned to the hotel, leaving Geia at the lagoon, my fellow attendees were already waiting in a large bus headed for the harbour. They must have packed up right away, eager to get out of there, even though the ferry didn't depart for hours. I passed by the Goddess™ Market. Staff members were already taking it down: white dresses packed away, all the vegan lipstick and glossy serums gone. I slipped past a worker packing up the last of the dildos and found myself back at the Goddess™ Library.

I retrieved my book from where I'd hidden it earlier. For the first time, when I looked at it I didn't feel like the world was shifting around me and I was struggling to keep my balance. I felt still, solid. Grounded. I looked closely at the cover. My name, Agnes Oliver, and the title I'd chosen, *Violets in Her Lap*. The vivid red of the cardinal caught my eye and I looked down at my nails, bare now, remembering my manicure on my way to New York: the same shade of red as the bird. I liked that colour, I realized. It looked good on me. I should get another manicure soon. There was nowhere to pay for my book, so I clutched it against my chest and walked out of the tent.

It was in my suitcase now. I planned to send it to my mother as soon as I got home. I didn't care if she read it or not; she should have a copy. She should know I wanted her to have one. I didn't want to hate myself anymore. My mother had always made me question everything about myself. Doubting what I liked, what I wanted, who I was. But that was only because she didn't trust herself either. She had made questionable decisions; she didn't want me to make the same mistakes.

Geia must have erased everyone's memories of the lagoon before we even left the island—I had expected to find a boatful of traumatized fans; instead, they were chatting and snapping selfies, capturing their last Greek sunset as it pitched lower in the pink and yellow sky. Clearly, no one would be telling Geia's secret.

"Hey," Ellen said, appearing next to me.

Pearl joined me on the other side, and the three of us rested our hands on the railing at the bow of the ferry.

"Anyone else feel like the last ten days are a total blur?" Ellen asked, frowning.

Pearl nodded. "I thought this trip would bring me clarity, but really, I feel a bit foggy."

They had no idea what had happened, but that was probably for the best.

"I'm thinking maybe it's a side effect of all the healing," I ventured. "You know, detox or whatever. We feel worse before we feel better."

Ellen nodded, but Pearl laughed.

"Agnes, you really are a different person from when we arrived. Who would have thought you'd be the one reassuring us about the benefits of the Summit?"

I smiled. She wasn't quite right. I wasn't a different person, but I did feel different. More content with the person I already was.

"I'm just glad we met," I said. "It's been a while since I made any new friends."

They both grinned as the sun descended on the horizon before us, blazing a fierce, shocking coral as it disappeared from view. A beauty fleeting, yet eternal.

Epilogue

VERMONT

I'd bought candy even though we wouldn't be getting any trick-or-treaters out here in the woods. From the grocery store, I texted Jack to see what he preferred: *Milk Duds or Reese's Peanut Butter Cups?*

Peanut butter is always the answer, he wrote back.

He was due to arrive any minute, having flown in from New York. I'd just come in from a walk outside. The leaves were ablaze with fall colour, so bright and vivid, I constantly wondered if I was dreaming. Nothing could be that beautiful, could it?

I'd finished the first draft of book two an hour ago, but I hesitated to send it to Zelda and Jessica. I needed a moment first, some fresh air. There was no rush. I was rushing less these days. Taking time to make sure I felt good about my choices, leaving less space for doubt.

I felt ready now. I opened a new email and attached the manuscript. Book two. It was inspired by my experiences on Mastika, but instead of writing about a glowing goddess of health and her trusty snake companion, I wrote about a sea goddess with a pixie cut, who had an appetite for mischief and a group of sea-creature friends. That's the thing about creativity: it's a meandering path; one stroke of inspiration leads to another. When I shared the premise with my publishing team, they had laughed and told me it was just the right amount of wacky.

I had dedicated the book to Pearl and Ellen, for their friendship when I needed it most.

I pressed send and exhaled deeply. My stomach started to twist, but I let the fear flow through me, breathing slowly until it faded. I'd been doing a lot of that lately, breathing and meditating, especially on my daily walks in the woods. Geia would be proud, I thought.

I heard a knock at the front door.

"Hello?" a familiar voice called as he let himself in. "Is this where Agnes Oliver, the famous author, lives?"

"In here!"

It was Jack's first time visiting my new place. I had asked him to give me a few months to myself to get this book done, and he had respected my space. We still talked on the phone every few days, but he didn't take over my thoughts like Owen once had. That's because I trusted him, and myself.

Jack appeared in the living room wearing a huge smile and holding up a bottle of champagne.

"To celebrate," he said, reaching for me. "You and your

first draft and your new cabin in the woods. It's perfect, Agnes. It feels like home."

"It does, doesn't it?"

It was strange to be back in Vermont after all these years. But it also felt right. It *was* home. I belonged here.

I kissed him deeply, breathing in his smell. When we pulled apart, Jack headed for the kitchen.

"Champagne, just like the first day we met. Do you have flutes?"

I laughed and told him no. I didn't even have wine glasses. I'd moved in at the beginning of September and I'd only unpacked boxes as I needed them. I'd bought nothing for the house so far except a can opener and a kettle.

"Mugs it is, then." He pulled two coffee mugs from the cupboard and filled them with champagne. "Cheers!" he said, and we clinked our mugs together.

"*Ya mas*!"

We both laughed. Then we wrapped ourselves in sweaters and headed outside. I had two chairs set up in front of the cabin with a view of the forest. The day was just turning. Evening crept in between the trees.

"So, are you happy with it?" he asked. "Last we talked you were feeling pretty confident about this draft."

"I am." I paused. "I think it's quite good for a first draft. It's weird...but you know, people probably need more weird in their lives these days."

Jack laughed and reached for my hand. "Very true."

"I have a proposition for you," I said. "I'd like us to work on something together."

"Yeah?" He looked intrigued.

"*Violets in Her Lap*. What do you think about us adapting it? We could write the screenplay together. I'm ready for a new challenge."

Jack grinned. "I've wanted to do that since I finished reading it."

"Why didn't you suggest it, then?"

"I didn't want to get in your way. I had the sense you were on your own path, and I knew if that was something you wanted to do, you'd arrive there in your own time."

I shook my head, amazed by him.

"So," I said, "how do we begin?"

"You want to start tonight?"

The breeze picked up around us, sending leaves flying in all directions, and I remembered what Ellen had said back on Mastika, about taking time to celebrate one's accomplishments. The cabin was for book one. My gift to myself: a home. Maybe this moment, the quiet, allowing Jack into my life like I'd never allowed anyone else, could be for book two.

I took a sip of champagne and gazed into the growing darkness of the woods.

"Well, all right," I said. "We'll start tomorrow."

Acknowledgements

To Geoffrey, for being my partner in all things and the best first reader I could ever ask for. Thank you for your love, generosity, and perfect ideas. You push me every day in all the right ways.

To Rufus, for being my whole world. Thank you for sleeping so soundly on my chest while I revised this book. Someday, I hope you'll read it.

To Mom, for reading to me before I was even born. And to Aunt Deb, for being my unofficial publicist.

To my community, local and otherwise, for the love and food when we were getting to know our brand new baby and I was revising this book. There are too many of you to name, but I'm eternally grateful for your support and kindness.

To Stephanie Sinclair, for early comments on this story and for introducing me to Paige Sisley and Suzanne Brandreth, my stellar agents. Paige and Suzanne, I'm so grateful for your enthusiasm and support. And Paige, your idea for the cover was genius!

To Doug Richmond, my incredible editor. Working with you was an absolute pleasure and a whole lot of fun. Thank you for your brilliant vision and belief in this story.

To Kate Juniper, your copy edits made this book so much better and your excitement about my writing was just what I needed. To Jenny McWha for ushering this book through production, Alysia Shewchuk for the gorgeous cover design, and Leigh Nash for stepping in while Doug was on leave. I always felt I was in excellent hands working with everyone at Anansi.

I first came up with the idea for this book on a bus ride to visit my late stepfather, George, in the hospital. It was March 13, 2020, and while the greater world was shutting down around us, my own world was ending because George was sick with pancreatic cancer and his time was limited.

I wrote this book in the months that followed. They were an escape from the pandemic but also from the anticipatory grief I felt about losing one of the great loves of my life. George died in December 2020. He didn't get to read this book but I'm endlessly grateful for the profound influence he had on me and my writing. George Walford was an extraordinary visual artist. His creativity and unique way of seeing the world will inspire me forever. Thank you, thank you, I love you.

© Geoffrey Whitehall

DEBORAH HEMMING is the author of *Throw Down Your Shadows*, which was a finalist for the 2021 ReLit Novel Award. She studied English at McGill University and the University of King's College, and Information Studies at Dalhousie University. She lives in Wolfville, Nova Scotia, with her partner and son.

deborahhemming.com
@deborah_hemming